The Cat of the Baskervilles

The Cat of the Baskervilles

A SHERLOCK HOLMES BOOKSHOP MYSTERY

Vicki Delany

CROOKED LANE

NEW YORK

Copyright © 2018 by Vicki Delany

Published in the United States by Crooked Lane Books, an imprint of The Quick Brown Fox & Company LLC.

Crooked Lane Books and its logo are trademarks of The Quick Brown Fox & Company LLC.

Library of Congress Catalog-in-Publication data available upon request.

ISBN (paperback): 978-1-68331-806-4
ISBN (hardcover): 978-1-68331-471-4
ISBN (ePub): 978-1-68331-472-1
ISBN (ePDF): 978-1-68331-473-8

Cover illustration by Joe Burleson
Book design by Jennifer Canzone

Printed in the United States.

www.crookedlanebooks.com

Crooked Lane Books
34 West 27th St., 10th Floor
New York, NY 10001

Hardcover Edition: February 2018
Paperback Edition: October 2018

10 9 8 7 6 5 4 3 2 1

For Pat, Karen, Leslie, and Jackie:
true friends of long acquaintance.

Chapter 1

"'The footsteps of a gigantic hound!'"

"More like one small cat," I said.

"That doesn't quite have the same dramatic impact," Jayne replied.

I ran the damp mop across the floor; the tiny prints faded and disappeared. Our shop cat went by the name of Moriarty, and although he stayed indoors all the time, I sometimes wondered what he got up to when the store was closed and he was (supposedly) locked inside. This morning, I'd arrived to find a trail of muddy paw prints that began beneath my desk, crossed the office floor, went down the stairs, wandered through the shop, and ended at the cat bed beneath the center table.

It had rained heavily in the night, but I found no broken windows or doors left ajar, and inside all was warm and dry. I eyed Moriarty, but he was curled up in his bed with his black nose tucked beneath his tail. As usual, he said nothing and ignored me.

I gave the floor one last swipe, and it was pristine once again. "What's got you so excited this morning?" I asked Jayne. "Apart from a visit by the Cat of the Baskervilles."

"Who says I'm excited?" She was practically bouncing on her toes. Jayne Wilson was a tiny bundle of energy at the best of times and a nuclear fusion when she was enthusiastic about something. Which happened a lot.

"Did your bread dough rise?" I teased, "or the price of sugar go down?"

"Come on, guess." She lifted one hand. "Although I know you never guess, Gemma, you can this time. To be helpful, I gave you a clue."

As Jayne said, I never guess. And I didn't have to today. Her supposed clue, the famous quote from *The Hound of the Baskervilles*, couldn't have been broader if she'd hired a plane to write it in sky letters. Rumors had been spreading through West London, Massachusetts, for weeks, many of them passed on by Jayne or her mother, Leslie. "'The play's the thing.'" I dropped a quote of my own. Although from Shakespeare, not Sir Arthur Conan Doyle. "Are you now saying that the worst-kept secret in town is going to be a reality?"

"Yes!" she squealed. "Mom called a few minutes ago. Nigel Bellingham himself—*Sir Nigel*, no less—will have the starring role in *The Hound of the Baskervilles*."

"Good news for the festival," I said. "And good news for the festival is good news for the town."

"And good news for the town is excellent news for us." She made a sweeping gesture to indicate my store, the Sherlock Holmes Bookshop and Emporium, as well as the business next door, Mrs. Hudson's Tea Room.

The West London Theater Festival is a small repertoire group perfectly suited to a Cape Cod town that fills with summer tourists. They mostly present the classics of American theater—Neil Simon, Eugene O'Neill, Tennessee Williams—but occasionally reach abroad. The year before last, they put on *The Importance of Being Ernest* by Oscar Wilde. It's not amateur theater: they employ professional directors and actors, those going up or coming down the ladder of fame, as well as ones content to spend most of their summer in Cape Cod rather than on Broadway or in Hollywood.

"Mom says they could use Arthur. He's the evil genius of fund-raising. When's he getting back from Greece?"

I shook my head. "You know Great Uncle Arthur. He comes, he goes." My uncle, founder and now silent partner in the business, had been invited to go sailing in the Mediterranean by an old Royal Navy buddy, and he'd been out the door of our shared 1784 saltbox house before he'd finished quoting Homer, "The wine-dark sea."

Theater isn't one of my interests, and summer's the busiest time in my shop, so I don't have much to do with the festival, despite Uncle Arthur's involvement. This year, I've been kept up to date with every development through Jayne's mom, Leslie, who's the chair of the volunteer committee.

"*The Hound of the Baskervilles*," I said, "is a departure from the festival's usual lineup. I'd hardly call it a classic play."

"It was suggested as a way of luring Sir Nigel," Jayne said. "He'll be reprising his role as played in the West End. It's going to be a huge hit! Everyone is beyond thrilled. We'll be packing them in all season. As well as theatergoers, Holmes fans and tea drinkers will be beating down our doors."

I smiled at her. Jayne was right. Not only the usual theater-going tourist crowd would come to West London to see the play, but Sherlock Holmes fans would be attracted as well. And where would Sherlock Holmes fans rather spend their pre- or postshow time but engaged in a shopping frenzy at the Sherlock Holmes Bookshop and Emporium followed by traditional afternoon tea at Mrs. Hudson's Tea Room?

I made a mental note to get in extra stock of *Sherlock Holmes: The Complete Novels and Stories, Volume II* (the volume containing *The Hound of the Baskervilles*), the second series of *Sherlock*, the contemporary BBC TV series, with the episode titled "The Hounds of Baskerville," and any related paraphernalia I could round up.

Located at 222 Baker Street, my shop is primarily a bookstore. As the name suggests, we specialize in Sherlock Holmes and Sir Arthur Conan Doyle, not only the original stories, but all the modern contributions to the pastiche, such as the Mary Russell series by Laurie R. King, the authorized novels of Anthony Horowitz, the series of young adult books by Angela Misri, and the myriad short story collections featuring the Great Detective or his imitators. The contemporary books on our shelves are new, but we carry second and later editions of the Conan Doyle books and the occasional first edition that falls into Uncle Arthur's hands, as well as bound copies of the *Strand Magazine* in which the stories first appeared. The Holmes books are supplemented by nonfiction about Sir Arthur, his contemporaries, and their lives and times, as well as what we call "gaslight": books and story collections set in the Victorian or Edwardian time frame. I'd prefer to keep the business strictly a bookshop, but times are not good for independent bookstores these days, particularly ones as specialized as mine, so I also stock DVDs, movie posters, mugs and dish towels, games, puzzles, and card sets. Anything and everything that might feasibly be related to the Great Detective.

Anything within the bounds of good taste, that is. I'm continually surprised how much is not.

Great Uncle Arthur and I own the Emporium, as well as half of the tea room next door at number 220. Jayne, a professional baker, owns the other half and runs the place. In keeping with the theme, Mrs. Hudson's specializes in afternoon tea and cream teas.

"I don't know much about the theater world," I said, "but isn't it getting late for them to add a new play? Opening night is only a few weeks away."

"Mom says Sir Nigel wasn't able to formally commit before now because he's been ill. The company's been rehearsing *The Hound* with an unknown young actor prepared to step in if Sir Nigel couldn't make it. Sir Nigel played the role for years in the West End, so he knows all the lines."

"Said unknown young actor can't be too terribly pleased," I said.

"Such is show biz," Jayne said dreamily.

"Don't you have enough to do with running the tea room, never mind taking up a part-time career in theater?"

She stared at me through narrowed eyes. "I swear, Gemma Doyle, sometimes I think you can read my mind."

People say I'm smart and observant. I don't know that I'm smarter than anyone else, but I know how to interpret what's right before my eyes. Jayne's been talking about the festival for weeks. When she thinks no one's looking, she makes dramatic sweeping gestures and practices bowing as though she's front and center at the Globe Theatre in London. Yesterday, I slipped into the kitchen to find her holding a giant ladling spoon in front of her face and studying it as though she were Hamlet and it the skull of Yorick. On that occasion, I rapidly tiptoed out and coughed heavily before coming back in to find her using the skull of Yorick to stir chocolate cake batter.

"Are you going to do it?" I said.

"Do what?"

"Volunteer for the theater group, of course. And before you ask how I can possibly know you're thinking about it, your mom asked me yesterday and said she'd asked you too."

"Are you?"

I leaned on my mop. "Certainly not. If there's one thing I have no interest in, other than being in the audience occasionally, it's the theater. A lot of people making a fuss out of pretending to be something they are not."

"I might. I finish work before five most days, so I have time in the evenings. Before they open, I can help with publicity, and Mom thought I could handle ticket sales; that way I'd be able to go home as soon as the play begins." Being a baker, Jayne lives an early-to-bed, early-to-rise lifestyle. She gets up at four AM seven days a week in tourist season to start the bread.

"I'm surprised you didn't try acting yourself," I said to her. "You're beautiful enough, and I know how much you love the theater world." Jayne's tiny and gorgeous with blonde hair and blue eyes, flawless dewy skin, and perfect bone structure. She looks far more like a typical English rose than I do. Jayne's a keen Anglophile, and I knew she wouldn't be able to resist taking part once she heard a real English Sir had been asked to join the theater troupe.

I'm an Englishwoman, born and raised in the heart of London. I used to own a mystery bookstore close to Trafalgar Square. When I first met Jayne, she gushed all over my accent, which she considered to be "so sophisticated." But now, I'm just Gemma, best friend and business partner. I never have told her that my mother's family is minor (although penniless and largely discredited) aristocracy.

She blushed at the compliment, making her even prettier. "Thanks, sweetie, but it takes more than looks to make it in acting."

"Not judging by some of the American TV shows you make me watch," I said.

"Live theater is different. Believe it or not, I did consider acting as a career for a while, but my mom dissuaded me. It's a tough life. Mom knows of which she speaks."

To me, being a baker and running a tea room was pretty much at the top of the tough scale. "Your mom was an actor? I didn't know that."

"She did some off-Broadway and summer stock before she married my dad. The pinnacle of her show-business career was a minor role in a Shakespearean production on Broadway that was a big hit. She loved being in that, but she wasn't able to withstand the constant competition for roles with

hundreds of other, hungrier actors, the endless discourage-
ment, the rounds of auditions, hopes raised and then shattered
when they never called back. When she and my dad decided
to get married, she was happy to give it up, and then Jeff
was born not long after. At least, that's what she says. I
catch her sometimes, watching a play with stars in her eyes
or humming a show tune and wonder if she regrets not
sticking it out."

Moriarty yawned and stretched and slowly—very, very
slowly—rose from his bed. He approached Jayne, and she
scooped him up. "What have you been up to now, you naughty
boy?" she murmured, scratching his favorite spot behind his
ears. "Prowling the moors in the night?"

I kept my distance. Moriarty might love to *be* scratched,
but his favorite place *to* scratch is the back of my hand. With
his claws fully extended. Moriarty seems to like everyone
who comes into the shop, but for some reason he's taken
against me. He and I live in a constant state of uneasy truce.
I try not to take it too personally. I get on fine with other
animals, and my cocker spaniel Violet loves me. "It's nice
that your mom's been able to be involved in the local festival," I said.

"It is."

"Now that you've broken up with Robbie," I said, "you've
got some free time."

Her eyes narrowed once again. She stopped fussing over
the cat, and he looked at me as though that was entirely my
fault. Their expressions of disapproval were almost identical.
"I didn't tell you I've broken up with Robbie."

I shrugged. She'd scarcely had to. Jayne hadn't mentioned him in days, and several times, I'd caught her checking the display on her phone and declining to take the call or ignoring the text. I could have said, "I'm glad you've come to your senses," but I didn't. I can be circumspect sometimes.

"It was a mutual decision," Jayne said.

Not judging by the number of calls she was getting from him, it wasn't.

I didn't say that either. What I did say was, "Why didn't you talk to me about it? You know I'm here for you, Jayne, always."

"I know," she said. "I was afraid you'd say something like you were glad I'd come to my senses. You never liked Robbie."

"I never said that."

"You never had to."

"Let's have dinner at the café tonight." That was not entirely changing the subject. My friend Andy, owner of the Blue Water Café, one of West London's best restaurants, was madly and (he thought) secretly in love with Jayne. After a string of layabout "artistic" boyfriends, I was determined to see Jayne achieve true happiness with the down-to-earth, responsible Andy.

"Sure. That'll be fun," she said. Bored with our conversation, Moriarty attempted to wiggle out of her arms, and Jayne put him on the floor. "I've made up my mind. I'm going to do it. I'll call Mom now and tell her to put me down as a volunteer. Catch you later, Gemma." She skipped back to her sugar-scented, flour-covered domain, and I flipped the sign on the street door to "Open."

Moriarty went back to bed for another nap.

*   *   *

When Jayne commits herself to doing something, she does it all out. The following day, the windows of the tea room and bookshop were plastered with posters advertising the festival. Sir Nigel Bellingham and *The Hound of the Baskervilles* had been given top billing. This season, the company would also be doing *Cat on a Hot Tin Roof* and *The Odd Couple*. I didn't recognize the names of the other actors, and Sir Nigel was not billed to appear in any other play.

It was the middle of July, and so far summer had been glorious. So glorious that tourists were flooding into the Cape. Business at the bookshop and the tea room was continually, and satisfyingly, brisk.

I glanced at the clock hanging over the sales counter next to a framed cover of *Beeton's Christmas Annual*, December 1887. That magazine was the first time Sherlock Holmes had appeared in print, in *A Study in Scarlet*. My copy was, of course, a reproduction of the magazine cover. The real thing would be far beyond my budget.

It's Jayne's and my habit to meet over tea in Mrs. Hudson's at three forty every day to go over business matters. "I'm popping next door," I said to Ashleigh, my shop assistant. "If you need me, come and get me."

"Okay," she said. "By the way, I've been meaning to ask, did you have a chance to read over those articles I sent you on establishing a franchise company?"

"No time," I said. Ashleigh was a good and conscientious employee, which made a change from what I was used to. She was continually making suggestions for what she saw as the improvement of my business, and I was continually attempting to politely discourage her. Such was the price I was prepared to pay to keep her happy with her job. I was also prepared to overlook her somewhat unconventional style of dress. Ashleigh dressed differently every day. Not just differently as in new clothes, but in a total change of style. I never knew what character she'd show up as. Today, she was a Japanese anime-girl in a short pink skirt lined with tulle, pink sneakers and socks, a glittery baby-blue T-shirt, and hair tied in two high pigtails with long blue ribbons.

I left the bookshop and settled onto my favorite seat in the window alcove of Mrs. Hudson's. Fiona served me English breakfast tea in a proper bone china pot along with a selection of tiny sandwiches and a raspberry tart. "All that's left today, Gemma," she said. "It's been busy for a Tuesday."

"Busy is good," I said.

Jayne came out of the kitchen, wiping her hands on her apron. She took a seat opposite me and poured herself a cup. Mrs. Hudson's closes at four, and Fiona and Jocelyn, the tea room assistants, were going about their end-of-day tasks. A group of laughing, sun-kissed women got up from their table, gathered piles of shopping bags, and departed, leaving nothing behind but empty jars of Devonshire cream and strawberry jam along with a few scone crumbs. They'd been in the Emporium earlier buying books and playing cards.

Jayne grinned at me from across the table with the expression of a child on Christmas morning.

"You're looking mightily chuffed with yourself this afternoon," I said.

"I am."

"Why?"

"Don't you know?"

"No, I don't know. And I won't ever know if you don't tell me."

"Can't you guess?"

As I have said, Jayne is my best friend. Which doesn't stop me from sometimes wanting to wring her neck. "No, I cannot guess! What?"

"This is so great. Sir Nigel arrives tomorrow to begin rehearsals. Everyone's really excited. It's going to be a big deal to have him here. We're hoping fans of *Roman Wars* will come to see him, the sort of people who don't usually go to live theater." Even I knew that Sir Nigel Bellingham's most famous movie role was the general in the hugely popular, cult-classic *Roman Wars* movie trilogy. That had been almost forty years ago, and he'd done nothing since but disparage the "sword and sandals" epic as being beneath him. No doubt as he counted all the money the movies had earned him.

"And . . . ?" I prompted.

"As with most artistic endeavors, ticket sales only fund a portion of the cost of putting on the production. The festival relies on donors and fund-raising efforts to foot part of the bill, and that's a lot of what Arthur and Mom and her team do for them. Raising money and all. Mom texted Arthur last night to ask for some input."

"And he replied? All the way from the Greek Isles? I can't get him to answer the mobile I gave him, never mind send me an SMS, even when he's in town."

"Maybe he doesn't think you have anything important to say to him."

While I pondered the significance of that, Jayne continued, "He suggested a major fund-raiser to introduce Sir Nigel.

Sort of a meet-and-greet thing for the big donors and long-time festival patrons, which will encourage them to put their hands in their pockets one more time."

"If I must," I said, "you can put me down for a hundred dollars. We'll be getting extra business over the summer because of this, so I suppose I can help out a bit."

"Thanks," she said, "but this isn't about the money. Not directly."

I was starting to get a bad feeling about this. There could be only one thing the West London Theater Festival would want from me aside from my hard-earned cash. And that would be work. I started to shake my head.

"Arthur suggested that the fund-raiser be a full afternoon tea. What could be better? Rebecca Stanton's the festival director and producer, and she's agreed to have the tea at her place. It'll be in her garden, under an event tent in case of rain. Guess who's been asked to do the catering?"

"I don't want to guess."

"We have!"

"We?" Oh, yes, I had a bad feeling about this.

"I'll need your help. It's on Saturday, which is a busy day in here, but it won't start until three. I'll close the tea room at two, and then you and me and Jocelyn and Fiona can get over there and set up. They're serving champagne when people arrive, and they'll sit down at four. We'll have to do all the food ahead of time, which won't be a problem if you help. You can come in early on Saturday before the bookstore opens to give me a hand. Mom and her volunteers will help with setting the tables, providing the flowers, and stuff like that."

"How many people are expected to attend?"

"One hundred."

"One hundred? Isn't that a lot?"

"One hundred paying guests, but more people because every table will have one of the actors or someone associated with the play seated at it."

I calculated. "If you don't want any empty seats and are using standard banqueting tables for ten, then you need one hundred and eight guests, plus one actor at each table, meaning twelve tables, one hundred and twenty teas."

"Right."

"As I said, that's a lot. Far more people than you serve in here at any one time."

"Sure it is, but we'll manage. As well as helping the festival, it'll be great publicity for the tea room. I'm planning to use the Sherlock pots and cups, although I don't have enough for everyone."

I eyed the pot my tea had been served in. It showed a hook-nosed man in a deerstalker hat peering through a magnifying glass, a pipe clenched firmly in his teeth. The accompanying cream pitcher and sugar bowl were adorned with smaller versions of the hat, pipe, and magnifying glass.

"We can put them at the head table," Jayne said.

"Are you sure about this? It's a big commitment."

"Afternoon tea with Sir Nigel Bellingham. Isn't that exciting? It's too bad he's not married. It would sound even better if we had Lady Pricilla or someone too."

"If he was married, his wife would be Lady Bellingham, not Lady Her-first-name, unless her father . . ."

"Whatever. I can never sort that stuff out. I'm meeting Mom at Rebecca's house after closing today to go over the menu. They're charging two hundred dollars a place, so they'll want the best."

"Two hundred dollars! For afternoon tea?"

"Afternoon tea with Sir Nigel Bellingham. Mom expects it to be so popular, they'll be turning people away." Jayne beamed.

"I trust someone's told Sir Nigel about this?"

"I suppose so," Jayne said. "Anyway, here's the plan. You arrive at eight on Saturday—"

"Eight in the morning?"

"Eight PM won't be much help with afternoon tea, will it, Gemma? You'll spend two hours helping me in the kitchen before you have to open the store. At two, you come back, and we'll take all the stuff to Rebecca's house."

"What about the shop?"

Jayne dismissed that trifle with a wave of her hand. "Ashleigh can take care of it. She is working on Saturday, isn't she?"

"Yes, but . . ."

"That's settled then."

I leaned back in my chair and took a sip of tea. In both our business partnership and friendship, I was the strong-minded one, and Jayne went with the flow. This was a new side of her, and I realized that I'd already lost any argument I might attempt to make.

"We don't have enough cutlery or plates for one hundred and twenty places," Jayne said. "So other than the Holmes cups and pots and a selection of teapots from here, we'll rent what we need and have them dropped off on Saturday before we arrive. I'm going to assign you and Jocelyn to be in

Rebecca's kitchen to arrange the individual trays and make the tea. Fiona and I will supervise the volunteers in the serving."

I considered making an emergency appointment at the dentist for a root canal on Saturday afternoon. But, I reminded myself, Jayne and I were partners, and partners helped each other.

"Eight o'clock it will be," I said.

Chapter 2

I didn't have to wait until teatime Saturday to meet the Great Thespian himself.

Shortly before one on Wednesday, I was shelving books in the section reserved for the Sir Arthur Conan Doyle stories when I felt the air move as the front door opened. The front door opens a lot during the day—we are a store after all—but this time the sheer crush of people had an almost physical effect. I straightened and turned to see what was going on.

Jayne's mother Leslie is an older and slightly rounder version of my friend, but she shivers with the same intensity of excitement. And she was certainly excited now as she held the door for Sir Nigel Bellingham.

I'll admit that I'd been curious, and on Monday night when I got home from dinner with Jayne at the Blue Water Café—sadly disappointed that Andy had taken the night off—I'd searched the Internet for information on the legend of stage and screen. Many years had passed since the role for which he was most famous: the *Roman Wars* trilogy as the heroic general inspiring the legions to rise up against the injustices of decadent, decaying imperial Rome. He hadn't been young then, and the years since had not been kind to him. He was jowly and pudgy and slow-moving, and the only color in his face was the network of red lines running through his nose and bloodshot eyes. His thin gray hair was worn far too long, curling around his neck in greasy strands. He wore a brown tweed suit, unsuitable for the heat of the day, and leaned heavily on his cane. I recognized the gold-topped cane as the sort with a screw-top handle and a hollow interior into which one could slip a glass container.

He stood in the doorway to my shop, red eyes blinking. No one said a word. "As marvelous as described," he said at last, and the man behind him clapped as though Sir Nigel had finished a particularly difficult Shakespearean soliloquy. His voice was deep and rolling, the English accent what we call posh. I knew from the other night's reading that although Sir Nigel hadn't appeared in a movie or on the stage for years, these days he did a lot of "voice work": speaking parts for commercials and animated movies or voice-over for documentaries. As soon as Jayne told me he was coming, I'd ordered a few CDs with the audio version of *The Sign of Four*, narrated by none other than Sir Nigel, and they'd arrived this morning.

Moriarty leapt off the sales counter, ears up, tail moving.

Sir Nigel swept into the shop, followed by his entourage. As well as Leslie, he was accompanied by a small man with dark darting eyes and nervous mannerisms who carried a large over-the-shoulder leather briefcase, a heavyset woman dressed in a flowing white dress dotted with pink flowers, an exceedingly handsome man who looked as though he was smelling something very bad indeed, and a pretty young woman hanging onto Sir Nigel's arm with a smile as fake as her tan and light blonde hair.

The shop was full of customers, and everyone stopped to stare at the new arrivals. Whispers spread rapidly through the crowd and heads popped in from the adjoining tea room.

Moments later, Jayne arrived in the shop at a rapid trot, eyes open wide, beaming with delight. Ashleigh—dressed today in her best ladies-who-lunch-at-the-yacht-club style—blinked in surprise. Clearly she, at least, didn't know who these people were.

I stepped forward. "Welcome, everyone. Good afternoon, Sir Nigel. Hi, Mrs. Wilson. If you need any help, be sure and let me know."

The actor extended a vein-lined, liver spot–encrusted hand. I took it in mine. His grip put me in mind of the last piece of cod at the fishmonger's at the end of a hot day. The scent of tobacco surrounded him like an aura. "An Englishwoman," Sir Nigel said in that rich, legendary voice. "Such a pleasure to meet you, my dear. You correctly surmised that I am Sir Nigel. Are you the proprietress of this fine establishment?"

"Gemma Doyle, recently of London, England. Currently of West London, Massachusetts."

"Doyle? Any relation?"

"You mean to the creator of Sherlock Holmes? No," I said. Uncle Arthur insists that he's a distant cousin of Sir Arthur Conan Doyle, but my father says that's nothing but the overactive, and hopeful, imagination of a Sherlock fanatic.

Moriarty rubbed up against the actor's legs, but Nigel ignored him. The cat then went on to check out the other arrivals. The younger man bent over and gave him a scratch. Moriarty purred.

"Delighted to make your acquaintance, Miss Doyle," Nigel said. "Such an interesting shop you have here."

Alone of the items in an actor's tool chest, the voice is immune from the effects of a lifetime of drinking, and rather than destroying it, tobacco often improves the timber of a voice. His hands shook, and that—along with the red-lined nose, the whiff of whisky on his breath, and the flask-containing cane—was a clear sign of an alcohol problem. The only reason he'd have to fortify himself with a drink before coming to the Sherlock Holmes Bookshop and Emporium would be because Sir Nigel needed to fortify himself for everything he did.

This man was going to play Sherlock Holmes? Maybe he'd suit in the movie version of *A Slight Trick of the Mind* by Mitch Cullin, although that had been done recently, and very well, by Sir Ian McKellen, but not Holmes in the prime of his life, at the height of his powers, bounding across the moor in pursuit of the great spectral hound.

I turned to the woman on his arm. "Hi."

"Hello." It's difficult to sound totally bored in one word, but she managed. Her accent was American. Californian, I thought. She looked very West Coast with her long blonde hair, blindingly white teeth, deep tan, and almost skeletal figure. She wore short white shorts and a tight blue T-shirt with silver sparkles spelling out the words "I Love Life."

Exclamation marks were added for good measure. Breasts of that size are rarely natural on a woman that thin. On closer inspection, I could see the network of fine lines under her eyes and around her mouth, which she'd tried to conceal with skillfully applied makeup. She was a good deal older than she first appeared. Mid to late thirties, no longer the ingenue she so desperately wanted to be.

"This is Miss Renee Masters," Sir Nigel said. "Miss Masters will be appearing as Miss Stapleton in our production of *The Hound of the Baskervilles*."

Miss Masters yawned.

"Let's not take up all these people's time, Nige," the large woman said. "They have a business to run here."

Sir Nigel didn't openly cringe at the diminutive of his name, but the small, nervous man with the briefcase did.

"I'm Pat Allworth," the woman said to me. "I'm directing the plays for the festival this year. Last night, Rebecca suggested Nige here should see this store, and I decided to tag along and bring some of the others. Sorta help us get into the Sherlock mood, right? It was nice of Leslie to offer to pick us all up."

Leslie's face was already tinged pink. The color deepened. She gave Nigel a hesitant smile, but he appeared not to notice.

"You're welcome to join us in Mrs. Hudson's Tea Room when you've finished shopping," Jayne said. "We serve a full afternoon tea, a cream tea, or a selection of tea sandwiches and pastries, if you'd prefer. We stock a wide range of teas."

The handsome man's eyes lit up as soon as he saw Jayne, and he straightened. She noticed him watching her and gave him a soft shy smile that was utterly charming, even more so because she didn't realize it. Unhappy at the sudden loss of attention, Moriarty hissed. The expression on his face was almost identical to that of Renee the actress.

"Sounds great," Pat said. "I—"

"I know the play version of *The Hound of the Baskervilles* inside and out," Sir Nigel said, as unhappy as the cat at losing the spotlight, "but I always enjoy catching up on the original. Do you happen to have it in stock?"

"I do," I said. "Later, if you wouldn't mind, we have a few copies of the audio version of *The Sign of Four*, which you narrated so well. Would you be so kind as to sign them for me?"

"I'd be delighted, my dear. Anything to help out an Englishwoman far from our shores."

Renee took the opportunity to tug herself free of Sir Nigel's arm and move closer to the younger man. "I'd adore a little prezzie, Eddie. Something Sherlock-like. Isn't that Benedict Cumberbatch a dream?" She smiled up at him, but he pointedly ignored her and continued grinning at Jayne. Renee huffed, spun on her excessively high heels, marched away, and pulled out her phone. Sensing dissent in the group, Moriarty followed her. Sir Nigel headed for the Conan Doyle bookshelf, and the small man scurried after him.

"I'd better get back to work." Jayne indicated her apron with the Mrs. Hudson's logo. "To the tea room, I mean."

"I suddenly have a real craving for a cup of hot tea and a scone," the younger actor said.

Jayne blushed to the roots of her hair, lowered her head, and scurried away to the mysterious depths of her domain.

"My daughter's the owner of Mrs. Hudson's," Leslie said to Pat. "She'll be catering the Saturday tea."

"Should be good then," Pat said diplomatically.

"I'll see if Nigel needs any help making his selection," Leslie said.

"As no one bothered to introduce me, guess I have to do it myself." The handsome man extended his hand. His grip was firm, his hand dry. "I'm Edward Barker. Everyone calls me Eddie."

"Pleased to meet you, Eddie," I said. "What role do you have in the play?"

"You recognized me." He smiled. I smiled back. I'd never seen the man before, on stage or off. Even if he hadn't been in the company of theater people, I'd instantly take him for an actor. Most middle-class Americans have good teeth, but only actors or models have that pure blinding whiteness. He was about five foot eight, slightly shorter than me, and his head was larger than average. He wasn't excessively muscular, but he was lean and fit. Clearly a man who worked out regularly, probably a runner. His voice was deep, his accent West Coast, his blond hair (dyed and highlighted) carefully arranged with a single lock falling over his forehead. He wore a black leather jacket over a plain white T-shirt and fashionably distressed jeans.

"I play Felix in *The Odd Couple*. I'm also . . ." His smile faded as his eyes wandered to where Sir Nigel was being helped by Ashleigh to examine the books while Leslie Wilson flitted about. "Understudy to the role of Holmes." Ah, yes, the actor who'd prepared for the part only to be bumped by Sir Nigel.

"The understudy might yet get to have his day. I've heard Sir Nigel's been ill." I attempted to be tactful. I needn't have bothered.

"In a rehab clinic, more like it," Eddie said. "I'm surprised they let him out early." He caught himself, and the smile returned. "I've had enough of this. I'm heading back to the B and B. I'll drop in another day and browse when the place is less crowded."

"Any time," I said.

"Do they do takeout coffee at the place next door?"

"They do."

"I'm not one for tea," he said, "although I might manage to develop a taste given the right incentives." He headed for the sliding door joining the two businesses.

Renee looked up from her phone and fixed her eyes on him until he disappeared. She did not look happy. Moriarty stood on the shelf beside her. She rubbed his head absent-mindedly. My customers went back to what they were doing.

Attracted by the crowd of people, Maureen, the owner of Beach Fine Arts situated across from us at 221 Baker Street, pushed her way into the shop. Avoiding my eyes, she slid up to a woman who was examining a framed poster of Robert Downey Jr. and Jude Law in *Game of Shadows* and said in a voice that wasn't nearly as low as she thought it was, "If you're looking for a souvenir of your visit, genuine Cape Cod art can be found across the street."

I've chased Maureen out of the Emporium more than once for trying to poach my customers. Without my having to say anything, Ashleigh headed toward them. "Can I help you?"

she boomed. Maureen slunk away, but she didn't leave the shop. She edged close to Sir Nigel, waiting for an opportunity to pounce and suggest he might like to purchase some art.

"Not that one, you stupid man." Sir Nigel was a trained actor with a powerful stage presence. Apparently he didn't know when to use his indoor voice. Everyone stopped what they were doing to look and then quickly returned to their own business, embarrassed to be so crass as to stare.

Sir Nigel loomed over the small man. He waved his cane, and the other man cringed. "I said I want *Volume II*, not *Volume I*. That's the one containing *The Hound of the Baskervilles*, you fool." The small man replaced the book he'd selected and pulled out another. "Frankly, I wonder sometimes why I bother with you, Gerald. Don't just stand there gaping—pay for the book!"

Gerald scurried away, his head tucked into his chest. His hair was thin, his eyeglasses thick, the bags under his eyes dark, and the lines on his face deep, from age as well as stress. He was in his early sixties, I guessed, and not a happy man.

"Poor guy," Pat said to me.

"The secretary, I assume," I said.

"Personal assistant is the modern term. I'd say general dogsbody and all around whipping boy, myself. I hope Nige is paying him well for what he has to put up with. Still, it's his neck; he can do what he wants with it. As for Nige himself . . ."

"He's not what you expected."

"Oh, he's exactly what I expected. I do my homework. Let's just say Sir Nigel Bellingham's best days are behind him. Far, far, far behind him. So far behind him, he can't see them in his rearview mirror. Rebecca Stanton wanted a big British name to play Holmes. She overrode my objections, so this is what we got. Still, he is a professional, and he's played the role many times before, so I'll cheerfully assume he'll rise to the occasion."

"Who's playing Watson?" I asked.

"Ralph Carlyle. Too young, really, to be Watson to Nige's Sherlock, but he's a good sort. Solid, respectable, reliable." Her eyes moved to the corner of the shop where Renee was standing in the bright sunlight pouring through the window of the reading alcove, her back to the room, laughing uproariously into her phone. Pat's eyes narrowed, and her face darkened.

The director's lot, I thought, *is not a happy one.*

"I'll be helping with the fund-raising tea on Saturday," I said. "Are all the actors planning to attend?"

With another scowl in the direction of Renee, Pat said, "If they know what's good for them, they will be."

"Did someone say tea? That would be just the ticket," Sir Nigel announced. "Gerald, secure us a table. It would appear that Edward has left. No matter. Pat will join me and Renee. You . . . what's your name again?"

"You don't . . . ? I'm Leslie. Leslie Wilson. I was an actress myself once, I used to be Leslie Montgomery?" I caught something in Jayne's mom's voice, the uptick at the end turning the statement into a question. She expected Nigel to react to the name. He did not.

"You're in charge of the volunteer committee, I've been told," he said.

"Yes, that's right. I've loved the theater ever since—"

"In that case, you can be my guest as well. A table for four," Sir Nigel said. Four meant no room for Gerald. I assumed he was expected to eat in the kitchen. Or in the back alley in the company of any stray dogs who might be passing. He scurried into the tea room to do his master's bidding.

"I'd love a cup of tea," Maureen said.

Sir Nigel ignored her. "Come along, people. Time we were off. Pay for your purchases, everyone. Renee!"

She glanced up from her phone. Her lips formed a rude word. Nigel noticed, and he bristled.

Pat had also noticed. "I think Renee has a costume fitting, don't you, dear?"

"Yeah. A fitting," the actress said. "Sorry about that." She walked out of the shop, still talking into her phone. "You won't believe what he said."

"I'll pop into the lavatory in the restaurant for a moment," Sir Nigel said. "And then I'll join you. Miss Doyle, I haven't forgotten about signing those recordings. Why don't you lay them out, and I'll do that in a moment. Gerald . . . Where is Gerald?"

"You sent him to get the table," I said.

"How long does that take?" he snapped. "I need my pen. I can't sign without my pen."

"I'll get the CDs," Ashleigh said.

"Unlike some people, I can't stand around chatting all day," Maureen said. "If this store seems too crowded, we'd be happy to serve you at Beach Fine Arts. Did I mention that our address is 221 Baker Street? Isn't that interesting?" When Uncle Arthur had first arrived in West London, he'd wanted to buy the building across the street, but it had not been for sale, so he'd had to settle on number 222. After giving me a smirk, Maureen left. No one followed her.

"Gerald!" Nigel bellowed. Gerald's head popped into the Emporium.

"I've found a nice table, Sir Nigel."

"Lay my pen out on the signing table. I'll be back shortly."

Sir Nigel might have needed to use the restroom, but that wasn't the only reason he wanted some privacy. When he returned to the Emporium, the scent of whisky on his breath had been refreshed.

The signing table was nothing but a spot cleared on the games and puzzles table with the comfortable red wingback chair from the reading nook hastily pulled up to it. I'd only bought four copies of the audiobook, and that made an unimpressive pile. But Sir Nigel sat down with great ceremony and extended his hand. With a slight bow, Gerald handed him a gold-plated fountain pen. The CDs came wrapped in plastic, so the best we could do was attach a sticker with the Sherlock Holmes Bookshop and Emporium logo onto the cover. Sir Nigel signed in large ornate script with a dramatic flourish.

"If those sell, I might get more in," I said to Gerald. "I'd be happy to bring them around to the theater or your hotel if Sir Nigel would be willing to sign them. Do you have a number where I can contact you?"

He put his hand into his jacket pocket and pulled out a small square of stiff white paper. "Be sure you ring first. Don't presume on Sir Nigel's time."

"I wouldn't dream of it." I swallowed a retort as I accepted the card. Sir Nigel couldn't be an easy man to work for, and if some uppity shop owner did "presume" on his time, poor Gerald would probably get the worst of it.

I slipped the card into my pocket, and Gerald hurried away to check if Nigel's pen was working or something.

"This is so great," Ashleigh whispered to me.

"Wouldn't have taken you for a fan," I said.

"I didn't recognize him at first, but then someone said his name. My granddad loves *Roman Wars*. He's seen it like a hundred times. Do you think it would be okay if I asked Mr. Bellingham for his autograph?"

"Normally, I'd say not, but as he's already signing, sure."

When he'd finished, Ashleigh cleared her throat. "Mr. Bellingham . . ."

"Sir Nigel," Gerald muttered.

"I'd love your autograph. Do you mind?" Ashleigh slid a piece of paper toward him.

"Not in the least, my dear. How do you spell your name?"

"Make it out to John, please. He's a huge fan of yours."

"John. Is that fortunate young man your boyfriend?"

"Oh, no. It's my granddad. *Roman Wars Part I* is his favorite movie of all time."

"Your granddad." Sir Nigel's smile faded. He hastily scribbled something indecipherable and shoved the paper at Ashleigh without bothering to smile again. I smothered a laugh.

"He's a lot older than I expected," she said to me once the theater people had taken their leave.

"Time does that. *Roman Wars* was made forty years ago."

"Sad," she said.

"Life," I said. "Now let's get back to work." Word had spread that actors were in the store and the tea room, and a substantial number of people had arrived to see what the fuss was about. I took one of the festival flyers out of the window and used to it make a display on the center table with *Volumes I* and *II* and the signed CDs. We don't usually sell audiobooks because they're so expensive, but two of these were snapped up quickly, and I decided to order another ten.

Yes, the West London Theater Festival was looking to be good for business indeed.

* * *

I was in Mrs. Hudson's getting a takeout cup of tea and a late lunch of roast beef with mustard and arugula on a Jayne-made baguette to eat in my office when Leslie Wilson returned. This time, she was with a woman I recognized from around town, although I didn't know her name. Fiona showed them to a table. Jayne's mom spotted me and waved, and I carried my cup and paper bag over to say hello.

"Having Sir Nigel in the shop was good publicity," I said. "We had a rush after he left."

"Glad it worked out—for you and Jayne, anyway," Leslie said. "I offered to bring them into town, as I was hoping to have a chat with Nigel, but we didn't get a chance."

"I'm sure you will later," I said.

"Gemma, this is Rebecca Stanton. Rebecca's the executive director of the festival. Gemma Doyle owns the bookstore."

Rebecca was in her late fifties, well put-together in tailored white trousers and matching jacket with a pretty pink silk shell beneath. Her makeup was subdued and perfect, her hair expensively cut and colored, her manicure fresh. The scent of Chanel No. 5, lightly applied, wafted around her.

She gave me a warm smile. "Pleased to meet you, Gemma. Thank you in advance for Saturday. Leslie tells me you'll be working with Jayne."

"Jayne's the one in charge of anything and everything to do with food and drink. I merely do what I'm told."

"The tickets are almost sold out already," Leslie said, "and it hasn't even been twenty-four hours since we made the announcement. I'm absolutely delighted. Some people were worried that we were charging too much, but Rebecca put her foot down. She knows her patrons."

Rebecca's smile was strained. "Have faith, Leslie."

"Right now, you don't," I said.

Rebecca gave me a look I've seen many times before. I keep telling myself that people don't like it when I seem to know what they're thinking, but if they want to keep things private, maybe they shouldn't have such expressive faces.

"Preopening jitters," she said. "It's common enough. In my long-forgotten youth, there were entire days when I couldn't keep anything I ate down, my nerves were so stretched. But then opening night came, and all would be well. Until next time."

"You were an actress? Broadway?"

"Oh, no, greasepaint and limelight were not for me. I can't bear to imagine what actually being on a stage would have done to my nerves. I worked for a production company for many years. Strictly confined to behind the scenes."

"Where the most important work's done," Leslie said. "Without people like Rebecca, there would be no plays being put on."

"Would you like to see a menu, Mrs. Wilson, Mrs. Stanton?" Fiona, the waitress, slipped quietly up to the table.

"I know it by heart by now," Leslie said. "I'll have a cream tea, please, with Lapsang Souchong. I was so nervous earlier, having tea with Nigel, I couldn't eat a bite. Rebecca?"

"The same for me, thank you," Rebecca said. Fiona left to get the orders. "I'm sorry, where are my manners? Won't you join us, Gemma? If you have the time. I see you have your food already."

"Thanks." I dropped into a vacant chair. I didn't really have the time, but I was curious. "It was good publicity for the festival for Nigel Bellingham and some of the cast to pop into the bookshop. Plenty of people saw them and the buzz began. Good for us too. We've been busy ever since."

"Nothing is spontaneous in this business," Rebecca said. "They went at my suggestion. The great man in town, we might as well make use of him. I paid for him to make a big show of treating some of the others to tea. I thought it would provide some advertising for the fund-raiser."

"I took a couple of pictures," Leslie said. "Before the tea was served, that is. I'd never take pictures of anyone eating. I got Fiona in the background with the tea room logo on her uniform showing, and a couple of Sir Nigel examining the books in your store."

"Is he up to playing Sherlock?" I asked.

"You get straight to the point, don't you, Gemma?" Rebecca said.

"The thought crossed my mind. I might as well express it."

"I have no worries at all." Her eyes shifted to one side, she patted her hair, and I knew she was lying. "He's played the role many, many times. He must know it so well, he can recite it in his sleep." She smiled at me. The fine lines around her eyes deepened. "Why, he'd barely arrived yesterday and immediately insisted on going into rehearsals. He knows most of the lines, of course, but our staging is different, and we have different actors for him to play off, not to mention a director with a fresh interpretation. It's going to be a marvelous production. Sir Nigel's age will add to the gravitas of Sherlock Holmes, don't you agree, Leslie?"

"He is known for his old world charm. Although . . ."

We didn't get to hear the rest of her thoughts as Fiona arrived bearing the tea things. She placed the pot in the center of the table along with two cups, the milk pitcher, and sugar bowl. The pot wasn't a Sherlock one but fine bone china in a soft pink dotted with red roses. The teacups matched the pot. Leslie Wilson poured, and Fiona soon returned with a plate containing four thick, warm, fragrant English-style scones and pots of strawberry jam, butter, and clotted cream. The women helped themselves, and I got to my feet. "I'd better get back. Nice meeting you, Rebecca. I'll see you at the tea on Saturday."

"It's going to be the perfect kickoff to a perfect season," Rebecca said. "I've no worries at all." Once again, she was lying.

I took my own tea, now rapidly cooling, and my sandwich into my office above the shop to work on the accounts while I ate.

* * *

Lunch over, and as much of the accounts done as I could bear (it's not my favorite task), I went down to the shop floor to give Ashleigh a hand. As is my custom whenever I've been out of the store, I surveyed the room and did a quick inventory as I came in. One copy of each of the latest two Laurie R. Kings were gone, as was *Bending the Willow: Jeremy Brett as Sherlock Holmes* and *The Sherlockian* by Graham Moore, three copies of the hottest new short story anthology, several of the mugs from the BBC series *Sherlock*, a DVD of *The Classic Sherlock Holmes Collection* (starring Basil Rathbone), and two of *The Abominable Bride*. Plus another one of the signed audiobooks, one jigsaw puzzle, and one *Sherlock: The Mind Palace* coloring book. We'd apparently had a rush on *Hudson House*, the third in the enormously successful Hudson and Holmes series by Renalta Van Markoff. The late Renalta Van Markoff, that was, as that lady unfortunately died recently not more than a few feet from where I was standing.

The store was busy as people browsed. Yes, I know browsing is a good thing, but I do wish they'd put things back where they found them. How am I supposed to keep track if the stock keeps moving about?

I was arranging the stack of puzzles, putting the tallest at the back where they belonged, when a woman approached me. "Excuse me. I saw the poster in the window for the theater festival. Are you selling tickets?"

"No," I said, "we're not. Sorry." I made a mental note to see about doing so.

"I'm so looking forward to *The Hound of the Baskervilles*," she said. "I love everything to do with Sherlock Holmes. When will tickets be on sale?"

I seemed to recall someone mentioning something about that, but I had to admit, I didn't know. I hadn't thought it a detail I needed to remember. Clearly, an oversight on my part. The theater poster contained a phone number for advance ticket sales. I ripped one down off the wall and handed it to her. She said thanks, picked up a *Mind Place* coloring book to add to her copy of *Hudson House*, and took it to the cash counter.

"I'm surprised at how well those coloring books are doing," I said to Ashleigh as we waved good-bye to another satisfied customer. "Who would have thought? Coloring books for adults. That's the second one bought this afternoon."

"I don't think so," Ashleigh said. "I've only sold one all day, that one just now."

"I sold one this morning before you arrived, and that left five on the rack. When I came back from lunch, I noticed one more had been taken, meaning four remained. There are now three. I hope someone didn't move it. I hate that."

"Do you always know what's on the shelves all the time?" Ashleigh said.

"Of course." I almost added, "Don't you?" but Jayne had once told me people didn't like that. If I was the only one working in the store, I also knew the contents of the cash drawer and the amount of the debit and credit card slips to the penny at any given time. When the business began to grow and I needed to hire an assistant, I hadn't liked losing control, but I'd decided that having something approaching spare time would be worth it. "Are you sure you didn't sell a coloring book from the time you arrived this morning until I came back after my lunch?"

"Positive." Ashleigh pushed buttons on the computer, "but I'll check anyway." She read the screen quickly and shook her head. "Nope. Only that one just now and the one from this morning."

"I don't see it misplaced anywhere. It's been stolen." I glared at Ashleigh.

She threw up her hands. "Hey, don't accuse me. I didn't take it. You can search my bag if you want."

"I'm not accusing you." Although I was accusing her of being careless, in which case I needed to blame myself as well. I'd been so distracted, first by the theater people and then by the crowd pouring in after them, I'd taken my eyes off the shop. Shoplifting wasn't much of a problem in the Emporium. Either the type of people who came into a bookstore weren't the sort inclined toward a life of petty crime or the steely-eyed glares of Benedict Cumberbatch and Robert Downey Jr. as the Great Detective put anyone off any inclination to engage in criminal activities.

"Maybe it'll turn up," Ashleigh said. "I'll keep an eye out for it."

"Thanks." The coloring book wasn't big, and it was soft-covered, meaning it could be rolled up. I thought back over the people who'd been in and out of the store this afternoon. It was a hot day, so no one had been wearing a coat, although a few had light jackets. Sir Nigel had been dressed in his Harris Tweed, suitable for a rainy autumn morning hunting grouse in the Scottish Highlands, but far too warm for a Cape Cod summer. Most people carried the usual assortment of handbags, a few beach bags, or shopping bags from other stores. A couple of the men had worn baggy shorts or loose pants with plenty of pocket room. And then there had been Gerald's leather man-bag.

I gave a mental shrug and put the loss down to the cost of doing business.

From the top of the gaslight shelf, Moriarty smirked.

Chapter 3

The forecast had been for a steady downpour all day, but to Jayne's infinite relief, and no doubt that of the West London Theater Festival fund-raising committee, Saturday dawned bright and sunny. A light breeze blew steadily off the Atlantic Ocean, and that promised to take some of the heat out of the day.

As I'd promised, and as I'd been reminded constantly to the point of receiving an unwelcome six AM phone call from Jayne, I was in the kitchen of Mrs. Hudson's Tea Room precisely at eight o'clock. Violet, Great Uncle Arthur's cocker spaniel named after Violet Hunter of the *Adventure of the Copper Beeches*, had been confused, although delighted, at being taken for such an early morning walk. We were so early that Stanford, the geriatric Bichon Frise who lived the next street over, hadn't been outside, nor had his equally aging owner. The highlight of their day, man and dog, seemed to be escaping through a hole in the fence of the otherwise enclosed yard to greet Violet (the dog) and hurrying to catch him, apologize to me for the dog getting out, and invite me in for a "cuppa" (the man).

By one minute past eight, I was rolling out biscuit dough. *Cookie dough*, I should say, being in America. Not to be confused with biscuits, which is what Americans call proper English teatime scones. What they call scones are something I'd never seen until I first came to West London. Meanwhile, Jayne rushed about and shouted orders at the staff. Jocelyn and Fiona had worked at Mrs. Hudson's since it opened and were more than capable. Today, under the rising barrage of Jayne's stress-induced anxiety, they were getting untypically frazzled.

"We have this, Jayne," I said once Jocelyn, distracted by Jayne's screech that they were out of sugar, had caught the tray of tart pastries ready for the oven before it hit the floor. "I moved the big sugar container. It's over there."

I complained about getting up at six, but it didn't look as though Jayne had even gone to bed. The tea room opened at the regular summer hour of seven to serve coffee and light breakfasts as well as fresh baked goods for takeout. In addition to all her usual chores, Jayne was a ball of nervous action preparing afternoon tea for one hundred and eight fussy, well-heeled theater patrons, twelve actors, and the six volunteers her mom had begged us to also provide for.

"Any more blueberry muffins?" Fiona's head popped into the kitchen. "I've got a takeout order for three blueberry and three bran muffins for a business breakfast meeting."

"On the cooling racks." Jayne didn't look up from the industrial-sized mixer currently churning a thick, deep chocolate dough.

"What are those going to be?" I asked.

"Brownies."

"Yum." We don't traditionally get brownies in England. They've become my favorite dessert treat. Particularly the way Jayne makes them with lots of walnuts and a light chocolate glaze topping. My favorite other than her pecan tarts, that is, with a melt-in-your-mouth short-crust pastry and thick syrupy filling packed full of the sweet nuts. Or maybe it's . . .

"Gemma, once you've finished the cookies, you can start on the sandwiches," Jayne said. I studied my handiwork. Cut into perfect circles, sugar cookies were laid out in neat rows on baking sheets. I'd dusted them lightly with sugar tinted Christmas-decoration red.

"Is it okay to make the sandwiches this early?" I washed sticky dough and red sugar off my hands.

"They're fine properly covered and kept in the fridge." Jocelyn dodged around me with a tray of almond croissants.

The kitchen behind Mrs. Hudson's is small. This morning, it was a scene of total chaos. Jayne checked recipes, wrote up sandwich instructions, and made dessert tarts and squares. Jocelyn pulled freshly baked bread and sweet rolls out of the oven and prepared soup for today's lunch between ferrying bagels and one-person-sized baguettes to the front counter. Fiona ran in and out, shouting for more cream cheese or demanding to know where the cucumbers were and somehow managing not to get in anyone's way. Me, I was in everyone's way pretty much all the time.

A kitchen, busy or not, is not my natural domain.

"Perhaps we should have hired extra help for today. Where's Lorraine?" I asked, referring to the part-time waitress.

"Sick. Don't worry; we're fine." Jayne wiped at a lock of hair that had escaped her net, leaving a streak of flour across her nose. Only Jayne could look delightful wearing a hairnet and flour. "We're hoping to make a fat profit out of this tea, remember."

"Right. Profit. Now sandwiches." I've helped at other times when the tea room has put on a special function. I can't be trusted, according to Jayne, to use my own initiative, so she prepares the sandwich ingredients herself and prints out directions for assembling them along with an illustration of the final product. This afternoon, we'd be serving smoked salmon and cream cheese on wheat bread cut into pinwheels, finger sandwiches of thinly sliced roast beef with locally made mustard and fresh arugula on light rye, cucumber with a touch of cream cheese on white bread triangles for the vegetarians, and egg salad, also on thinly sliced white bread.

I liked making the sandwiches; it suited my orderly mind. I cleared everything off the back countertop and laid out the slices of bread in a long row. I went up and down the line following Jayne's instructions: buttering the bread, laying on the filling, adding pretty herbs and fresh greens as required, putting the tops on, cutting them into the proper shapes with a careful eye for uniformity of size. Then I carefully placed the tiny, gorgeous sandwiches onto platters and covered them tightly in plastic wrap. Jocelyn ferried them to the fridge.

I made five hundred small sandwiches. I was rather pleased with myself, but Jayne, being Jayne, wouldn't allow me to rest on my laurels. "Fiona's overwhelmed out front. Jocelyn, take off your cooking apron and go and help. Gemma, you'll have to finish the cupcakes."

"Me?"

"Yes, you. They need frosting." One hundred and twenty-five tiny, perfect coconut cupcakes were cooling on a high shelf. The kitchen, as I have said, is small. We were running out of room to put all the food. "The frosting's made. All you have to do is use an ice cream scoop as a measure. One scoop on each cupcake. Don't worry about covering the tops to the edges. When that's done, give the frosting a little swirl with a knife to make it look pretty and sprinkle coconut on top." While she talked, Jayne mixed the dough for the next batch of scones. I set about icing coconut cupcakes in the same assembly-line fashion I had with the sandwiches.

"A swirl, Gemma. Just a swirl," Jayne said. "If you're trying to make a work of art out of each one, you'll be here all day."

I studied the cupcake at hand. I hadn't been trying to re-create the London office tower nicknamed the Gherkin in coconut icing, but it did bear a slight resemblance.

"I'll finish up," Jayne said. "It's almost ten."

"It is?" I glanced at the wall. "So it is." Time to open the Emporium. "Are we done?" I surveyed the kitchen. Mixing bowls and baking pans and spoons were piled in the sink in a stack that also bore a resemblance to the Gherkin. The contents of sugar and flour and nut containers appeared to have been emptied onto the counters and spread across the floor.

"We made good progress," Jayne said. "Time to begin lunch prep."

I took off my apron and hung it behind the door. Before leaving, I took a moment to admire it. It resembled a Jackson Pollock painting: spatters of cream cheese, a streak of the pink salmon spread, a dusting of flour, an explosion of icing sugar, and a few drops of chocolate brownie dough (although I'm sure I didn't go anywhere near that mixing bowl). "Perhaps I could frame this and ask Maureen to sell it at Beach Fine Arts," I said. "It's no worse than some of the so-called art she tries to unload on innocent tourists."

"Bye, bye, Gemma," Jayne said. "Remember, we're leaving at two o'clock on the dot."

I dodged around Jocelyn, bringing in a tray piled high with still more dirty dishes, and escaped Jayne's realm.

Once again, I thanked my lucky stars that I'd decided to become a bookseller and not a professional baker.

* * *

Jayne closed the tea room at two after politely but firmly shoving two women lingering over a late lunch out the door, and I prepared to leave the Emporium in the capable hands of Ashleigh for the remainder of the day.

"Break a leg," she called after me.

"I don't think that's an appropriate saying for nonacting people," I replied.

Moriarty hissed at me from the top of the gaslight shelf. No doubt he was also telling me to break a leg. But in his case, it was more likely to be the literal meaning.

"Whatever," Ashleigh said. "While you're out, I'll continue my survey of the customers as to their paperback preferences."

That I had not asked my assistant to survey my customers on their paperback preferences, or anything else, appeared to be of no consequence. I waved good-bye.

Jayne, Jocelyn, Fiona, and I carried the food and drink preparations to a catering van rented specifically for the occasion. Earlier, I'd changed into dark slacks and a dark long-sleeved shirt in my office. Jayne handed me a clean, highly starched Mrs. Hudson's waitress apron, white with the tea room logo of a steaming teacup next to a pipe.

"Why are you giving me this?" I asked. "You say I can't be trusted to serve our guests. Not after what happened that other time."

"Times," Jayne said. We paused for a moment in memory of past disasters. "I might need you out front today. Mom's organized volunteers to do the serving, and that means anything can happen. She told me Mrs. Franklin wants to help. Mom's the type who can't say no."

"What's wrong with Mrs. Franklin?"

"She's a marvelous woman, and I love her to bits. But she's ninety-four, uses a walker, and won't admit that she needs glasses."

"You're saying even I'm a better waitress than her?"

"That's exactly what I'm saying. I've changed my mind and decided it would be best if I stay in the kitchen with Jocelyn. Fiona will supervise the serving, and you're backup in both of those roles in case of emergencies."

Jayne opened the tea room a year ago, when she returned to her hometown of West London after learning her trade in Boston. Over the course of that year, I've come to know her very well. I reached out and placed my hand lightly on her arm. "It's all under control. Don't be nervous."

"Nervous. I'm not nervous. Jocelyn! Did you remember the napkins? Quick, run back and check."

"Yes, Jayne, I remembered the napkins. Along with every-thing else you had on the checklist, and some things you didn't."

"Perhaps I'll drive." I plucked the keys out of Jayne's hand.

* * *

Guests were due to begin arriving at three. They would be served Prosecco while wandering the spacious lawns, admir-ing the gardens and the view of the Atlantic Ocean, exchang-ing air kisses, and backbiting mutual friends. Rebecca had provided the sparkling wine as well as one hundred and twenty tall crystal flutes and silver trays with which the vol-unteer servers would circulate. Guests would be called to sit down to afternoon tea at four.

I hadn't been to Rebecca Stanton's home before, and I let out a low whistle as I turned into the driveway. I'd expected it to be nice—she was hosting afternoon tea for one hun-dred and twenty people, after all—but it was indeed spec-tacular. The long driveway curved between two rows of tall pines through which I caught glimpses of perfectly main-tained lawns and carefully cultivated perennial beds. The forecourt was wide, ending at a staircase with huge black iron urns planted with yellow begonias, tall ornamental grasses, and trailing purple-and-green vines. The house itself consisted of two levels of pale-gray siding and a dark-gray roof.

A large sign with the words "West London Theater Fes-tival Afternoon Tea" had been erected in front of the three-door garage. A big black arrow directed ticket holders to the path at the right of the house. Jayne told me to pull the van left, around to the kitchen entrance. I parked and clambered out of the van, feeling the fresh salty breeze on my face and hearing the soft pounding of surf against the shore.

Rebecca came out to greet us. She was beautifully dressed for the party in a sleeveless teal-and-navy dress that flowed around her slim ankles. Long strands of silver draped from her ears, and a chucky turquoise and silver necklace circled her throat. "Welcome," she said. "If you need anything at all, be sure and let me know."

Leslie Wilson stood behind her with something resembling a manic grin on her face. I recognized that grin: I'd seen it a few minutes earlier when Jayne had climbed into the passenger seat of the rented van and said, "Isn't this going to be fun?" Mrs. Wilson wore a pale-pink summer dress with a white apron over it. The neck, hem, and pockets of the apron were trimmed with pink appliqué. "The tables and chairs have been set up on the lawn," Leslie said. "The dishes have arrived and are in the kitchen, and my volunteers will be here any minute to help set the places."

"That's all good then," Jayne said. "Not a thing to worry about."

"Absolutely not a single thing," her mum replied.

They grinned at each other.

With Leslie's help, we carried our cartons of supplies into the kitchen. Rebecca stood to one side and supervised.

The kitchen was all modern and high-tech. So high-tech, I doubted anyone ever did any cooking in it. The marble and soft-stone countertops were polished to a high gloss, the black-and-white ceramic tiles showed not a speck of dirt or stray crumbs, and the glass doors to the cabinets sparkled. There were no containers of jumbled cooking utensils within easy reach of the stove, no drying rack, no dirty dishes piled in the sink, no paper towel holder or spice container, no sticky finger marks on the microwave door, no dish towels tossed over the oven door handle. There weren't even any pictures and postcards or yellowing newspaper articles stuck haphazardly to the stainless steel, ice-machine containing, double-door fridge. The only countertop appliance in view was a huge black Cuisinart coffeemaker.

This room was about three times the size of the kitchen in Mrs. Hudson's Tea Room.

"Nice place," Jayne said in the understatement of the year.

A breakfast bar—black marble countertop and red leather stools—separated the kitchen from the entertainment room. Comfy-looking couches (also looking like they were never used), gas-burning fireplace, enormous flat-screen TV, tasteful art. The far wall was all glass, looking out over a patch of lush lawn lined by woods better groomed than would be found in nature.

"Use those doors," Rebecca said, pointing to French doors leading off the kitchen, "to get to the patio and the garden. Jayne, do you have my phone number on you?"

"Yes."

"Call me if you need anything." Rebecca slipped out.

"She must be worth a few bucks," I said. "Do you think she made this kind of money as a theater promoter?"

Leslie laughed. "She married the boss. He was quite a bit older than her, and he died a few years ago. Neither of them had any children, so everything he had went to her."

"That's my goal," Jayne said. "Marry a rich man, and take up a life of good works."

Leslie smiled at her daughter. "I knew her husband, Ron, well. He was an absolutely marvelous man, and he and Rebecca were totally devoted to each other. Sometimes, honey, it does work out."

A rap at the kitchen door announced the arrival of the first group of volunteers, interrupting our contemplation of marrying for love *and* money. Leslie admitted two women, all gray hair and excited giggles. "I've made us matching aprons," she said, digging into her tote bag. "Put these on. Our first task is to set the tables. Jayne, do you have any special instructions?"

"Nope." Jayne pointed to the boxes of plates, teacups, and cutlery delivered earlier from the rental supply place. A wheeled cart stood nearby to move everything around. "Have at it. Oh, one thing. The Sherlock Holmes teapot and matching cups go on the head table. If there's no head table, then wherever Sir Nigel will be sitting. Do you know which table that is?"

Leslie pulled a piece of paper out of her apron pocket. "I have a seating plan. The guests will sit randomly, but the actors and other theater people are assigned to specific tables." The new arrivals put on their aprons, and they trooped off.

"Gemma," Jayne said, consulting her list of things to do. "The champagne glasses are supposed to be set up outside already and the Prosecco chilling in the outdoor fridge. Can you check, please?"

"Sure," I said. "I have to go to the loo first. Where do you think it is?"

Jayne shrugged, and I wandered off in search. A passage-way led off the entertainment room and I took it, assuming the facilities would be close to the kitchen and the telly. I opened a small door. What in this sort of house was no doubt called "the powder room" was tiny and gorgeous in feminine shades of peach and teal with a floral scent not at all overpow-ering, as artificial restroom scents usually are. I washed my hands with sea-green soap carved into the shape of a rose and dried them on a fluffy peach towel. I refrained from running the soft towel across my cheeks.

Instead of heading back through the TV room, my curi-osity got the better of me, and I decided to take a quick peek into the next room, which appeared to be a library.

It was coming up to three o'clock, almost show time, but I forgot all about my errand and the impending arrival of a hundred and eight ticket holders the moment I stepped into the library. I sucked in a breath. Sherlock Holmes himself would be comfortable in a room exactly like this one when visiting an estate in the "green and pleasant countryside," perhaps even Baskerville Hall itself. Floor to ceiling shelv-ing filled two walls, and those shelves were crammed with books. A third wall was occupied by an enormous fireplace, not gas but wood-burning, and the fourth was all glass, look-ing out over the gardens to the sea. Red cedar floors gleamed, a red-and-gold Aubusson carpet filled the center of the room, and the paint on the walls was a shade of soft gold. A big couch of well-seasoned brown leather punctured with brass hobnails faced the fireplace, and two wingback chairs upholstered in red damask stood on either side. About the only thing Sher-lock wouldn't have encountered at Baskerville Hall was the huge chandelier hanging from the twenty-foot-high ceiling. The light fixture was made of glass, a multitude of sweeping, intertwining yellow-and-green strands. So pure was the glass and so brilliant the colors that this chandelier barely needed electricity; it caught the sunlight and glowed from within. I stepped closer and looked up. It was either a Dale Chihuly or a darn good imitation. Great Uncle Arthur had taken me sailing two winters ago in the Gulf of Mexico. We'd stopped at St. Petersburg and visited the Chihuly Center, where I'd fallen in love with the man's stunning masterpieces of imagination, glass, and color. I'd wanted to take something home, but even the smallest Chihuly pieces were well beyond anything I could afford. I glanced around the room, taking in the rest of the details. A display cabinet tucked into a bookshelf contained another glass piece, this one a large bowl of intertwined green and yellow inspired by the inside of a sea shell. A smaller version in blue and yellow, about two inches long and an inch wide, lay beside it. Another display case held two cute glass sculptures resembling chocolate kisses.

Stunningly beautiful.

"Gemma!"

I tore myself away from admiration of the sculptures. Jayne stood at the entrance to the library, hands on hips, scowl on face. "What on earth are you doing in here? Did you check the wine?"

"Wine? I thought we were serving tea."

"The Prosecco. I sent you outside to make sure the wine's chilled and the glasses ready. For heaven's sake, Gemma, you've been gone so long, I thought I'd better look for you."

"Sorry," I said. "Got distracted. I'll do it now."

"Never mind. I called Mom to ask if you were out there, and she said she'd do it. I need you in the kitchen."

"Coming, boss. Did you notice the chandelier? If it's an original, it's gotta cost in the twenty to fifty thousand range. If they have a piece like this in the library, I wonder what they have in the front hall and living room."

"Don't you dare wander off for a peek. We haven't been invited to make ourselves at home or to admire the decor, you know. The rest of the volunteers are here, including Mrs. Franklin, walker and all. Mom intercepted her before she could reach the kitchen and assigned her to a table at the gate checking tickets. So that's one potential disaster avoided."

I peeked out the windows. People had begun to arrive, among them Pat Allworth, the director, and Eddie Barker, the understudy. I didn't see Sir Nigel or his shadow, Gerald. Smiling women in pink-trimmed aprons circulated with Prosecco.

"What do you need me to do?" I asked Jayne as we went into the kitchen.

"Start arranging the trays. You know the layout, sand-wiches on—"

"Sandwiches on the bottom tier, scones in the middle, tarts and cookies on the top. As immortalized by Anna, Duchess of Bedford, in—"

"Thank you, Gemma. I am aware of the history of after-noon tea."

I harrumphed. I'd once suggested that rearranging the contents of the trays into consistency of shape rather than according to tradition would be more visually appealing, and

Jayne had bitten my head off. Sometimes Americans could be more tied to English traditions than we British.

We worked in silence for a while. I couldn't see the garden, but I could hear the increasing sound of excited chatter as guests arrived. The food would be served all at once on the three-tiered trays, so as soon as everyone sat down, all we had to do was keep the teapots refreshed. To simplify things, Jayne had selected only two types of tea. Earl Grey and Darjeeling. Then reluctantly, she'd added a decaf green tea. Reluctantly, because it was unlikely Queen Victoria or Anna, Duchess of Bedford, had worried about their caffeine consumption.

"We're good here for now," Jayne said once the trays were all neatly assembled, the kettles full, and the china pots ready with fresh loose tea leaves. Jocelyn poured herself a glass of water from the dispenser on the fridge.

"Gemma," Jayne said. "Do you know where my mom is?"

"She went out to see if Mrs. Franklin was okay at her table, but I haven't seen her since."

"You can do something for me then. Take a look outside, and make sure the tables are set correctly. Take my camera, will you? It's in my tote bag. Snap some pictures of the tables and the place settings. Close up as well as panoramic pictures. Things we can use for advertising."

I rummaged in her bag and pulled out a compact camera. "Got it."

"Start counting to five. Now."

"Why am I counting to five?"

"Because when you reach five, I want you standing outside. Not wandering around the house gaping. Got it?"

"One," I said. I was through the French doors, out of the house, and on the back patio by the time I reached four.

As if the kitchen in the house wasn't enough, there was a full outdoor kitchen as well. Stainless-steel barbecue approximately large enough to grill a whole ox, rows of fancy (and spotlessly clean) cooking implements hanging on hooks, countertops, cabinets, fridge, a table that would seat twelve, and a fire pit around which more chairs were arranged. Presumably this kitchen and outdoor dining area was used only in the summer months, but it was a heck of a lot better equipped than the one in my house.

Fortunately, considering the heat of the day, the fire pit was not lit. The barbecue was covered, and the cabinets closed. One of Leslie's white-and-pink-aproned volunteers poured drinks at the long bar counter. Three other women, wreathed in huge smiles, circulated with crystal glasses on silver trays. Some of the elderly guests had taken chairs on the patio, but most milled about, holding glasses of Prosecco or sparkling water. Everyone was dressed in their best as suited a summer afternoon. The women wore colorful dresses, and a few even sported wide-brimmed hats; the men were in sports jackets or open-necked shirts over well-ironed trousers. One or two of the older men wore suits and ties.

"Nice turnout," said a voice beside me. I turned to see a smiling Eddie.

"We're lucky with the weather," I said. A canvas event tent had been erected on the lawn, but it wouldn't be necessary. The only clouds in the sky were light and white and fluffy.

"Is your friend here?" Eddie asked.

"My friend?"

"The woman from the tea room. Jayne, is it? I, uh . . . wanted to say hi."

"She's in the kitchen but super busy, as you can imagine."

"Do you think she'd mind if I popped in to say good luck?"

I hesitated. Rebecca hadn't said anything about not allowing people into the house, and no one was standing guard next to the French doors. "I suppose that'll be okay. The kitchen's through there."

He gave me a wink and slipped inside after taking a quick detour to nab a glass of Prosecco off the bar.

I crossed the lawn, heading for the tent, taking pictures as I went. The twelve round tables were covered in crisp white cloth, their edges fluttering in the breeze. Ten chairs surrounded each table. The flower beds were a riot of carefully controlled color. The property sloped downward to end at a cliff overlooking the ocean, and a patch of woods ran along the right side of the perfectly maintained lawn. In the distance, boats skimmed across sparkling blue waters, their colorful sails running before the wind.

"Hey, Gemma!" Irene Talbot broke away from the pack around the bar and trotted toward me, a black Nikon camera slung around her neck.

"Are you here working?" I asked her. Irene was a reporter for the *West London Star*. In these days of declining newspaper subscriptions and budget cuts, she was the only full time reporter they had, so she covered everything from murder to high school sports games to society events.

"Yup. This is a big shindig. It's got it all. Sir Nigel Bellingham, representatives of some of Cape Cod's oldest—not to mention richest—families, and the Stanton house, which is never opened to the public. I'm only allowed to take pictures until the group sits down to tea, and then they'll release the hounds if I'm not off the property, so I'd better get busy. Smile!" She lifted her camera, but I didn't bother to pose. With all the beauty, natural and human, around me to photograph, my scowling visage would not be used to grace the pages of the *West London Star*. Irene trotted off. She wasn't the only one snapping away. Many people had phones or cameras out and were asking friends to take pictures of them with the actors.

I spotted Pat Allworth, dressed in wide-legged capri-length black trousers and a navy-blue cape, chatting to a cluster of blue-rinsed, diamond-ringed matrons. She wore black mesh shoes with four inch heels that flared out at the bottom to make a gold star. Rebecca would not be pleased if Pat marched across her perfect lawn, stamping stars into the grass as she went. Sir Nigel had arrived, and he was standing at the bar, accepting a glass while Gerald hovered at his elbow and a group of women milled around them, wondering if it was appropriate to approach the great man. Eddie was probably still chatting up Jayne in the kitchen. Renee was hiding in a patch of shrubbery smoking, phone to her ear. She'd apparently not gotten the memo about circulating with the guests or about suitable attire for afternoon tea. She wore short (very short) white denim shorts, a low-cut red T-shirt tucked into a wide black belt, and sunglasses that covered half her face. A giant red beach bag was tossed over the shoulder, and her shoes were red espadrilles with cork platforms.

I was about to continue on my way when Rebecca hurried up to the actress, her face like a thundercloud. She snapped at Renee, and the younger woman glared at her. Rebecca made angry gestures to the cigarette, and Renee dropped it and ground it beneath her shoe. Rebecca then pointed to the crowd of people behind her. Slowly and deliberately, Renee said something into her phone before switching it off and dropping it into a side pocket of her bag. She patted her hair and sauntered across the lawn, straight toward a circulating waitress. She snagged a fresh glass of Prosecco. Rebecca caught me looking and gave me a grimace.

"Everything okay?" I asked.

"I hate actors. Every single one of them. It's why I left the theater world. I don't know why I took this on."

"It all seems to be going splendidly," I said.

"Are you ready in the kitchen?"

"I'm doing a last minute check of the table settings, and then we're good to go."

"At least Nigel got here on time. Might have had something to do with the serving of drinks. He's another one I had to tell not to smoke on my property. Aside from the fact that my husband was a two-pack a day smoker who died of lung cancer and every whiff I catch of tobacco reminds me of him, my guests do not want cigarette-breath in their faces. I'll do the welcome in five minutes. Thank everyone for coming, introduce the cast, and ask them to be seated." She headed toward the house, her own heels digging into the immaculate lawn, and I continued on to the tent.

"Quite the do," a man's voice said behind me.

I turned with a smile. "So it is. I'm surprised to see you here. I didn't know you were interested in theater."

"Not particularly." Grant Thompson fell into step beside me. "As I'm new in town, I'm interested in making the acquaintance of the sort of people who have money to buy what I sell."

Grant had dressed for today's event in slim-fitting khaki Dockers, beige belt, and a recently ironed blue-and-white checked button-down shirt. A trace of black stubble showed on his strong jaw, and the damp air had curled his thick brown hair. He was a rare book dealer who specialized in Victorian and Edwardian detective fiction. We'd met when a potentially extremely valuable item had come (briefly) into my possession. The Emporium is strictly retail and doesn't handle rare books, but Grant and I had continued our friendship.

Was it more than friendship? Grant was a charming, handsome single man. We had a lot in common. We both loved books and made our living from them. He'd lived in England for a time. He seemed to like me. But I wasn't entirely sure what our relationship was, or even what I wanted it to be.

"Good luck then," I said.

"Everything looks great," he said.

And it did. Crisply ironed white linen cloths, white paper napkins printed with the Mrs. Hudson's logo, china teacups with matching plates, silver polished to a high shine. A local florist had donated the flowers, and Mrs. Wilson's volunteers had arranged centerpieces of miniature pink and yellow roses accented with a touch of greenery inside teacups. Each of the twelve tables had one place card, marking the table's host, an actor, or a person otherwise involved in the production, such as the director, the wardrobe mistress, and the set designer. I took more pictures.

Some of the guests were already checking out the seating, no doubt planning to nab a place at the best table. One woman put her handbag on a chair to mark her place. It was the head table, the one for Sir Nigel, with the Sherlock Holmes-themed dishes.

"I'll catch you later," I said to Grant. "If I don't report back for duty, Jayne'll have my guts for garters."

The green flakes in his brown eyes twinkled. "I do miss those English expressions some times."

I gave him a grin and then headed back to the kitchen to report to Jayne that we were about to begin. Before I reached the house, I was waylaid by Donald Morris, a prominent and somewhat eccentric Sherlockian. Today, Donald had dressed the part in an ulster—a calf-length overcoat with cape and sleeves—and his habitual deerstalker hat. Ulsters are mentioned in *A Study in Scarlet* and *The Blue Carbuncle*, neither of which were set in North America in the middle of summer.

"Aren't you hot in that getup?" I said somewhat rhetorically, as if beads of sweat weren't forming at Donald's temples and a drip hesitating at the end of his nose, ready to drop off.

"Somewhat," he admitted, fumbling in his pocket for a handkerchief. "I thought we'd be inside the house." He wiped his face.

"I'll take your coat into the kitchen if you want," I said.

With a sigh of relief, he pulled it off and handed it to me. Underneath the coat, he wore a clean button-down shirt and pressed trousers. "I have an item you might be interested in purchasing, Gemma."

"Not now, Donald. I'm kinda busy here. Jayne and I are doing the tea, you know."

"This won't take but a moment. I have a playbill from Sir Nigel's run of *The Hound of the Baskervilles* at the Shaftsbury Theater in London. It's been signed by Sir Nigel and others of the cast. Do you want to buy it?"

"No," I said, and I walked away, carrying Donald's ulster. He'd quit his law practice prematurely to concentrate on his love of all things Holmes. Whereupon he found out that Sherlock doesn't provide much of a living. I was surprised Donald had been able to afford the two hundred dollars for a ticket to this tea.

Nigel Bellingham was surrounded by guests, and Gerald hovered nervously at the edges of the circle. As I passed, two people broke away, and Nigel spotted me through the gap. "There she is!" he cried. "My English rose. You don't have a drink in hand, my dear. Gerald, see to that."

"No, thank you." I remembered to smile. "I'm working."

"Working? That will never do." Sir Nigel had dispensed with the Harris Tweed and wore a white seersucker suit with a red-and-gold paisley cravat tied jauntily at his throat. He waved his glass at me. His hand shook, his eyes were tinged red, and his baritone voice trembled.

"I think we're about to sit down, Sir Nigel." Gerald blinked through his coke-bottle glasses, and he shifted his leather bag. He was not holding a drink.

"In that case, get me another glass to take to the table," Nigel said. "This lady will be seated next to me, of course."

I shook my head. "Working. Have a nice time." I wasn't going to stand there arguing.

I turned and almost collided with Renee. She ignored me and spoke directly to Nigel. "Speaking of working, buddy, that's why we're here, don'cha know. We're no better than any of the other working stiffs. These folks have paid a lot of money to meet you. Not to watch you drinking up most of the champagne single-handedly." A few of the onlookers began to edge away; others moved in closer. Someone lifted their phone and snapped a picture. Renee was not smiling, and she was not attempting to keep her voice down. The harsh sun shone fully on her face, revealing the network of small lines radiating from the edges of her mouth. Her eyes were hidden beneath her sunglasses. Rebecca had told her she was here to work the crowd and she'd better get to it, and Renee was now determined to pass her anger on.

Gerald plucked at his boss's sleeve. "Why don't we move along, Sir Nigel?"

"Sir Nigel," Renee barked. "Lord Muckety-Muck. Prince Broadway. I'll try to act impressed."

I glanced quickly around. I didn't see Rebecca or Pat anywhere. I did, however, see Irene crossing the lawn at a rapid clip, heading our way. Reporter's instinct for trouble, I guessed. Leslie had reappeared, and I could tell that something had happened. She'd been bubbling with excitement when we'd arrived, but now her face was drawn and her eyes dull. Bickering between the volunteers, I thought. I had other things to worry about right now.

I touched Renee's arm. "Why don't I show you . . . ?"

She shook me off. "Plenty of good *American* actors could have taken the part," she said. "We didn't need some aging has-been from England."

Nigel's top lip curled up in a sneer. "I was surprised to hear you'd be playing the role of Miss Stapleton. I mean, really, my dear, at your age, wouldn't you be better in the part of Mrs. Hudson?"

Renee tossed the contents of her glass in Sir Nigel Bellingham's face. Gerald squealed. A woman screamed. A man said, "Hey, there!" Irene snapped a picture. Nigel stood in the sun, blinking. He made no move to wipe the liquid from his eyes. Leslie pulled a tissue out of her apron pocket and started to dab at the actor's face. Nigel pushed her roughly away. "Will you leave me alone, woman. Stop pestering me."

I thought Jayne's mom might burst into tears. "I'm only trying to help."

"When I want your help, I'll ask you for it. And that is unlikely to happen."

Irene took another picture as Leslie turned and ran toward the kitchen door.

I grabbed Renee's arm and almost jerked her off her feet. "That was totally uncalled for. Come with me and cool down."

She pulled herself out of my grip. "Shouldn't you be in your kitchen?" Spittle flew. "Haven't you got pots or something to scrub?"

I kept my voice low. "You can insult me all you want—or all you think you are, because to my mind doing an honest day's work to earn an honest wage isn't at all a bad thing."

"Don't you think you'd be better off minding your own business?"

"It is my business to see that this tea is a success. And let me remind you, yours as well."

I had no interest whatsoever in this woman and her insecurities, but as long as she was arguing with me, I was able to lead her away from Nigel and the crowd of onlookers.

"Good afternoon, everyone." Rebecca stood at the bar, clapping her hands. "Can I have your attention, please?"

Conversation drifted to a halt. Renee gave me one last poisonous glare, and then she switched on her professional smile as though someone had flicked the switch to the Chihuly chandelier. She stood taller, straightened her shoulders, and crossed the patio to where the rest of the actors were joining Rebecca. Renee gave Nigel a warm smile, and he offered her a slight bow.

Theater people are weird. Almost as weird as Sherlock Holmes people.

"I was about to send another search party out for you," Jayne greeted me as I came into the kitchen. "Where have you been?"

"Performing other duties as assigned." I threw Donald's ulster over the back of a barstool and slipped Jayne's camera back into her tote bag. "Everything looks good, and they're doing the welcoming thing now. I think I got some usable shots."

Jayne's mum stood by the fridge, sipping a glass of water. I gave her a reassuring smile and was pleased to get a small one in return. She put the water down, wiped at her eyes, blew her nose, put her tissue into her pocket, and took a deep breath. She then joined her four volunteers, who were lined up like soldiers on parade. I almost expected Leslie to walk up and down the line inspecting them. "The five of us will serve. I've asked Mrs. Franklin to remain at the gate in case of late arrivals."

"Good to know." Jayne pointed to the twenty-four three-tiered trays, piled high with food. "Place two trays in the center of each table. They're all the same, so it doesn't matter which one goes where, but put the first two on the head table. Do you have your direction sheets?" The volunteers checked their apron pockets and nodded. "I've written out the list of ingredients in case you're asked, but if you have any questions at all, ask Fiona."

Fiona waved.

"Take the tea out first and then come back for the food. The Earl Grey is in the pots with green or red flowers and the Darjeeling in the blue ones. Tell them that, so they can choose the flavor they want."

A woman put up her hand. "What's the difference?"

"Darjeeling is thinner, lighter in color, and slightly spicier," Jayne said. "We have decaf green tea as well, but it won't be on each table. Gemma will circulate with it for anyone who wants it. Tell them that too."

"I will?"

"Yes, you will. Try not to pour tea down anyone's cleavage, Gemma."

"That only happened once," I reminded her. "And it was toward the end of the meal, so the tea was getting cool."

"It lives large in my memory." Underneath her nervous anticipation, Jayne was smiling ever so slightly. "Stay alert and keep watch on your assigned tables, but don't hover. Once the teapot is empty, bring it back in and Jocelyn will fill it."

This time it was Jocelyn's turn to wave.

"Break a leg," Jayne said, and the women headed out, gripping their teapots, chattering like excited birds.

I picked up the pot Jayne indicated for me. "Dare I ask what's got you so pleased?"

"Me? I'm pleased because everything's going well." Her blue eyes twinkled.

"Everything was going well before I went outside. I wonder what might have happened in the short time I was away. Oh, yes. Edward Barker came in looking for you. Date tonight?"

Her face fell. "Nothing ever surprises you, does it, Gemma?"

"Sometimes it does." Renee Masters acting like a spoiled diva in front of a hundred and eight well-heeled donors certainly had. As had Sir Nigel Bellingham, legend of stage and screen, publically insulting both her and Leslie Wilson.

I reminded myself that their behavior was none of my business. I had tea to serve.

Chapter 4

The tea went off without a hitch. All the actors, even Renee and Nigel, were charming and entertaining, and the guests seemed to be enchanted. A place had not been prepared for Gerald, and he'd taken a seat at the patio table. As I passed, having refilled my pot, I suggested he go into the kitchen and ask Jocelyn for a cup of tea.

"Can't leave. I have to be here at his beck and call. Yup, there he goes. Another Prosecco is needed." I glanced down the lawn to see Nigel holding his glass aloft. From here, it looked as though he was waving his arms about to illustrate a point.

"Those eyeglasses you're wearing are good," I said. "I can't tell that it's empty."

"It's always empty," Gerald said. "Except when it's full." He shifted the bag across his chest and got to his feet. No one was staffing the bar, but a bottle sat in a silver ice bucket. Gerald grabbed it, poured a glass, and carried it across the lawn.

Shortly after, people began pushing back their chairs and getting to their feet. A number of the guests were regulars at the tea room, and some of them slipped into the kitchen to offer Jayne their congratulations. No one congratulated me on the precision of the slicing of the sandwiches or on the excellent pouring of decaffeinated green tea (no mishaps this time), but I basked in their praise nonetheless.

On Jayne's instructions, the workers cleared the leftover food from the plates—sea gulls were already circling—but the rest of the cleanup would wait until the guests had left.

"Drat," said one of the volunteers as she carried in a tray on which nothing remained but crumbs, and not many of those. "I was hoping to snag one of those brownies."

"Mmm," said another around a raspberry tart.

Rebecca's head popped into the kitchen. "We've one more special moment planned. Come out, all of you. You've worked so hard and done such a marvelous job, you deserve to enjoy it." Rebecca noticed that Jocelyn had begun laying out the extra sandwiches held back for the volunteers. "Bring your food with you. You've done so much in support of the festival, and it's much appreciated."

Most of the crowd had gathered around the patio. Prosecco was being served again, but there weren't many takers. Everyone was stuffed to the gills with scones, sandwiches, pastries, and tea.

Rebecca clapped her hands for attention, and conversation died.

"I hope you all enjoyed that," she said. Loud cheers. "I'd like to thank Jayne Wilson from Mrs. Hudson's Tea Room in West London for that delicious repast." Jayne blushed and bowed to much applause. Eddie was the most enthusiastic clapper of all.

"My thanks also to Leslie Wilson and her team of marvelous volunteers. Without the hard work and support of people like them, like you all, the festival would not exist." More applause. "Leslie, ladies, take a bow."

Someone had dragged a patio chair to the bar area for Mrs. Franklin. She punched the air in triumph, and the audience applauded enthusiastically. Two of the volunteers curtsied deeply with practiced flair. The older one of the pair staggered as she tried to straighten up and had to be helped. She blushed and giggled and said something about "not as young as I once was." Rebecca hesitated for a moment, giving Leslie a chance to accept her thanks. Everyone looked around, but Leslie was nowhere to be seen.

"She's still working, I assume," Rebecca said. "Now for a special treat, I've asked our honored guest, Sir Nigel Bellingham, to recite a few lines from *The Hound of the Baskervilles*. Sir Nigel." She smiled broadly and extended her right arm, palm up in invitation.

Nigel stepped forward. He tripped over his own feet and almost fell into Rebecca. Her smile didn't falter one inch, but the lines around her eyes tightened. She plucked the half-empty champagne flute out of his hand.

He turned to face the crowd and blinked rapidly. Then he composed his face into serious lines. It was amazing, I thought, how an actor could seemingly change his physical appearance with nothing more than a shift of posture and a few small gestures. The years melted off Nigel, he grew several inches, his eyes hooded and blazed with a fierce intelligence. I could almost smell the scent of pipe tobacco, feel the damp fog, and hear the clop of horses' hooves and the rumble of carriage wheels across cobblestone streets. "Bear in mind, Sir Henry," he rumbled in his deep resonant voice, "one of the phrases in that queer old legend which Dr. Mortimer has read to us, and avoid the moor . . . when . . . I mean, in those hours of darkness when . . . when . . . the powers of evil are exalted." He hiccupped, and the entire edifice crumbled and the pretense disappeared as though into that London fog. His mouth opened, but no further words came out. He closed it again. He hiccupped again.

Gerald shouted for a glass of water.

"That is to say . . . when the powers of evil . . ." Nigel swayed. He might have fallen had Pat Allworth not grabbed him by the arm. "Are you unwell, Sir Nigel? Dear me, is it the heat of the day? Jet lag, maybe? Why don't you rest for a few moments?"

Sir Nigel Bellingham burped. Pat recoiled. Whispers ran through the crowd.

"Bear in mind, Sir Henry," said a deep voice from the midst of the onlookers. People stepped aside to let Eddie through. I'd thought him too modern and too handsome, with his playful California-surfer-boy looks, to play Sherlock Holmes, but gravitas settled over his shoulders like an Inverness cape as he recited the lines.

People turned from watching Sir Nigel being led away to Eddie performing.

I glanced at Jayne beside me. She was beaming, and the light of love—or at least the light of momentary infatuation—shone in her eyes. *Oh, dear.*

Nigel was helped to a chair at the patio table. Someone produced a glass of water. Gerald leaned over him, while Pat and Rebecca, each more furious than the other, watched. I edged closer in a brazen attempt to listen in.

"Quite all right now," Nigel said.

"Give him a few minutes," Gerald said. "He'll be fine shortly."

"He'll be fine," Pat said, "when he sobers up. Although that doesn't appear to ever happen."

"Perhaps it's the heat." Rebecca saw me watching. "Gemma, do you have any food left over? I expect Sir Nigel didn't have a thing to eat, he was so involved in chatting to his guests. One of those nice sandwiches would help settle him."

"I'll find something," I said.

The kitchen was quiet. I put two roast beef sandwiches on a plate, tucked in a napkin, and carried the food outside. Gerald took the plate out of my hand and mumbled something that might have been, "Thank you." Then again, it also might have been, "Get lost." Pat and Rebecca had left the two men alone.

Thunderous applause, appreciation mixed with relief that the climax of the afternoon had been saved, broke out. Eddie took a deep bow. "Let's hear it once again for the master chef herself, the source of our delightful tea, Miss Jayne Wilson."

Blushing furiously, Jayne stepped forward. Eddie swept up her hand and pressed it to his lips. More applause, more clicking of cameras and smartphones. Irene had cleared out before the tea, so at least the tale of Sir Nigel's fumbling failure at acting wouldn't make the front page of tomorrow's *Star*. Renee stood on the sidelines, ignored, phone in hand, glaring at Eddie and Jayne.

Gradually, people began to leave. The bar was closed and the food cleared away, but a handful of guests lingered. A young couple walked hand in hand across the lawn to the water's edge. Eddie and the other actors, some of whom I hadn't met, continued chatting to admirers. Renee had put her phone away and was flirting playfully with two elderly gentlemen. Donald was talking to Grant, no doubt asking him if he wanted to buy a playbill. Jayne and Jocelyn had melted back into the kitchen, and Fiona herded the volunteers as they gathered up the rest of the dishes and table linens. Rebecca stood at the side gate, bidding her guests good-bye, and Pat was deep in conversation with a man I'd noticed earlier. He was in his late forties, permanently tanned, with manicured hands and perfect teeth. His few strands of graying hair were pulled off his face and tied at the back of his head into a man-bun. The watch around his left wrist was a Rolex Oyster, and a thick link of gold chains circled his right. He wore pink Bermuda shorts, a white golf shirt, and handmade Italian loafers without socks. He didn't appear to have come with anyone and had spent most of the party by himself, simply observing everything. Other than a casual greeting or polite exchange, he'd engaged in conversation only with Pat, who spent a lot of her time with him. Fussing around him, I would say.

Sir Nigel sat at the table, all alone, nursing a glass of water. Even Gerald had momentarily disappeared. I was heading in Nigel's direction, planning to ask if he needed anything, when Leslie Wilson marched across the patio with strong determined steps, her face set into hard lines. She stopped in front of Nigel and stood close, very close, to him. "It's time for you to hear a few truths," she said.

I left them alone and went into the kitchen to help Jayne pack up her dishes. The volunteers were gathered around the table, enjoying their sandwiches and the leftover pastries and chattering about the day. "You did good," I said.

"I did. Oh, and the tea went okay too." Jayne laughed. "Isn't Eddie an absolute dream?"

"Only if you like the handsome, charming type," I said, and she laughed again.

Before much longer, the rented dishes were packed away, the leftover food either eaten or wrapped up as a treat for husbands, and the volunteers said their good-byes. Fiona and Jocelyn collected Mrs. Hudson's serving trays and most of the special tea sets and placed the boxes by the back door, ready to be taken out to the van, while Jayne put leaves of Darjeeling into the Sherlock Holmes pot and added freshly boiled water. She then produced a plastic container with a secret stash of scones and poured the tea into four of the Holmes cups she'd held back. "I don't know about you," she said, "but I'm starving."

Fiona, Jocelyn, Jayne, and I lifted our cups in a toast.

After the chaos of the past three hours, Rebecca's kitchen was almost as sterile as it had been when we entered. We talked about highlights of the afternoon as we sipped tea and ate. "I hope they do this again next year," Fiona said. "A couple of out-of-town guests asked me for the address of the tea room."

"Good publicity for sure," Jayne said.

Pat came into the kitchen, her star-shaped heels clattering on the ceramic tile. "Has Nigel been in here?"

"No. Not all day as far as I know," Jayne said. "Is he lost?"

"I've ordered a van to take the cast to their hotels, and we're ready to go. But I can't find him." She swore heartily.

"Perhaps he took a taxi earlier," Jayne said.

"Gerald didn't call one for him. I'm starting to get the impression that Nigel doesn't do a thing, can't do a thing, for himself."

"He's probably ashamed of fluffing his lines," Fiona said. "So he snuck off without telling Gerald or anyone else."

Pat looked doubtful.

"Where did you see him last?" I asked.

"I left him at the patio table. I was so furious I didn't dare stay a minute longer."

Jayne got to her feet. "I'll check the library and the living room. Perhaps he . . . uh . . . dozed off in there."

"Passed out more like it," Pat said. "I'll get Rebecca to search upstairs. He might have decided to go for a nap. Did you see anyone talking to him after I left him?"

Leslie Wilson. Who, I realized, also hadn't been seen since. She hadn't joined the volunteers in the kitchen for their snack. I put my teacup down. "I'll have a look outside. Maybe he went for a stroll in the woods."

Pat muttered a bad word and stomped out.

Jayne and I exchanged a look and headed in different directions.

The cast and crew, minus Sir Nigel, were milling impatiently in a group. "Leave him to find his own way back," the iron-haired woman who'd been introduced as the wardrobe mistress said. "I've already lost most of a day on this nonsense."

Renee was checking her phone. One of the male actors tapped his watch. "I'll wait in the kitchen," Eddie said.

"Call me when we're ready to go." He gave me a wink as he passed me.

A handful of guests, unwilling to see the party end, lingered. The bar was closed, the patio table empty. The party tent, with its bare tables and pushed back chairs, looked sad and lonely. A few sea gulls hopped about on the ground in search of fallen crumbs.

I stood at the edge of the lawn, debating which way to go to start my search. Grant saw me and hurried over. "Everything okay, Gemma?"

"Hard as it is to believe, they appear to have lost Sir Nigel."

He laughed. Then he read my face. "You're not joking."

I plunged into the woods to the right at a rapid clip, and Grant followed. The property was extensive, but it wasn't exactly in a wilderness. The surrounding woods were tame and well-maintained. In the shelter of the pine trees, all was cool and quiet. "Nigel!" I called. "It's time to leave. They're also searching the house," I said to Grant. "He's probably fallen asleep on a couch or something."

"Nigel!" Grant shouted. "Come out, come out wherever you are." He dropped his voice. "I'm glad I caught you before you left, Gemma. Are you free for dinner tonight?"

"That would be nice," I said. "After today, I need someone to cook for me. As long as it's a late one—I just finished a couple of scones."

He patted his flat belly. "I stuffed myself with scones, sandwiches, and cookies. Wow, they were good. I lucked out and got a table with a couple on a gluten-free diet. While they plucked the grapes and strawberries off the display, scooped the filling out of the fruit tarts, and pretended they weren't at all desperate to dive into those sandwiches, I gorged."

I laughed. "Gluten-free, afternoon tea is not."

"And," he said, "as an added bonus, they showed genuine interest in collecting rare books, and I gave them my card."

We walked through the woods toward the sea, calling Nigel's name. Frankly, if not for the fact that the last time I'd seen him he'd been confronted by Jayne's mum, who seemed prepared to take no more nonsense (and what did she mean, *hear a few truths?*) from him, I wouldn't have bothered with this search. Let his PA and the theater people deal with him.

I was dead tired, but before going home and putting my feet up (and now getting ready to go out to dinner), I still had to pop into the shop, check with Ashleigh on how the day had been, and go through the end-of-day routine.

The trees ended abruptly, and we stepped out of the woods onto a rocky cliff. The sparkling blue waters of the Atlantic Ocean spread before us.

"Beautiful spot," Grant said. Below, waves crashed on the rocky beach.

"Sure is." I was about to turn away when something caught my eye. A scrap of cloth, caught on the branches of a thin bush. A paisley cravat. Grant reached out to pluck it off the bush. "Isn't this . . . ?"

I grabbed his hand. "Don't touch." A patch of grass had been pressed down, as though trodden on. A dying bush at the edge of the cliff was bent over, it's branch half-broken. "Something happened here."

"I don't see anything," he said.

Out of the corner of my eye, I caught a glimpse of another scrap of cloth lifted on the breeze. A torn piece of pink ruching was caught on the sharp thorn of a bush. I made no move toward it and didn't point it out to Grant.

"Stay there. Don't move." I stepped carefully toward the edge of the cliff, watching where I put my feet. It hadn't rained in a week, and the ground was dry, but the mark of a man's shoe print was visible in the dirt, and tuffs of grass were compressed.

I stood at the edge of the cliff and looked down. The tide was coming in, and the surf was rough. The cliff wasn't very high—they aren't along this stretch of the coast—not more than twenty feet. Not high, but high enough. The rocky beach was only a couple of feet wide, and water crashed against a row of boulders.

A man lay on the beach below me. His face was pressed into the ground, and the incoming waves lapped at his head. He wore a seersucker suit, and he was not moving.

Chapter 5

Grant pulled out his phone. While I looked around for the best way of getting down to the beach, he calmly and efficiently told the 9-1-1 operator what we'd found.

"Go up to the house and meet them," I said.

"We have to check on him. He might still be alive. There must be some way down."

"I can do that," I said. "You run for help."

"I'm not leaving you here alone, Gemma."

"Whoever did this, if anyone did, is long gone. Someone has to tell Rebecca Stanton and the others what's going on and lead the emergency personnel here. We don't want them crashing around in the woods, wasting time trying to find us."

"You go up to the house then, and I'll stay here. It looks as though he fell by accident, but that might not be the case. If someone . . . pushed him, you can't be sure they've left."

Actually, I could be sure. The woods were cleared of brush and undergrowth; trees in reach of freezing salty spray were too thin and scraggly to conceal a person. Sea gulls flew low over the beach, and a crow cawed at us from the top branches of the dying pine that had snagged the edges of cloth. Pink ruching that I'd last seen on the aprons made by Leslie Wilson for her volunteers. Otherwise, all was quiet. Nothing but Grant and me, and the body below, to attract the attention of the birds.

"Please, Grant," I said. "Don't argue. Time's passing. The police will be arriving any moment and putting everyone into a panic." I pulled my phone out of my trouser pocket and held it up. "I'll keep this in hand in case I need to call."

Doubt crossed his eyes, and for a moment, I thought he was going to argue. Instead he gave me one last look before turning and running into the woods.

I wanted to take some pictures of the scene, but I feared the police would want to check my phone. I studied my surroundings, trying to take it all in as quickly as I could. Then I snatched the ruching off the tree and stuffed it into my pocket along with my phone.

I was well aware that I had interfered with a crime scene, and that that was a crime in itself.

Was it a crime scene? Perhaps not. Nigel might have gotten too close to the edge of the cliff and, in his drunken state, slipped and fallen. He might have done himself in, driven by shame at the botched performance. But until I found out who'd been wearing the torn apron, I'd keep that detail to myself.

I didn't have time to examine the area around me. Among the dirt and rocks and a few dead leaves blown in on the wind, only the single print of a man's shoe seemed significant. About thirty yards away, the cliff edge softened and sloped, rather than plunged, down to the beach. I ran toward it and picked my way carefully down, slipping and sliding on loose rocks, disturbing the ground and snapping small branches as I grabbed them for support. Nigel wasn't moving, but the incoming tide was beginning to wash his face.

I dropped to my haunches beside him. I touched the side of his neck and felt nothing stir. I knew I shouldn't move him, but with the water rising, I had no choice in case he clung to life. I turned him over.

His eyes were so blank, I knew immediately he was dead.

"Gemma Doyle!" Someone shouted my name. I got to my feet and yelled back. Grant's head popped over the cliff edge first, followed by that of a man in uniform, as well as leftover party guests. I pointed to where I'd found access to the beach. The first uniformed officer on the scene was Officer Richter. He was overweight, underexercised, and had suffered a minor heart attack recently. I'd heard he was off sick and had hoped he'd slip gently into retirement. No such luck. I prepared myself to give chest compressions if he tried to get down that cliff, but wisely he stayed back while others clambered down.

Two paramedics reached me first, equipment bags thrown over their shoulders. "You're too late," I said.

"Still gotta try," they replied and got to work. I left them to their task. It was impossible to tell if anyone had recently walked across these rocks or through the rapidly filling tidal pools. Not even a trace of my passing showed. As I scrambled back up, thankful that I'd worn trainers today rather than sandals or heels, I passed a young female officer climbing down. "You were the one who found him?" she asked me.

"Yes. I had to turn him over. His face would soon have been completely in the water."

"The detectives will want to talk to you." She continued on her way.

By the time I reached the top, Richter was stringing a line of yellow police tape from tree to tree, and telling the onlookers to keep back. This was a respectable group, so most of them did as they were told. The actors, including Eddie and Renee, stood together, whispering among themselves, while Rebecca pushed her way through the crowd. I didn't see Gerald. "Nigel! Is it Nigel? Has something happened to Nigel?"

"I can't say," Richter told her. "Step away, please." Rebecca did so, but Renee left Eddie and attempted to cross the tape. Richter grabbed her arm. "I said stay back."

I hurried over. "Nigel's had a . . . fall." I kept my voice low, speaking only to the two women.

"Is he okay?" Rebecca asked.

I gave my head a slight shake. Renee groaned, and Rebecca visibly paled under her light tan and perfect makeup.

Jayne and her mum stood among the onlookers. Jayne's face was curious, Leslie's stricken. She was not wearing her apron. I headed toward them, intending to get the heck out of Dodge, but Richter shouted at me. "You! Doyle! Don't move. The detectives are on their way. They'll want to talk to you."

I put my hand on my heart and swayed slightly. Grant wrapped an arm around me, and I gave him a weak smile, making sure my face was turned toward Richter so he could see my distress. "I . . . I," I said.

"Let me take her up to the house," Grant said. "She's about to faint."

"My orders are to keep the witnesses here," Richter replied.

"We aren't witnesses," Grant said. "We didn't see what happened."

Richter hesitated. If he couldn't make a decision, then I'd have to do it for him. I swayed once again. "She needs to sit down," Grant said. "Either here or at the hospital. Your call, buddy."

"Okay, take her to the house. But no farther."

Grant half-carried me into the woods. Jayne and her mum hurried after us, and curious onlookers watched us go. From out on the lawn, I heard Pat cry, "Nigel! What's happened to Nigel?" as she hurried across the grass toward the cliff.

As soon as the trees closed around us, I pulled myself out of Grant's arms. I felt a slight tinge of regret at having to do so. It had felt very nice indeed to be there.

"Okay," I said. "Nigel's dead. It might have been an accident, but then again it might not have been. Leslie, you're coming with me. Grant, stay here and find out what the police are saying, if anything."

"You're okay?" Leslie said. "You scared me there."

"Scared me too," Grant said. "That was all an act?"

"I don't care to be involved in police investigations," I said. "When I tell them what I have observed, they have a tendency not to believe me. It would appear as though I, once again, have no choice. If I have to wait for them, I prefer to do it in comfort. Jayne, stay with Grant."

"Why?"

I didn't answer. I headed toward the house, making sure Leslie followed. I hoped to have a few minutes in private to ask her about the apron ribbon. Leslie and all five of her volunteers, including Mrs. Franklin in her walker, had worn the same style of homemade apron, so the one that had snagged on a dead tree branch might not belong to Leslie. But as far as I knew, the last person seen with Nigel had been my best friend's mother.

We weren't fast enough. As we emerged from the woods, who did I see approaching but two West London PD detectives.

The only thing I hate more than police incompetence is police efficiency.

One of the approaching officers was Ryan Ashburton. When I think of Ryan and me the word that comes to mind is "toast." And not in the sense of enjoying hot buttered toast and marmalade on the balcony wearing dressing gowns, sipping coffee or tea, and reading the morning papers while watching the sun come up over the ocean. But toast, as in finished.

Ryan gave me a wide smile, but Detective Louise Estrada groaned and said, "Not you again."

"Me again. Don't worry, I'm not involved. I just happened to be here, serving tea. You'll want to go that way." I pointed. "He's . . . it's on the beach at the bottom of the cliff. You can either cross the lawn or take the path through the woods."

At that highly unfortunate moment, police radios crackled, and Richter's voice, efficient for one dratted time, said, "Detective Ashburton, I've said Gemma Doyle could go up to the house because she didn't look well. She's the one who found the body."

Police radios usually sound as though aliens are using them while attempting to speak to us from the farthest reaches of outer space, but this time the voice at the other end came over loud and clear. We all heard it. Leslie gasped. "Is it a body? I . . . I hoped . . . Are they sure?"

Ryan gave her a sympathetic look. "It would seem so, Mrs. Wilson."

I placed my hand on her arm. "I'm sorry."

Her face crumbled, and tears began to flow.

Estrada gave me a look that would frighten small children. "Not involved?"

"You look perfectly well to me," Ryan said.

"A temporary fainting fit," I said.

"I doubt you've fainted a day in your life," Estrada said.

"What's been going on here?" Ryan asked. "Looks like a wedding or something."

"An afternoon tea fund-raiser for the theater festival. Mrs. Hudson's catered." I pointed to my apron. "I helped."

"Mrs. Wilson," Ryan asked, "were you a guest here?"

It came as no surprise that they knew each other. Like Jayne, Ryan was West London born and raised.

"I'm on the volunteer committee." Her voice trembled, but it was no act. I could feel her body shaking. "I . . . I can't believe it. Nigel. We were just . . ."

"It's been a heck of a shock," I said. "Can we go somewhere and sit down? Please?"

"If you found the body, then we need to talk to you," Estrada said. "Before you and your friends can get your stories straight."

"I have no *story* to get straight, Detective." Other than the removing evidence from the scene part, that is. "If you ask me a question, I'll answer it."

The first time we met, Louise Estrada and I had not exactly got off on the right foot. She thought I'd killed a woman and wanted to arrest me. Our relationship had gone downhill from there. She didn't like me and she didn't trust me, and I didn't fully understand why.

"I need an officer here," Ryan said into his radio. "I want to check out the scene first, then I'll talk to you, Gemma. The initial call said two people discovered the body. Were you the other one, Mrs. Wilson?"

She shook her head. "I didn't . . ."

"I was with Grant Thompson," I said.

Ryan's eyes narrowed ever so slightly. Ryan and I had once been . . . close. Our relationship had ended, and he'd moved to Boston. He'd come back a few months ago, but we hadn't taken up where we'd so abruptly left off. Maybe that's why Estrada didn't like me. I'd never gotten the sense of any chemistry between them, other than as work colleagues, or the impression that she liked him more than she should. He didn't appear to have personal feelings for her one way or the other. Irene Talbot told me Estrada had expected to be offered the promotion to lead detective when that post became available, but then Ryan abruptly returned to West London and got the job over her. Maybe the reason she didn't like me was that she thought he'd come back to be with me. Which he hadn't.

All of that was neither here nor there at the moment.

"Grant and I were together because everyone was searching for a missing guest. Sir Nigel Bellingham, star of this summer's theater festival, had disappeared after the tea. That's all."

"You don't have to explain to me, Gemma," he said.

"Actually, you do," Estrada said. "As the two of you just happened to come across the body."

"Is it this Nigel fellow who you found, Gemma?" Ryan asked. I nodded.

"Was he a friend of yours, Mrs. Wilson?" Ryan said.

"No. I mean . . . no, he wasn't. But I admired his acting so very much."

Officer Stella Johnson broke out of the woods at a trot, and Estrada waved her over. "Take these women into the house. They're not to talk to anyone until we've had a chance to interview them."

"Mrs. Wilson can go home," I said. "She didn't see anything. She just followed everyone else who followed the paramedics and the police through the woods."

"Mrs. Wilson," Estrada said, "can go home when I say so. No one leaves here until we talk to them."

"How many people were at this fund-raiser, Gemma?" Ryan asked.

"One hundred and eight ticket holders, twelve members of the cast, crew, or festival office, six volunteers, including Leslie here, Jayne, me, and two staff from the tea room."

"That would be . . ." Estrada tried to count. She struggled not to tick the numbers off on her fingers.

"One hundred and thirty people. Most of whom have left already," I said.

"One hundred and thirty." Ryan groaned. He gave his head a shake and spoke to Officer Johnson. "See that Gemma

Doyle stays put until I can talk to her." He headed into the woods. Estrada threw me another poisonous look before following him.

Leslie and I headed for the house in the company of the uniformed police woman. Leslie pulled a tissue out of her pocket, blew her nose, and wiped her eyes.

Gerald came around a corner as we reached the patio. "What's happening? Why are all these police here?"

"Where have you been?" I asked.

"Making a call to my mother in England, if you must know." He eyed the policewoman with us and shifted the weight of his bag. "She likes me to check in regularly when I'm traveling with Sir Nigel."

"When did you last see him?" I asked.

"Not since he was . . . uh . . . overcome with vertigo after the tea and needed a private moment to compose himself. What's going on?"

"Let's go," the policewoman said. "You were told to wait in the kitchen. And no talking. Sir, you are not to leave the property until one of the detectives has spoken to you."

"Detectives!" He clutched his bag closer. "What . . . ?"

"Find Pat or Rebecca," I said to Gerald, "and get them to explain."

We went into the house, leaving Gerald standing open-mouthed on the patio.

"Would you care for a cup of tea, Stella?" Leslie asked the officer. "I'm going to have one."

"Okay, thanks. That would be nice."

No, it would not. I needed to get Leslie away from the listening ears of the police before she said anything she might regret. "Why don't you go and get Jayne," I said. "She can help me with the things. Perhaps all the officers would like something."

"Detective Ashburton said she was to stay here," Johnson said.

"No, he said I was to remain here. And I will do so."

Leslie twisted the tissue in her hands and stared off into space. *Was she upset at the death of Nigel Bellingham or upset at having killed him?* I shoved the thought away. It was entirely possible Leslie had argued with Nigel, and either she'd shoved him in the chest, tipping him over the edge, or he'd backed up and gone over accidentally. If that had happened, she would have run to the house, screaming for help.

Leslie Wilson would not have walked away, leaving a man lying alone at the bottom of the cliff in the face of the incoming tide, and pretended to know nothing about it.

I rubbed at the scrap of cloth in my pocket. "Leslie," I prompted. "You're going to fetch Jayne?"

Johnson opened her mouth as if to argue, so I said, "Uncle Arthur's trip is lasting longer than he expected. I hope your grandmother was able to find another euchre partner."

"Card partner, yes," Johnson said, "but she does love your uncle's company. An unmarried man isn't so easy to come by at her age."

My attempt at distraction failed, as before I could get rid of Leslie, the French doors opened and Rebecca and Jayne came in.

"Detective Ashburton told me I could make tea and lay out some of the leftover food," Jayne said. "He and Estrada are down at the beach, and they've said no one can leave until they've given a statement."

"Got it," Johnson said.

"Brilliant!" I said. "Leslie, give Jayne a hand."

"As you've packed up the catering dishes without washing them," Rebecca said, "you might as well use mine." She opened a cupboard door to reveal white mugs perfectly arranged, all the handles pointing in the same direction. Next, she opened the fridge. Aside from a couple of condiment bottles in the door racks, a container of milk, and a single bag of coffee beans, it was as empty and glaringly white as the High Arctic in winter. She pulled out the coffee and handed the bag to me. Presumably it would be my task to prepare the drinks. I wondered if Rebecca even knew how to use the machine.

I certainly didn't. I'm mostly a tea drinker, but I make coffee on occasion. When I do, I use a French press and pre-ground beans, not one of these space-age contraptions. I studied it carefully, searching for the on switch. Officer Johnson pushed me aside. "I'll do it."

"We're to set the things up outside," Jayne said. "Ryan doesn't want anyone coming into the house."

And possibly sneaking out the front. I had to admit, the thought had crossed my mind.

"If they want me," Rebecca said, "I'll be in the living room. This has all been most difficult. Leslie, why don't you join me? I'm sure your daughter and her friend can handle the refreshments."

Leslie hesitated, and I jumped in. "Good idea. You need to sit down, Leslie."

"Thank you," Leslie said. "It has been a shock."

We didn't have much left in the way of food, but we made big pots of tea and coffee. I helped Jayne carry everything outside. A group of party guests and some of the actors were seated at the patio table. Eddie leapt up to help Jayne with her tray. "I wanted to come inside and see if you're okay, but he"—Eddie nodded to an officer guarding the door and listening in on potential witnesses—"said no admittance."

"Not even to us," Fiona said. Jocelyn took the tray from Eddie, and they set out the mugs and plates.

"Thanks," Jayne said. "I'm fine. It's upsetting, but it has nothing to do with me. You must be devastated, Eddie. You must all be. What will this do to the production, do you think? Will they continue with the play?"

Eddie shook his head. "I don't know." He swallowed a sob. "It's up to Rebecca and Pat and the festival directors. Right now, it doesn't seem to matter much." He looked grief-stricken, and I reminded myself that Eddie was a professional actor. One who had a great deal to gain from the death of Sir Nigel Bellingham. If the play continued, the understudy would take the main role.

Word that refreshments were being served must have drifted down to the cliffside, and people started coming back to the house.

Rebecca was inside with Leslie. Most of the remaining members of the festival had gathered on the patio and around the bar, as had a handful of guests and Leslie's volunteers, except for Mrs. Franklin, whose son had picked her up before the drama began. It made a lot of people for the police to get statements from. I watched Louise Estrada moving through the crowd, taking down names and phone numbers. I overheard someone say Pat was at the cliffside, insisting on remaining until Nigel was taken away. Donald had left earlier, forgetting his coat, and I hadn't seen the chap with the pink shorts and the man-bun in a while. Estrada turned her head and looked directly at me. I went back to the kitchen.

Jayne stood at the sink filling a kettle. Johnson had been called outside to help Estrada.

"What's the matter?" Jayne whispered to me.

"What do you mean, what's the matter? A man's dead. Quite possibly murdered."

"You're as jumpy as . . . well, as a cat on a hot tin roof. Eddie's got a role in that play."

"I am not jumpy," I said. "I'm tired, and I want to go home."

She studied my face. I forced out a smile. "Gemma, do you know something about this?"

"What would I know?" I was horrified that she seemed to be reading my thoughts. That would never do.

"You seem to be awfully concerned about Mom."

"Not concerned, just . . ."

"When you're at a loss for words, Gemma, I know something's up. What?"

I was saved from having to find an answer when the door opened once again and Ryan and Estrada came in.

"Will you leave us, please, Ms. Wilson?" Estrada said.

Jayne fled.

The detectives didn't look at each other as they crossed the kitchen floor and pulled stools up to the breakfast bar.

The air between the two of them was so electrified, the coffeemaker was in danger of a power surge. They'd been arguing, and it was easy to guess what they'd been arguing about. Me. Not long ago, Ryan had been taken off a case when Estrada had told their boss that Ryan and my past relationship had destroyed his impartiality. I suspected she'd tried the same tactic again and had been overruled on the grounds that I was not a suspect this time but the person who came across the body, and that in the company of another person. Although, in Estrada's mind, I probably was still a suspect. Fortunately, I had not the slightest reason to want to kill Sir Nigel Bellingham.

I kept my hands out of my pockets and took a seat.

"We've spoken to Grant Thompson," Ryan said. "He told us his version of the story. Do you want to tell us what happened?"

I quickly related the sequence of events. Pat reporting that they couldn't find Nigel. People heading off to search the house and grounds. Me volunteering to search the woods. Grant joining me. I didn't say he'd asked me out to dinner, as that was not the least bit relevant, only that he'd volunteered to accompany me to help with the search. We discovered the body, Grant called 9-1-1 immediately and then ran to guide the first responders to the scene. I climbed down to the beach, realizing that if Nigel was alive, his face had to be taken out of the approaching water.

"Why did you look over the cliff?" Estrada said. "You could see from the woods that he wasn't standing there."

"We saw the cravat caught on a bush. You did find it, didn't you?"

"Yes, we found it," she said. "Hard to miss. It has been identified by several people as the one Bellingham was wearing all afternoon."

I didn't pretend to be grieving or in shock. I kept my voice calm and neutral and my English accent level. I suspect Estrada thought I sometimes put on airs. I wondered if she watched *Downton Abbey*. I try hard not to sound like Lady Mary Crawley at her snootiest, but my mother's influence does sometimes slip through.

Ryan asked me if I'd seen anyone in the woods, and I answered truthfully, adding that I hadn't heard anyone either.

"Did you see signs of any tensions or disagreements among the people here today? Particularly between Bellingham and anyone else?"

"That would be an understatement," I said. I told the police everything, leaving out only the few angry words I'd overheard Leslie say to Nigel.

"That's what we've been told," Estrada said. "He drank too much and made a fool of himself in front of a hundred people who'd paid two hundred bucks each to meet him."

"That's about it," I said. "Have you met his PA, Gerald . . . ? Sorry, I don't know his last name."

"Greene," Estrada said.

"Tell me about him," Ryan said.

"I've nothing to tell. His job was to follow Nigel around and do what he was told to do. He'll be the person here closest to Nigel, and the one most likely to know if he had any problems or was worried about anything. Have you considered that this might be a suicide? Maybe Nigel realized his glory days are long past and decided to end it all. Gerald might be able to tell you about Nigel's state of mind these days."

"I don't need you to tell me how to do my job," Estrada said.

"We're considering all possibilities," Ryan said. "Including that he got too close to the edge and slipped, although that's unlikely. That cliff edge is solid; I tested it myself. But as several people have told us, the man was falling-down drunk. Did you see any sign of drug use, Gemma?"

"No," I said. "Alcohol was his poison. It was obvious he'd been drinking before coming into the bookshop on Wednesday early in the afternoon, although everyone politely pretended not to notice. This afternoon, it probably didn't help that he was a heavy smoker, and Rebecca ordered him not to light up. He might have drank even more than usual to compensate."

"Was Bellingham given the same food and drink as everyone else here?" Ryan asked.

"If you're asking if he might have been deliberately poisoned," I replied, "that's not possible. The food was prepared by Jayne and her staff, including me, at Mrs. Hudson's, brought here, and laid out on three-tiered trays about this big." I illustrated with my hands. "The trays were carried down to the tables by our volunteer helpers. All the trays contained the same food and were distributed randomly. Nothing was prepared separately for Nigel or anyone else. Two trays were put on each table, and the guests picked off the trays themselves. The tea was served in pots made in the kitchen, not prepared in individual cups." I'd been wandering from table to table with my pot of decaf green tea. I called up a mental image of the head table. "Nigel Bellingham didn't eat a thing. Nor did he have any tea," I said.

"How do you know that?" Estrada asked. Always with the suspicions. *Must make for a very tedious life.*

"Because I observed, Detective. You might try doing that someday."

She bristled, and Ryan said, "Gemma," in a low voice.

"All I mean," I said, "is that's what I saw. He put no food on his plate, and his teacup remained empty."

"With a hundred and eight guests, you can tell me what one person ate," Estrada said.

"In this case, it's understandable," Ryan said. "Nigel Bellingham was the star of the show."

Estrada grumbled something that I decided to take as an apology.

"He drank instead," I continued. "Pretty much constantly, but as with the food and tea, the Prosecco was shared. Bottles were kept in the fridge, and when opened, they were put in an ice bucket on the bar. Glasses were circulated by volunteers acting as waiters before the tea, but wine was not served at the tables. After they sat down, if anyone wanted a glass, they had to go to the bar to fetch it for themselves." I called up the scene again. "I don't think anyone did, except for Nigel, who had Gerald running back and forth with a fill-up."

"So this Gerald was in possession of Nigel's glass?"

I nodded.

"The glass is . . . ?"

"They'll be by the outside bar, waiting for the rental company to collect them. We didn't wash them. There was, I'll add, nothing individual about Nigel's glass. They were all the same."

Ryan nodded to Estrada, and she spoke into her radio, telling someone to collect the glasses.

"You must have set the tables before everyone sat down, and I noticed place cards," Estrada said. "People would have known where Bellingham was going to sit, and which would be his cup and plate."

I really didn't want to give up Jayne's beloved Sherlock Holmes-themed tea set, but I had no choice. "The dishes at Nigel's table were ours—I mean, from Mrs. Hudson's. The rest were rented because we don't have enough for a crowd of that size. We used our special china for the head table." I nodded toward the box by the door. "But as I said, he didn't have anything to eat or drink."

"As you said," she repeated. "We'll take that box with us."

"Does anything else here belong to you? To the tea room?" Ryan asked.

"The plastic containers, serving trays, and teapots are ours."

"Leave them here. You can take your personal belongings, such as your purses, but nothing else. I'll let you know when you can pick them up."

"We can't operate a tea room without teapots," I said. "We brought almost every one we have."

"Can't be helped," Ryan said. "We may not need to analyze them, but I won't know if that's necessary until I finish interviewing the witnesses."

"The man didn't die by poisoning," I pointed out. "He fell to his death."

"Right now, Gemma, I don't know what I'm dealing with. As you pointed out, he might not have been murdered at all. I'm not going to secure the dishes, but I don't want them leaving the premises until I'm sure I don't need them."

I didn't bother to argue. My main aim at the moment was to keep them from searching *me*. And finding the pink ribbon hidden at the bottom of my pocket.

"Did you take any pictures today?" he added.

"Yes. I used Jayne's camera because we hoped to get some photos we could use for advertising. I didn't take any of specific people though—mostly the tables and the place settings."

"Where's the camera now?"

I pointed toward Jayne's bag on the floor by the back door. Next to her mother's.

Estrada rummaged around inside it and found the camera. She didn't look at Leslie's bag. "We'll take this. What about your personal phone?"

"I didn't use it."

She held out her hand. *Suspicious sort.* "Let me see."

I could have put up an argument, told her she'd have to get a warrant, but I didn't. I'd save my rousing defense of the law for a more suitable time. Still, I wasn't going to have her pawing through my phone. I unlocked it and opened the photos app. The most recent picture was of Violet playing in the backyard. She'd been caught in midair, her long ears flying, as she leapt for a ball. Outside of the warm light cast by the carriage-house lamps over our garage, all was dark. I held the phone up. "As you can see, this is the most recent picture. It was taken at night. Nothing today."

"You might have deleted them."

"I've been kinda busy here, Detective. I didn't take any photographs."

"We have plenty," Ryan said. "Lots of people took pictures."

At last, they told me I could go home, as could Jayne, Fiona, and Jocelyn. I hopped off the stool.

"Don't leave town without checking with us first," Estrada said. "We'll have further questions."

"I'm not going anywhere. It's the busiest time of year in the shop."

"See that you don't."

I avoided rolling my eyes. Ryan hefted the box containing our themed tea sets and carried it outside, leaving me alone in the kitchen.

Leslie's tote bag, the one she'd brought the volunteer aprons in, lay on the floor next to the back door. I picked up a box full of the plastic containers we'd used to bring the food to the house, and carried it across the room to the back door. I put it on the floor, neatly in place for the police and scooped up Leslie's bag to put it on the counter next to the sink. I glanced around the kitchen, making sure all was clean and organized. And not at all incidentally, checking that no one was peering in through the windows. I opened Leslie's bag and went quickly through it. There were six white aprons with pink ruching. Five of the aprons had intact appliqué, but on the sixth, a section of the ruching along the hem had been torn off, leaving the remaining end hanging loose. I stuffed all the aprons back in the bag and went to tell Jayne we were ready to leave.

Chapter 6

My phone had buzzed with an incoming text while I'd been talking to the police, but I'd refrained from checking it. As soon as they left and I'd examined the volunteers' aprons, I pulled it out of my pocket. Grant, telling me the police said he could leave and he'd made a reservation at the Blue Water Café for eight thirty.

I found Jayne standing with her mom on the patio, watching the police activity. Most of the guests had left, and the police were taking statements from the few remaining stragglers. I didn't see any of the theater people. Yellow crime scene tape fluttered in the breeze, sealing off the entrance to the woods.

Jayne and Leslie turned as I opened the French doors and stepped onto the patio. Leslie's face was very pale and her eyes, so like those of her daughter, were rimmed red. Jayne had her arm around Leslie's shoulders. They gave me identical sad smiles. "Can we go now?" Jayne asked.

"Yes."

"Thank heavens," Leslie said. "I don't remember when I've last been so exhausted. Rebecca was kind enough to let me sit with her, but I couldn't stay still so I came back outside."

"They've taken the Sherlock tea set," I said.

"Who has?" Jayne asked.

"The cops. They want to check for poison or something in Nigel's cup. They're also going to analyze every one of the champagne flutes. I told them that's a waste of time. All the food and drink came from shared sources, and nothing Nigel used was separated ahead of time. Still, it's their time to waste."

Leslie lifted a hand to her mouth.

"He wasn't poisoned," Jayne said. "He jumped off a cliff, isn't that obvious? He made a fool of himself in front of a hundred of Cape Cod's most influential people. Are you okay, Mom?"

Leslie didn't look okay. If anything, she'd turned even paler and fresh tears threatened to flow.

"Did you come on your own?" I asked her.

"What?"

"I asked if you drove here."

"Oh, yes. I did."

"I'll drive you home. Jayne can follow us and pick me up."

"It's out of your way," Leslie said.

"I don't mind." I will admit I had an ulterior motive. I wanted to get Leslie on her own and find out what happened between her and the late Sir Nigel Bellingham.

She shook her head and gave me a weak smile. She pulled a tattered tissue out of her pocket and wiped at her eyes. "I'm perfectly fine. Heavens, Gemma, you were the one who found the body. You need someone with you more than I do. Jayne, be sure you look after Gemma. As for me, a hot shower followed by a glass of wine on the back deck will be just the ticket. I won't even cook tonight. I have some things in the freezer I can reheat."

The issue had been so neatly deflected, I couldn't have done better myself. I couldn't now continue to argue that Leslie needed me to accompany her.

Jayne called to Fiona and Jocelyn. "Let's get our things and get out of here."

"Uh . . . about that," I said. "The police said we're not to remove anything except our personal bags."

"What?" Jayne said. "I need my teapots."

I shrugged. "Detective Ashburton's orders."

"He can't do that." Jayne looked around. "Where is he? I need to talk to him."

"Leave it," I said. "I have a couple of teapots at my house. I'm sure we all do." Fiona and Jocelyn nodded. "We can manage with borrowed pots for a day or two."

"I'm not using that ugly Brown Betty of yours in my tea room, Gemma Doyle."

"It's a teapot, Jayne. It will suffice to serve tea. Let's not stand here arguing. We do not want any more police attention directed our way."

We went into the house, gathered up the last of our personal belongings, and left by the back door. Leslie Wilson swept up her tote bag containing the aprons.

Jayne walked her mom to her car and then we drove off. Police cars, cruisers and unmarked, filled the wide driveway in front of the house. Officer Johnson was stationed at the front gate, preventing the curious from entering. She gave us a wave as we drove slowly past. We turned left, back to town. In the rearview mirror, I watched Leslie Wilson peel off to the right.

"That was fun," Jocelyn said.

"You think?" Jayne said. "A man died, I'll remind you."

"Well, it was fun up until then. I didn't get much of a chance to have a look around the house, but what I saw was absolutely fabulous. What an amazing kitchen. I'd love to have a garden like that."

"And have garden parties," Fiona said.

"Too much work keeping up a place that size," Jayne said.

"If you can afford a house and garden like that, Jayne," Fiona said, "you can afford to hire staff."

"Instead of being the staff." Jocelyn sighed. "Like me."

"Like us," I said. "We all work for a living."

"All except for Moriarty," Jocelyn said. "In my next life, I want to be a shop cat." In this life, Jocelyn was a young mother with two kids and a husband known to be a frequent visitor to McGillivray's Irish Pub.

"Anyway," Jocelyn said. "It was fun until the end. I hope we can get more gigs like that."

"Rebecca was pleased," Jayne said. "She's going to pass our name on to some of her friends."

Jocelyn squealed in delight. I was delighted too, although I refrained from squealing. Jayne had worked hard to make Mrs. Hudson's a success, and referrals among the well-connected, afternoon-tea-party-giving set would be a nice bonus. As long as she didn't try to rope me into helping.

"It was great meeting the actors too," Fiona said. "They were so polite and friendly, even to us. They didn't have to be nice to us."

"It's too bad that guy, Sir Nigel, died," Jocelyn said, "but he wasn't nice."

"No," Fiona agreed.

"What do you mean?" I asked.

"He smiled at the guests and was oh-so-charming," Jocelyn said, "but the minute they walked away, he'd have something snarky to say about the way the women were dressed or the men talked. I heard him call that woman in the red print dress and matching shawl a fat cow."

"She wasn't fat," Fiona said, "but her dress was way too tight. I wasn't there when he insulted that actress by saying she was too old, but I heard all about it. I wasn't surprised. He was sure rude to me. He snapped at me to get him a glass of wine, and when I said we were serving tea and the wine was self-serve at the bar, he made a crack about not getting good help in the colonies. The people at his table laughed, but you could tell they were embarrassed."

"Rebecca Stanton kept her eye on him all afternoon," Fiona added. "She looked absolutely furious most of the time. He was drunk. I bet he'd been drinking before he even arrived."

"Come on, guys," Jayne said. "The man's dead. Give him some respect."

Jocelyn and Fiona were momentary chastised, and then they went on to gossip about the other guests.

I cursed Jayne under my breath. *What's wrong with speaking ill of the dead anyway if you'd have no problem speaking ill of them in life?* I wanted to hear more about Nigel Bellingham's last hours on this earth, and it seemed as though not much of it was going to be favorable.

We pulled into the alley behind the bakery.

"I cannot believe you let the cops take my Sherlock tea sets," Jayne said.

"What was I supposed to do, throw myself on them? Grab them and take off, pursued by a pack of howling dogs? I'd have been unlikely to get far, running down the street lugging a box of bone china teapots and cups while taking care not to break them. The police take whatever they want from a murder scene. They didn't need my permission."

Jocelyn and Fiona whirled around. "Murder!" Jocelyn said. "We thought it was an accident. He was so drunk, I figured he'd walked off the cliff without noticing it right under his feet."

"Or rather, *not* right under his feet," Fiona said. "Kinda like Wile E. Coyote."

"I only mean they're investigating all possibilities, as is normal procedure in a suspicious death," I said. *Was it murder?* I was pretty sure it was. Unlikely Nigel would have headed off into the woods for a solitary walk, not in his state. The woods were too far from the bar, for one thing. He had to have been lured there, by someone wanting a private chat perhaps. *Someone like Leslie Wilson?* I shoved that thought aside. The possibilities were just about endless. Nigel had not been a popular guy.

Then again, perhaps I have a suspicious mind, and it had been an accident after all.

"I sure hope I get my pictures back," Jayne said. "I had a quick peek at the ones you took, Gemma, and they were great. If we ever want to expand into catering parties, pictures from today will be good promotion."

"Why'd they want them?" Fiona asked. "Do the cops want to learn the proper setting of afternoon tea?"

"They asked everyone for their photos," I said. "In case someone caught an image of something significant. Maybe without knowing what they were seeing."

Fiona and Jocelyn bade us good-bye, and Jayne headed for the kitchen to do whatever she had to do to get ready for opening the tea room tomorrow. I went into the Emporium.

By now it was half seven. I'd phoned to tell Ashleigh I was delayed, although I hadn't said why. Obviously, that hadn't been necessary. She greeted me by saying, "Wow! Sir Nigel Bellingham died at your high tea thing."

Moriarty jumped onto the counter. His ears were up, and his intelligent amber eyes shone with interest. Even the cat wanted to hear all the details.

"Afternoon tea," I said, "is not the same as high tea."

"Whatever. Do the cops know what happened?" Her eyes opened wide. "Do you think that piece of paper he signed for my granddad will be worth something now? It might be the last time he wrote his autograph."

"I don't know, but I wouldn't go around suggesting his death has been to your advantage, if I were you."

Her mouth snapped shut.

"Not until it's all cleared up, anyway."

"What are the cops saying?" she asked. "Do they think he was murdered? Who do they think did it?"

"I don't know. Have you been busy?"

"Do you think they'll want to interview me?"

"Why would they do that? Do you know anything?"

"I was here Wednesday when he came in. I can tell them how the other people around him acted. Like his PA, that skinny guy? You could tell that he and Sir Nigel were really close."

"You could tell that, could you? How has business been today? The bookshelves look quite undisturbed."

"A lot of people came in between when you left and dinnertime. They bought plenty of books. I found more upstairs and put them out. I hope that's all right?"

"Perfect. Thank you. I'm dead beat, and I want to go home. Do you think you can close up by yourself tonight?"

"Sure! No problem."

Moriarty nodded his agreement.

I dragged myself the few blocks home. Not only had it been a long day and I'd been kept on my toes serving tea, but I find sparring with the police not a relaxing activity. The West London Police Department and I have what might be called a history. A professional one in addition to my personal relationship with Ryan Ashburton. Ryan and I had met a few years ago—before Uncle Arthur, Jayne, and I opened the tea room—when a string of arsons plagued the shops on Baker Street. I attempted to help the police by telling them the minor details I'd observed among my fellow business owners, one in particular. West London's finest had repaid the performance of my civic duty by marching me down to the station, fingerprinting and photographing me (in highly unflattering light), and accusing me of being the guilty party because apparently I knew too much about details the police had not released to the public.

All I knew was what I had observed and the logical conclusions I had come to.

I'd been able to persuade Ryan, if not his superior officers, to act on my tip, and the next time the arsonist attempted to burn down a store, he was caught red-handed.

Thoughts of the past faded as I turned onto the path to my house. It was coming up to eight o'clock, but even in my tired state, I felt myself smiling. I share the house with Great Uncle Arthur, and it's big enough for the two of us to lead separate lives when we want to. He keeps a private apartment on the second level, and I fill the much larger ground floor. It's far too much house for the two of us, but we love it. Built in 1784, it's a classic colonial saltbox, meaning two stories at the front and one at the back. The exterior of the house could be used on the set of a historical movie, but the interior is thoroughly modernized, although the renovations had maintained many of the house's best features: the wide-planked redwood floors, foot-high baseboards, and a dramatic, sweeping oak staircase. The yard is small, and the lovely garden is maintained by a friend of Arthur's who moved into an apartment when her husband died but then found she missed her favorite hobby.

I went around the back and through the mudroom as usual, to be greeted by a wildly enthusiastic Violet.

Now I was home, the last thing I wanted was to go out again. One of Uncle Arthur's rich beef stews with thick gravy and plenty of plump mushrooms, pulled out of the freezer and reheated, followed by a long read curled up in the den, was exactly what I needed tonight. I'd brought *The Whole Art of Detection* by Lyndsay Faye home from the bookstore and was eager to dive into it. I'm not a Sherlock Holmes fanatic. I can't discuss at length every bit of minutiae of the Great Detective's (fictional) life or debate (with quotes from the books) whether he was a woman in disguise (I thought that highly unlikely), but I do enjoy a well-written novel, and many of the pastiche books were just that.

Now that I was home, I only wanted to stay home. But I'd accepted Grant's dinner invitation, and it would be impolite to cancel at the last minute.

I didn't have time to take Violet for a walk, so I promised her one later and let her into the enclosed backyard. I kicked off my trainers, took off my black clothes suitable for serving tea and tossed them into the laundry hamper, and hopped into the shower. I didn't worry too much about what to wear for dinner. Summer in Cape Cod is very casual, and we were dining alfresco.

My phone rang, and Irene Talbot's name popped up on the display. I let it go to voice mail. She'd want the scoop on what I knew about the death of Sir Nigel Bellingham, and what little I did know, I wasn't planning on telling anyone, particularly not the newspapers.

Irene's call reminded me: I dug through the laundry basket and pulled out the trousers I'd been wearing this afternoon. I took the scrap of pink ruching out of the pocket and placed it in the palm of my hand. Any one of the six volunteers could have worn the apron it belonged to. They appeared to be identical, and all were the same size. The aprons themselves had been mass-produced and store-bought: plain white, knee length with a bib and a sash that tied at the back. Leslie had bought the aprons and added the pink trim to make them more attractive. The aprons were plain cotton. It might be possible to get fingerprints off the surface, perhaps even some DNA. Leslie's fingerprints would be on all the aprons, as would many others. I'd seen some of the women tying each other's sash or helping to adjust the bib. The police would have no way of knowing who'd worn the damaged apron. At the end of the party, the volunteers took off their aprons and left them in the kitchen, where anyone passing would have had access to them.

I thought back over the volunteers. Highly unlikely Mrs. Franklin and her walker had gone for a stroll to the cliff, never mind shoved a man over. That left, aside from Leslie, four others. I'd not seen any of them interacting with Nigel or showing any undue interest in him. They'd done their jobs efficiently and had seemed to be enjoying themselves. Only one apron-wearing woman had argued with Sir Nigel: Jayne's mother. The same woman who was the last person I'd seen with him before his death. Leslie had been distracted and upset most of the afternoon.

I did not believe Leslie had killed Nigel. Therefore my reasoning was sound: this scrap of pink cloth torn from a mass-produced white apron could not provide a clue to the identity of Nigel's killer. Assuming, that is, he had been murdered.

My reasoning was sound. But the police were highly unlikely to agree with me. They tended to want to draw their own conclusions.

I decided to look at it this way: I'd be helping the police by not allowing them to get distracted by a triviality that would lead nowhere. I wasn't, however, prepared to destroy the evidence. Not yet.

I went down the hall to my office and found a plain white envelope. I slipped the cloth into the envelope, took it to the den and locked it inside the safe. Uncle Arthur and I don't have anything that needs to be protected by a safe, but it had come with the house, embedded in the thick brick walls. We'd hung a portrait over it.

I fed Violet, told her not to wait up, and walked down to the harbor. The summer night was approaching, and the sky over the ocean to the east was inky black; behind me, it was streaked with shades of red, pink, and gray.

The Blue Water Café sits on the edge of West London's small boat harbor close to the fish pier. In the off-season, it's warm and cozy and small. In summers, it more than doubles in size when the doors are thrown open to a spacious deck resting on pylons jutting out over the water. I pride myself on being punctual, but tonight I'd been delayed, debating what to do about the pink cloth, and arrived five minutes late to find Grant already seated. He jumped to his feet with a wide smile as I made my way across the deck. The restaurant was full tonight, as it would be most evenings for the next few months. Lights shone from tiny bulbs wrapped around the railing, and on the tables, white candles flickered in hurricane lamps.

"Quite the exciting afternoon," Grant said as I took my seat.

"More excitement than we would have liked."

"The tea was great though. Everyone I spoke to enjoyed it very much. As they say, there's a silver lining in every cloud, and in this case, you can be sure people will remember you when they're planning an event."

"It has also been said, there's no such thing as bad publicity. About that, I disagree. We don't want to be remembered as people who catered an event where someone died."

The water arrived and we placed drink orders. Grant accepted a menu but I waved it away. I always have the same thing at the café. The fish doesn't get any fresher than here: from the restaurant's deck, you can watch the day's catch being unloaded and the sleek gray fur of seals bobbing through the water searching for scraps. "I thank you for the sentiment and for trying to cheer me up."

"Do you need cheering up?" Grant asked.

"No. I didn't know Nigel, and I didn't much like what little I did see of him."

We leaned back to allow the waiter to place our drinks on the table. A frosty mug of Nantucket Grey Lady for Grant, a New Zealand Sauvignon Blanc for me. Grant ordered Caesar salad followed by a steak, medium rare. I asked for clam chowder and the stuffed sole.

We clinked glasses and said, "Cheers."

"I heard the word murder bandied about this afternoon," Grant said. "What do you think happened?"

"I have no idea."

"Are you going to get involved?"

"Involved in what?"

"In the case. You did those other times."

"The first time, I was directly affected. Detective Estrada thought I'd done it. The second time, Donald Morris asked me for help. This time, I'm not even a witness. Merely the person unfortunate enough, as were you, to come across the body. No, it has nothing to do with me. If you don't mind, I'd rather not talk about it." I was thinking of little else, but talking was another matter altogether. The pink ruching would remain in my safe, tucked away in the wall behind the portrait of a glamorous opera singer I believe had been Uncle Arthur's one true love. I remembered Leslie's words to Nigel: "It's time." Plenty of people spoke to Nigel that afternoon, and not all of them were friendly. It meant nothing. So I told myself. Nothing other than the pink ruching connected Jayne's mum to the dead man; I had no reason to get involved.

"There's Jayne now," Grant said. I turned to see my friend crossing the deck, following the hostess. To my surprise, she was with Eddie Barker, the actor. I knew they'd arranged a date for tonight, but I would have expected him to cancel it after what happened this afternoon. I wasn't happy to see him out with my friend. He had a lot to gain from the death of Sir Nigel, and that put him pretty high on my suspect list.

Not that I was keeping a suspect list.

Jayne saw us and waved. She said something to the hostess, and they changed direction to come our way. The people at the table for two next to ours were fumbling with their wallets and laboriously calculating the tip.

"Mind if we join you?" Jayne said. She looked lovely and fresh in a blue dress the color of her eyes with a thin white belt and low-heeled sandals.

Grant hesitated. He obviously didn't want the company but didn't know how to say so politely. Understandable if he thought we were on a date. *Were we?* I didn't know. In order not to have to make a decision about that, even to myself, I waved to the nearly vacated table. "Good timing."

"I'll get this cleared away," the hostess said.

The other couple left and Jayne sat down. Eddie looked about as thrilled as Grant at the change in seating arrangements.

"How's everyone handling the death of Nigel?" I asked him.

"Gemma," Jayne said, "that's a bit blunt."

"It is? It's what we're all thinking about."

"I'm not thinking about it," Eddie said.

"Sure you are," I said.

"Gemma," Jayne said in that warning voice I know so well.

"I'm thinking it's a nice night in a beautiful place, and I'm with a beautiful woman." Eddie smiled at Jayne. She smiled back. I mentally rolled my eyes. "Two beautiful women," he added politely.

"You're not really from California," I said. "Mississippi would be my guess. Louisiana, maybe."

Grant smothered a laugh with a mouthful of beer.

"You've a good ear," Eddie said. "I've worked hard to get rid of that accent." His smile didn't reach his eyes.

"Sorry about your marriage breaking up," I said.

"What the . . . ?"

"Gemma's observant," Jayne said quickly. "I bet she noticed a tan line on the ring finger of your left hand or something." She involuntarily glanced across the table; Eddie slipped the guilty hand into his lap. *Guilty because his marriage wasn't entirely over?*

"Good evening," the waiter said. "Can I get you something to drink?"

"Will the play go on?" I asked once the waiter had left with their orders, as well as a request for another round for Grant and me.

"Pat wants it to," Eddie said, "as a memorial to Sir Nigel, and Rebecca agrees." He lowered his eyes for a moment in a gesture of respect.

"With you in the lead role," I said.

He lifted his head, and his eyes bored into mine. The carefully arranged length of sun-kissed (in a hair salon) blond hair moved in the breeze. "That will be up to the director. She knows best."

"Have you been to Cape Cod before, Eddie?" Grant asked. "If not, I can recommend some places worth a visit on your days off."

"We won't be getting many days off, I'm afraid, but I'd like that. No, I've never been here. I'm from the west"—a glance at me—"I mean, the south."

"Where are you staying?" Grant asked.

Eddie sighed. "We're at a B and B for the duration. The Sailor's Delight. What a chintzy name. Nice enough, I guess, but I hate B and Bs. You're expected to make friendly with a bunch of strangers over breakfast. Nigel and Gerald got themselves put up at the Harbor Inn. Now that Nigel's not using it, I might ask if I can move in."

"Did he get a particularly nice room?" I asked.

"Nothing but the best suite. With an adjoining room for Gerald. I'm surprised they bothered with that."

"Why?" I asked.

"I'd have thought they'd roll out a camp cot in the hall-way for Gerald. Guy's a wimp if ever I saw one."

"I'm sure you've seen a lot of them in your time."

"What's that supposed to mean?"

"Nothing." I sipped my wine.

Jayne stood up. "I'm going to powder my nose. Gemma?"

"What?"

"Do you need to come also?"

"No."

"Yes, you do."

"I do?"

She glared at me and jerked her head toward the back.

"Oh, right. I need to powder my nose. I totally forgot to do that before leaving the house." I pushed myself to my feet and followed the angry tap of Jayne's heels on the wooden deck.

"Why don't you just say you're going to the loo?" I said to her back. "They know we don't need to apply face powder in unison."

The moment we walked into the building itself, Jayne turned on me. "What do you think you're doing?"

"Doing? In regards to what?"

"I'm used to you deducing things about people they'd rather you didn't know, but tonight you're being out-and-out rude. If Eddie wants people to think he's from California, what does it matter? Why did you challenge him on it? Never mind that bit about being divorced."

"I don't think you should be going out with him."

"Why on earth not? And why on earth should I care what you think?"

"For one thing, I doubt he's divorced. Easy enough to check. He'll have a bio on IMDb. I'll look him up on the Internet when I get home."

"You'll do nothing of the sort, Gemma Doyle. I like him, and he seems to like me, and I want it to lead where it might. I do not want your interference. Do. You. Understand?"

"Jayne, he's a possible suspect in a murder."

"He's not a suspect. Yes, he was there, but so were a lot of people. I was there. You were there. Even my mom was there."

"Uh, right. I don't think it's wise for you to get involved with an actor." We were standing in the hallway leading to the restrooms, close to the open kitchen. Staff passed us with trays piled high with food. I saw my clam chowder and Grant's Caesar salad sail past. "There's Andy." I called out, and he glanced up from a sizzling frying pan. I gave him a wave. He waved back. When he saw Jayne with me, his face lit up. He said something to a young woman, and she took over the frying pan. Andy wiped his hands on his apron and came out of the kitchen.

"Nice to see you, Gemma. Hi, Jayne. Are you here for dinner?"

"Why, yes," I said, "we are. I bet you could use a break right about now. Why don't you and Jayne take a few moments for a quiet drink? We're here with a couple of friends; they won't mind."

Andy looked hopeful. Jayne looked shocked.

"Don't try to change the subject." She turned to Andy. "Will you take a rain check? I hope you don't mind, but

Gemma and I are having an important business meeting here, and she's trying to weasel her way out of it."

Andy tried not to look too downcast. "Rain check it is. Any time at all." He slunk back into the mysterious depths of his kitchen.

I hadn't been changing the subject at all. I simply thought Andy a far better match for Jayne than some passing actor, who may or may not be divorced.

"Gemma, please don't get involved in my love life."

"Would I do that?"

"Repeatedly and constantly. I'll admit Robbie might have been a little bit of a mistake."

"A little bit."

"But Eddie is not Robbie. He's sooo good looking for one thing, and he's doing really well as an actor. He's met all sorts of great people. Leonardo DiCaprio, Johnny Depp, Kristen Stewart."

I considered pointing out that his career wasn't exactly on the path of DiCaprio and Depp if he was playing the under-study for a summer repertory theater in Cape Cod, and that "met" didn't mean "working beside," but I bit my tongue. Jayne didn't often get angry with me, but she was heading there now, and at a rapid clip.

All I had at heart were her best interests, particularly if Eddie was going to be involved in a police investigation. "Okay," I said.

"What?"

"Okay. You win. I'll let you make your own mistakes. I mean, your own decisions." I smiled at her.

She did not smile back. "I don't know what you're doing here with Grant, anyway. Suppose Ryan sees you."

"What would that matter?"

"If you don't know, Gemma, I am not going to tell you." She headed back outside. Apparently her nose didn't need powdering after all.

Chapter 7

Once again, I was woken by the ringing of the phone at some ungodly hour.

I hadn't gotten to bed too late, perhaps because our dinner hadn't been entirely comfortable. Eddie and Grant didn't want to be seated with another couple, and Jayne was still cross with me. Only I seemed to be enjoying my meal. When I finished my coffee and announced that it was time for me to be off home, Eddie barely restrained himself from punching the air in delight.

Grant walked me home, but I didn't invite him in, and he didn't seem to mind. I didn't know what my feelings were for him, if I had any beyond friendship, but that wasn't the only reason. It had been a long, emotional day.

I took Violet for a turn around the block and then went to bed, where I read *The Whole Art of Detection* until I fell asleep, looking forward to tomorrow. Sunday's my favorite day of the week. I love to swim, and I live minutes away from the ocean, but the summer's so busy at work I rarely get a chance to enjoy the beach in the heat of the day. On Sundays, the shop doesn't open until noon, and it closes at five, making it the one chance I get to have a swim at a reasonable hour. I planned on enjoying a leisurely cup of tea and a proper English breakfast over the online papers before heading to Nantucket Sound with my chair and umbrella, swimming costume, and book. After work, Violet and I would enjoy a long walk along the wilder section of the coast.

Instead, I fumbled for the phone, almost knocked it off the night table, and finally mumbled, "Hello." The bedside clock said it was quarter to eight.

"Gemma!" Jayne yelled. "You have to come. Now. The police have arrested my mother."

That woke me up all right. I sat up. "What! Why? When? Where are you?"

"She just called me. They were on the doorstep first thing, and they've taken her down to the police station."

"Did they actually arrest her—read her her rights and everything—or just ask her to come with them?"

"I don't know. She didn't say. I'm heading to the station now. Can you meet me there?"

"What do you want me to do?" I shoved the covers aside and jumped out of bed. Violet watched me with great interest.

"Maybe you can talk to Ryan—Detective Ashburton. Tell him my mom doesn't know anything about this."

"I don't think he'll listen to me, Jayne."

"Sure he will." She hung up.

I dressed quickly in whatever clothes happened to come to hand. I ran a comb through my unruly curls and tied my hair back with a clip. I couldn't leave without letting Violet out, so I tapped my foot impatiently while she checked behind all the bushes and through every patch of impatiens for signs of invading squirrels or other unwelcome nighttime visitors. Finally, she finished her morning ablutions and security check and trotted back inside. I don't normally drive into town, but I didn't know what else I might be expected to do today, so I decided to take the car. Uncle Arthur's prized blue 1977 Triumph Spitfire 1500 was safely stored in the garage, and my red Mazda Miata sat in the driveway.

I found Jayne pacing up and down in the lobby of the police station, still wearing her gray baking apron. A streak of flour ran across her left cheek, and flakes of dough stuck to her fingers.

She greeted me with a wail and a huge hug. When I finally freed myself from her death grip, I said, "What's happening?"

"They won't let me see her." Jayne sobbed. "They told me she's not under arrest 'at this time.'" She made quotation marks in the air with her fingers. "She's answering questions."

"Do you know a good solicitor?"

Her blue eyes opened wide. "You mean a lawyer? Do you think we need one?"

"I don't know what's going on, Jayne, but you might. It wouldn't hurt to find one and put him or her on standby." I led her to a row of cheap plastic chairs against the wall. We were in the outer area of the police station, watched over by a scowling officer seated behind a glass partition. The air conditioning was turned up so high, if we had to stay here very long, I might have to go home to get my winter coat. "You need to get back to work," I said. "I can stay here and let you know as soon as I hear anything."

She shook her head. "No. I'm good. Thanks for coming down." She slipped her hand into mine. "I'm sorry I got mad at you last night."

"What happened after I left?" I asked. Believe me, I didn't want to know, but I lit on the first available subject in an attempt to distract Jayne from her worries.

"It was lovely." Some of the worry cleared from her face. "We had another drink, then some coffee. We talked and talked for ages. He's so nice, Gemma. And so interesting. Makes me almost wish I hadn't let Mom talk me out of going into acting. We went for a walk along the boardwalk. So romantic. Then he walked me home. He kissed me goodnight on the doorstep. Wasn't that sweet?" She sighed happily. But then she remembered where we were, and why, and the blissful look disappeared from her face. "I'm sorry I panicked, Gemma. This is routine, I suppose. The police will be asking everyone who was at the tea to come in for questioning."

That, I doubted. They had to have some reason for focusing on Leslie Wilson.

It wasn't the torn apron, so it had to be something else.

Had someone seen her and Nigel at the edge of the cliff? Overheard them arguing? Had Leslie threatened Nigel?

If Leslie was charged, I'd truly be in a pickle. I'd removed evidence from a crime scene. Should I confess now or wait to see what happened next?

I reminded myself that the person I needed to worry about right now was Jayne. Jayne and her mum. Any pickle I might find myself in would be incidental.

At that moment, we heard voices coming from the inner sanctum. Jayne and I leapt to our feet. Detectives Ashburton and Estrada walked on either side of Leslie. Ryan was six foot three, and Estrada not much under six feet. Leslie looked like a schoolgirl between them. A very frightened schoolgirl.

The door opened and she rushed into Jayne's arms.

"What brings you here, Ms. Doyle?" Estrada said. "I don't see that this is any of your business."

"Of course it's my business," I said. "Jayne's my friend as well as my business partner. I am here to provide support. I assume Mrs. Wilson is free to go."

"For now," Estrada said. I didn't care much for the tone in her voice. I glanced at Ryan. He returned my look, but I could read nothing in his face. And that, I feared, was not a good thing.

"Mrs. Wilson has been told she's not to leave the town of West London," Estrada said, "as we will no doubt have further questions for her." She turned and walked away. She pointedly held the door for Ryan. "Detective Ashburton, a moment of your time, please."

"If I know what the problem is, perhaps I can be of help," I said.

"If I want your help," Estrada snapped, "I'll ask for it."

"Stay out of it, Gemma," Ryan said, his voice low. The last time murder had struck our little town, Ryan asked me for my unofficial help. He trusted me and my observations, even if his partner and his chief did not. I searched his face, looking for a sign that he didn't mean what he was saying now, but I didn't see it. He turned and walked away.

"Let's go home, Mom," Jayne said.

We walked outside, Jayne's arm around her mother's shoulders. The inside of the police station was so cold, literally as well as figuratively, that I was momentarily taken aback when the hot sun hit our faces. I pulled my sunglasses out of my bag. "I brought my car, so I can drive you home, Leslie."

"Thank you, dear. It was good of you to come down."

"There isn't room for the three of us in the Miata," Jayne pointed out.

"You have to get back to work anyway," I said. "Isn't Sunday morning one of the busiest times of the week at Mrs. Hudson's?"

"Well, yes. Tourists like to stock up on treats to take on the road or indulge themselves with a nice breakfast before leaving. But . . ."

"As the Emporium doesn't open until noon today, I have the time."

"I can't ask you . . ." Leslie began.

"Of course you can. I'm happy to help," I said. Jayne held one of her mother's arms. I took the free one and pulled. Jayne held on, and I feared we were about to get into a tug of war with Mrs. Wilson as the rope.

"Gemma's right," Leslie said. "You need to get back to work, honey, and stop worrying about me. The detectives had a few questions about what I might have seen yesterday. That's all. They'll want to talk to everyone. I can imagine Rebecca Stanton's face when she's asked to report to the police station." She laughed. It came out more like a strangled howl, and Jayne didn't look entirely convinced.

"That's settled then. See you later, Jayne." I had to stop myself from breaking into a run, dragging Leslie Wilson behind me.

"I . . ." Jayne's feeble protest faded behind us.

As the Miata roared out of the police station parking lot, I caught a glimpse of a tall, lean figure standing at the window of one of the offices watching us. Ryan Ashburton.

The top of the car was up, but Leslie didn't seem inclined to engage in conversation. She sunk low in her seat and stared out the window at the passing scenery. I doubt she was appreciating the view or the beauty of the day.

Her house was about ten miles outside of town on a residential street not far from Nantucket Sound. The house had been built sometime in the 1960s, a small home on a big piece of property.

I pulled into the driveway.

"Thank you, Gemma." Leslie unbuckled her seat belt. "You're a good friend to Jayne."

"I hope I'm a good friend to you too."

She touched my hand, and then she opened the car door and swung her legs around. She had not invited me to come in. I'd have to handle that myself. "I'd love a cup of tea."

"Pardon me?"

"I ran out of the house when I got Jayne's call and didn't have time for so much as a mouthful of water, never mind a cup of tea. I'm absolutely parched."

Good manners. How I love them. I watched the struggle on Leslie's face. She didn't want to talk to me, but she couldn't bluntly tell me to go away.

I opened my own door.

"Do come in, Gemma," she said. "I'd enjoy a cup also."

The side door of the house opened directly onto the kitchen. A dog—a big, shaggy, drooling, friendly mutt—ran to greet us. I gave him a hearty pat.

"That's Rufus," Leslie said. "Don't let him jump on you."

"What breed of dog is he?" I asked. He sniffed at my legs, catching traces of Violet.

"Heaven only knows. There might be a standard poodle in there somewhere. Maybe some labrador or golden retriever. He was a rescue dog. Take a seat, and I'll get the tea."

The room was spotlessly clean, everything neat and tidy, but it was seriously out of date. Linoleum flooring, turning up slightly at the edges, a scarred round pine table with matching chairs, laminate countertops, tiles on the backsplash featuring pictures of Dutch windmills and fields of tulips. The decor in this room might be old, but it was lived in, far more than Rebecca Stanton's cold, forbidding, ultramodern kitchen. I found it comforting; this was the sort of kitchen in which you knew you'd be served a good, satisfying meal along with plenty of laughter and intelligent conversation.

I sat on one of the pine chairs, and Rufus wandered away to see what Leslie was doing. The kitchen wasn't intended to be stylishly retro. It needed some money spent on it. I hadn't been concentrating too much on the outside of the house, but I had noticed leaking downspouts, paint chipping from window frames, weedy cracks running through the driveway paving, and the edges of tiles lifting off the roof of the detached garage.

Leslie plugged the kettle in and bustled about with mugs and milk and sugar. I sat back and let her bustle. "If you haven't had breakfast, can I make you some toast?" she asked. "A boiled egg?"

"No, thank you. Tea will be fine."

Tea was eventually made and served, and Leslie couldn't put it off any longer. She sat down opposite me and sighed. Rufus dropped to the floor beside her.

"'Double, double toil and trouble,'" I said.

"'Fire burn, and cauldron bubble,'" she replied automatically.

"So it would seem. The police are not bringing everyone who was at the tea yesterday down to the station to take their statements," I said. "That would take far too much time. Why you?"

"It's all a mistake." She kept her eyes on the contents of her teacup.

"Tell me about it."

"You know the police took people's cameras and phones to check pictures that had been taken over the afternoon?"

"They confiscated Jayne's camera, which I used to photograph the table settings."

"Someone had taken a picture of me."

"Go on."

"Of me and Nigel."

"Nigel talked to a lot of people. Working the room was the only reason he had for being there. Therefore something had to be very significant about this one picture."

She lifted her head. For the first time, Leslie looked me in the eye. "We . . . he and I . . . were . . . going into the woods. The background showed that the tea had finished, meaning it was . . . shortly before he . . ."

"Were you wearing your apron in this picture?" I asked.

She studied her tea again. "What do you mean?"

"Just asking. Were you?"

"Yes. It was after he'd embarrassed himself by not remembering his lines. I hadn't taken my apron off yet."

"Who suggested this walk in the woods? You or him?"

"It was my idea. I . . . admired him. As an actor, I mean. I wanted the chance to tell him so privately. The tea was over; our job was finished. I took the opportunity to tell him how much I love his acting. I told the police that. It was nothing. Really, it was nothing! Anyone there would have done the same. It was nothing but sheer bad luck that I was the one caught on camera."

"You wanted to talk about the old days. Your days together on Broadway. Maybe discuss some unfinished business between you."

Her blue eyes, so like Jayne's, stared at me. "How do you . . . ?"

"Jayne told me you'd been an actress in New York. You had a small speaking part in a Broadway production of Shakespeare. But you left the stage abruptly, came home to Cape Cod, and married Jayne's dad. It was obvious, to me anyway, that something lay between you and Nigel. The way you told him your maiden name, as if expecting him to react, how his casual insults and rebuttals offended you on what was obviously a deeply personal level. You and he are of the same generation, although you're few years younger. I read the other night that he appeared on Broadway in the early eighties. He played Macduff in a hugely successful production of Macbeth. Macbeth has few minor female speaking parts, three of which are the witches."

"'Something wicked this way comes . . .'" she mumbled. She twisted her mug in her hands. "Jayne says you're very smart."

"I can put two obvious facts together, that's all."

"Why did you ask about my apron?"

"I noticed yours was torn. I was wondering when that happened." I hadn't noticed any such thing. I hadn't even seen Leslie between observing her and Nigel at the patio table, when she was wearing the apron, and then her joining the crowd at the cliff without the apron. I sipped my own tea and waited.

She said nothing for a long time. "I must have snagged it on a bush or something. I didn't notice until I came back to the house to get ready to leave." She shuddered, and then she began to spill her secret, as I knew she would if I waited long enough.

"You're right, Gemma. Nigel and I. . . . I thought of him as my boyfriend during that run of Macbeth. I played the part of the third witch. I was incredibly lucky to get the role. My first time in a major production. I can't tell you how exciting it was. All my dreams were coming true. And to top it all off, I fell in love with Nigel. Best of all, to have Nigel, the great Nigel Bellingham, fall in love with me. He wasn't a knight then, but he was incredibly famous after *Roman Wars*. Could anything have been more perfect?"

I didn't bother to reply. She snorted. "Of course it could. I knew he was married, but he told me they were in the process of getting a divorce. The line every innocent young actress with stars in her eyes wants to hear. One day, his wife arrived unexpectedly in New York. *Surprise, darling!* He was married to Georgette Raeburn at the time. She was making a movie in Morocco. The desert set was flooded out during unexpected rains, disrupting filming, so she took the opportunity to hop a plane to New York and drop in on *darling* Nigel."

"There was no pending divorce."

"No. Georgette showed up at the theater during Sunday matinee. Nigel made such of fuss of being absolutely thrilled. He totally ignored me. At first, I thought he was pretending, keeping up a front with Georgette, not wanting her to make a scene. When I tried to speak to him the next day, he wouldn't let me into his dressing room. He wouldn't answer the phone if I called. I was frantic. I desperately needed to know what was going on. I needed him to tell me he loved me and we were going to be together forever. There are no scenes between Macduff and the witches, so we were never so much as waiting in the wings together. I caught some of the cast and crew exchanging snickering glances when I passed, but I thought they were just jealous. Then one night, I managed to find out where Nigel and Georgette were going for dinner after the show with the major actors and the producers." Her voice trailed off.

"You followed them."

She nodded. "I can't believe I was ever so young and naïve. So stupid. My plan was to arrive after they were seated and ask the maître d' to summon Nigel to the phone. This was the time—seems so long ago—before cell phones. When Nigel saw me waiting for him, he'd declare his undying love for me, reassure me that it was all a pretext with Georgette, and we'd be together as soon as she went back to Morocco. Nigel didn't come out. He sent Georgette in his place. It wouldn't have been so awful if she'd been angry. Instead, she laughed at me. She said Nigel had a habit of collecting silly little actresses when they were apart, but most of the girls knew how the game was played. She really did think it was terribly funny." A single tear dripped down Leslie's cheek. She made no move to wipe it away.

"He's been married several times since," I said. "I assume their game ended soon enough."

"Oh, yes. Last I heard of Georgette, she married an earl and is now Lady Something-or-other. No loss to stage or screen, I'm sure."

"Did you finish the run of the play?"

"No. Like so many foolish girls before me, I walked for hours that night, thinking about throwing myself into the East River after leaving a dramatic note tucked under a rock on the grass. Instead, I left New York the next morning and came home."

"Because you were pregnant."

She stared at me. "How did you know?"

"That happened thirty-five years ago. You've got a nice life here, I think." I held out my arms to indicate this kitchen, the house, West London. "You have great children—Jayne, anyway. I've never met your son. From what Jayne tells me, you had a happy marriage before your husband's death. But simply thinking about what happened between you and Nigel still has the ability to bring you to tears. We've all been there. Bad relationships, bad men. I left my husband five years ago because he was a lazy, cheating, no-good layabout, but I've gotten over it. I accepted his friendship on Facebook a few months ago, although it came as a surprise that he wanted us to be virtual friends. If you're still upset about what happened all that time ago, it has to be because you were left with something to constantly keep the affair fresh in your mind."

As I talked, I'd done the math. Jayne was thirty-two, the same age as me. The Broadway run of Nigel's Macbeth had ended thirty-five years ago. Nigel Bellingham was not Jayne's father. That came as an enormous relief to me. That was not a secret with which I wanted to be burdened. Jayne had an older brother, however.

The dog sensed something of Leslie's distress. He sat up and laid his big head on her lap while she cried silently. A steady stream of fat tears spilled out of her eyes. She pulled a tissue out of her pocket and blew her nose. "He doesn't know."

"You mean your late husband?"

"No, I mean Jeff, my son. I was pregnant with Jeff when Rick and I married. Rick knew it wasn't his child. He knew about Nigel. He always said it didn't matter. He was a good husband and a good father. Better than I deserved."

"Don't say that," I said sharply. "You did nothing wrong, but it seems to me that you were badly wronged. You never had any contact with Nigel again?"

She shook her head. "Never. Rick and I had dated in the last year of high school. He wanted us to stay together, to make plans to get married in a few more years, but I was convinced I was destined for bigger things than marriage to a West London boy. I broke it off the summer after graduation. He went to college and got a business degree, and I hit the footlights and greasepaint. When I came back to West London, pregnant, ashamed, despondent, we ran into each other. He was still in love with me, he still wanted to marry me, and I"—the edges of her mouth turned up ever so slightly—"discovered that, wonder of wonders, I was still in love with him. We were very happy together."

"And then, all these years later, Nigel, now Sir Nigel, arrives in West London."

"The worm in the apple. Don't get me wrong, Gemma. I had no feelings for Nigel any more. I wasn't about to suggest we run away together and live happily ever after in our declining years. Perhaps all I wanted was for him to acknowledge that he'd hurt me. I wasn't planning to tell him about Jeff. What possible good would that do? If he'd so much as said, 'Nice to see you again, Leslie, as beautiful as ever,' I'd have been content. At first he didn't recognize me. We all age, don't we? Some better than others, and some of us have better memories than others, so I didn't mind too much. I sought him out at the tea, before most of the guests arrived, and I told him who I was. Even then, he didn't remember me at all. He didn't even pretend to remember me. He sneered and said something like, 'One in a long line.'"

"He was not a nice man."

"I was hurt, Gemma. All the horrible, terrible pain that man caused me came rushing back. I cornered him after he made a fool of himself at the tea. I told him we had things to discuss, and I demanded he listen to me. He was drunk; anyone could see that pretty clearly. I saw him for the mess of a man he'd become, but I wanted him to acknowledge that I was more than 'one in a long line.'"

Her attempt at keeping herself composed burst apart, and Leslie began to cry. Great gulps of air, racking sobs, cascading tears. I sipped my tea and waited quietly and patiently for her to compose herself.

Eventually she blew her nose and wiped at her face. "I wasn't going to say anything about Jeff. I didn't even want to. But I did. I threw it in his face. The son he'd never known he had. His only child, who he'd never get to know. You can understand why I wanted us to go into the woods, get away from prying ears, particularly that strange little man who followed him around everywhere."

"Gerald, the PA."

Leslie nodded. "Nigel and I walked into the woods. It was cool, and it was quiet. Nigel listened to what I told him and seemed to sober up right before my eyes. He told me he hasn't had a good life. Four marriages, too many affairs to count, no children. His parents are long dead, and he's estranged from his only sister. Now at the end of his life, he's left with nothing. A dying career, no wife, no family, not even the respect of his peers. I felt sorry for him."

"You shouldn't have," I said. "He managed to turn your story into a pity party for himself."

"Jayne also says you're blunt."

"When I need to be. Allow me to be even more blunt. Did you shove him off the cliff?"

"No, Gemma, I did not. We walked through the woods toward the ocean. The bushes tugged at my clothes, so that must be when my apron tore. We watched the sea and the tide coming in. I said my daughter was waiting, and he said he was glad we'd talked. And he said he was sorry. I told him not to be. I went back to the house and left him standing there. All alone."

"Was he wearing his cravat when you left him?"

She shook her head. "He took it off as we walked and carried it in his hand. He said it was hot. He was holding it when last I saw him."

"Did you see anyone else in the woods, anyone else out for a walk?"

"No. I suspect if a herd of wild elephants stampeded past, I wouldn't have noticed them, I was so deep in thought."

I believed her. I can't say why I was sure, but her story rang true for me. She'd made her peace with Nigel and left him standing alone at the cliffside. If it had not ended well, if they'd quarreled, she'd have aired her grievances to me. She might not confess to having killed him, but she'd want me to know she had reason to do so.

"Did you tell the police all of this?"

"My life story? No. I kept it short and simple, that I admired his acting and wanted to tell him so. That I told him I'd had a minor part in one of his plays many years ago, and we went for a walk to get away from the party and have a little stroll down memory lane." She shifted in her chair and once again studied the mug, now full of cold tea.

"That could be interpreted as simply omitting some unnecessary facts. What did you outright lie to them about, Leslie?"

She was quiet for a long time, and then she said, "I told them we didn't get as far as the water's edge. That we only talked for a minute or so, and I had to get back, so Nigel carried on alone, wanting to see the view from the cliff."

"That was a mistake," I said. "Don't lie to the police. You can decide not to tell them some things, but don't out-and-out lie." Leslie was probably as bad a liar as her daughter.

"Are you going to tell them?"

"It's unlikely they'll ask me." Now I, on the other hand, am an excellent liar. But I try not to make a habit of it.

"If they do, and if it's at all possible, I'd rather you didn't mention what I said. About Jeff, I mean, and about my shotgun marriage to Rick."

"That I'll keep to myself. I promise." It's not my place to tell the police how to do their jobs, particularly when they make it clear they don't want my help. Leslie didn't tell me about her pregnancy until I surmised it. Let the cops do the same. Ryan could, given the right circumstances. Estrada, maybe not. Estrada preferred the blunt approach.

"Thanks for the tea." I stood up. Leslie walked me to the kitchen door. I bent over and gave her a hug. She felt so frail in my arms. When we separated, her eyes were wet once again.

"Don't worry," I said. "Everything will turn out okay."

"I was thinking about Nigel," she said. "Poor Nigel. I loved him once, Gemma, I can't pretend I didn't. He wanted too much. He wanted everything, and he ended up with nothing. Such a sad, sad ending." She rubbed at Rufus's head, and the dog pressed against her leg, providing comfort.

Chapter 8

I'd never been a pet owner until Uncle Arthur showed up one day with a rambunctious six-week-old cocker spaniel. We had no pets as children because my mother is highly allergic to animals, and when I was married and living in London, we were too busy and didn't have room to house a pet larger than a mouse at any rate. I don't care much for rodents.

I'd always told people I didn't see the appeal of pets. Dumb creatures that never grow up, constantly demanding attention and needing feeding and watering and exercise and visits to the vet, along with all the expense that involved. Pets were props, I declared, for emotionally needy people.

The moment Violet gazed at me with her adoring brown eyes, wagged her stubby tail, and licked my outstretched hand, I understood what all the fuss is about.

One benefit of having a dog, I'd learned, is that long walks are a great way to get some thinking done. When I got home from Leslie's, I abandoned the idea of going for a swim and instead laid out the things I'd need for my delayed Sunday breakfast and took Violet for a long walk.

While she sniffed under bushes, ran ahead as far as the leash would allow, or tried to dash across the street to greet a Jack Russell straining at his own leash, I thought about what Leslie had told me. Originally, I'd dismissed the idea that Nigel might have thrown himself off the cliff. He hadn't seemed the suicidal type—whatever type that might be. But now I was reconsidering. He'd drunk far too much, and Leslie had left him sad and dejected, bemoaning his lot in life. Had he decided to end it all in a spectacular leap off the cliff to the rocky shore below?

Possible.

I couldn't take this new theory to the police. According to what Leslie had told them, she and Nigel had a pleasant chat about the good old days, and he'd carried cheerfully on his way when she went back to the house. If I told them that wasn't true, I'd have to say why I knew and then I'd break Leslie's confidence.

I wasn't prepared to do that.

Not yet, anyway.

My phone rang as Violet and I were turning into our driveway. When I saw the caller was Jayne, my heart fell, fearing that the police had arrested her mum properly this time. "What's happened now?"

"Happened? Nothing's happened. Nothing new, anyway."

I let out a sigh of relief. "Glad to hear it. What's up?"

"Are you at home?"

"I'm back from walking Violet and looking forward to the breakfast I didn't get as I had to run out in such a hurry." Sausages, eggs, tomatoes and mushrooms, and toast and marmalade. Yummy. In a nod to healthy eating, the sausages were turkey, not pork; the eggs would be scrambled, not fried; the bread would be out of the toaster, not soaked in melted fat; and the tomatoes and mushrooms would be lightly sautéed in olive oil. But it was still a proper English breakfast, and it was my occasional Sunday indulgence.

"I need you to go around to Rebecca's house," Jayne said.

"Why?"

"Estrada called to tell me they're finished there, and they aren't going to have my serving dishes and teapots forensically examined, so I can have them back. She said other witnesses also testified that Nigel didn't eat or drink anything specially prepared or served to him. Thank heavens for that. I bet you forgot you were going to bring your own teapots in for me, hadn't you?"

"Not at all," I lied. "They're by the door, ready to go."

"We can't have the Holmes dish sets unfortunately. As Nigel was specifically given one of those, they're still at the lab awaiting forensic examination. I hate to think about whatever chemicals they use being spread all over my plates and teacups."

Time was rapidly passing. As it was, I had barely enough time to cook my lovely breakfast and relax over it and the British papers online before dressing for work and heading into town to open the shop. "Can't you go and get them after the tea room closes?"

"I don't want to leave my things there any longer. You have a car. It's just after ten, so you have time before work."

I let myself into the kitchen. Violet made a beeline for her water bowl while I studied the breakfast preparations. The sausage was laid out on the counter next to two extra-large eggs; a thick, ripe red tomato; and a handful of plump white mushrooms. The bread was the heel of a crusty baguette, made by Jayne herself.

"Thanks for taking Mom home," Jayne said. "It was upsetting to both of us, and I don't know why they had to make such a big show of it, but at least that's over and done with. Estrada said she still wants to talk to me. I said I was busy, but I could find a few minutes after the lunch rush if she didn't mind talking in the kitchen. When are they going to interview you?"

I hesitated. That no one had called saying they wanted to talk to me was, I thought, not a good sign. "What time are you meeting with Estrada?"

"One thirty."

"I want to be there. Don't start without me, no matter what she says." I intended to be early, in case Estrada tried to pull a fast one and get Jayne alone.

"Okay. See you later." She hung up, not having given me a chance to tell her I wasn't going to pick up her dishes.

I put the sausage and eggs back in the fridge, and then jumped into the shower and dressed for work. If I got talking to Rebecca, I'd not have time to come home before opening the store.

At the big house overlooking the sea, I parked by the kitchen door. I rang the bell. I hadn't seen any cars in the driveway, but the garage doors were all closed. I tapped my foot and rang again. The tinny sound of the bell echoed back at me. I was about to go around to the front when the door opened.

"Sorry," Rebecca said. "After all these years I still can't tell the ring of one bell from the other in this house. I assume

Jayne sent you to get the last of your things." She was dressed in the summer uniform of a wealthy Cape Cod matron. White capris, blue-and-white striped T-shirt, loads of gold jewelry. Her feet were bare and her toes painted a soft pink.

She stepped back and waved me inside. Before leaving yesterday, we'd returned the kitchen to its immaculate (and apparently never used) state. Our boxes were stacked by the door where I'd left them. Other than that, the only sign of human habitation was a small container of fat-free milk sitting on the counter beside the coffeemaker. Catching sight of the left-out milk, Rebecca hurried to put it away. In the cavernous depths of the fridge, I glimpsed three-quarters of a pizza, wrapped in plastic wrap, all alone on a shelf.

"You have a lovely home," I said politely. "I hope you don't mind, but I noticed some beautiful glass art yesterday when I was hunting for the loo. Chihuly?"

She smiled. "Do you know Dale's work?"

Dale. As though the two of them were great mates or something. Then again, maybe they were. "I know of it. I've been to the Chihuly Center in Florida. Gorgeous stuff."

"Would you like a quick tour?"

"If you have the time, that would be great," I said, as though I hadn't engineered the invitation myself. I didn't know what I hoped to find in Rebecca's house. Nothing probably. But it never hurt to have a look around the vicinity of a crime scene in case the police had missed something.

She led the way out of the kitchen and into the family room. Her home was beautiful, the furnishings and decorations expensive, the taste exquisite, the views unbeatable, but the never-lived-in look made it cold and impersonal.

We went into the library and stood for a few moments, not speaking, simply admiring the blue-and-green chandelier. "It's like living light," I said.

She beamed. "Exactly. I have another in the main hall. It's bigger, but I think I like this one the best. It's the ocean, brought indoors. My late husband bought the first few pieces, and since his death, I've been fortunate enough to acquire more. As you know, Dale works large. Large and flamboyant, like the man himself. Most of his art is enormous, but he does occasionally create some smaller objects. Like this . . ." Her voice trailed off.

We were standing in front of the display case. The large bowl I'd admired yesterday, the one resembling the inside of a sea shell, was still there. It's much smaller companion was not. Nor were the two glass "kisses."

Rebecca's face was a study in shock.

"It's possible," I said. "That one of the guests picked them up to admire and put them back in the wrong place." A quick glance told me that was unlikely to be the case. Everything in this room, probably everything in Rebecca's life, was a picture of order. The books were in a straight line on the shelves, filed in alphabetical order by author name, the rugs perfectly parallel to the walls, the log in the fireplace placed dead center. I checked anyway. I opened cabinets, finding only lead crystal glasses, decanters, and liquor bottles; writing paper, pens, and envelopes; and an iPad in a purple leather cover. No misplaced glass bowl or whimsical ornaments.

Rebecca dropped into one of the wingback chairs. "It's been stolen."

"A smaller version of that bowl and two glass pieces in the shape of chocolate kisses. I noticed them yesterday."

She nodded. "Can you pour me a drink, please, Gemma? There's whisky in that cabinet. My late husband always said a good dram would calm one's nerves."

I took out the bottle of Laphroaig and one heavy crystal glass and poured. "Ice? Water?"

"A drop of water brings out the flavor," she said. "Thank you."

I trotted into the kitchen and poured water directly from the tap. I didn't like leaving her before I'd had time to search the room, but I didn't see that I could refuse the woman a drop of water. When I got back, she was sitting exactly as I'd left her. I handed her the glass, and she twisted it in her perfectly manicured fingers, studying the smoky depths.

"Is anything else missing?" I asked.

"Not that I can see. Not in this room, anyway. We'll have to search the house. I have some nice pieces in the living room."

"The iPad wasn't taken."

"Perhaps the thief only had an eye for art." She groaned and sipped her drink. "I can't believe that I opened my house for charity, and someone came in and stole from me."

"It might turn up," I said, although I didn't believe it.

Rebecca tossed the contents of her glass down her throat, and then put it onto the table beside her with a solid thud. She stood up. "Call the police. I'm going to check the rest of the house."

I didn't call 9-1-1 but instead punched in a very familiar number.

"Gemma. This is a surprise," Ryan said. "What's up?"

"I'm at the Stanton home, and it appears as though there's been a robbery." I trotted after Rebecca as I talked. "You'd better come over. I know you're busy with the Bellingham death, but if this happened yesterday during the tea, it might be connected."

To Ryan's credit, he never said, "Are you sure?"

"On my way," he said. He also didn't bother to tell me not to touch anything. First of all, that wasn't necessary, and second, it wouldn't have mattered. I'd touch what I wanted to touch, thank you very much, and I wouldn't touch anything else. He knew that too.

We walked quickly through the dining room, which accessed the kitchen via another door, down the hallway, and into the living room. My taste agreed with Rebecca's. As lovely as the red-and-gold Chihuly chandelier in the front hall was, it wasn't as beautiful as the smaller one in the library. The paintings on the walls, soft watercolors of ocean views mostly, looked original and expensive. They hung as straight as though they were measured with a plumb line every morning, and there were no gaping spaces with a nail in the center indicating that anything had been taken. A tiny bronze statue of a woman resting on a garden bench with her book sat on a table by the front door. It was small enough to fit into a handbag, and I found it significant that it hadn't been pinched. Either the thief hadn't gotten this far into the house or they were only interested in Chihuly.

Rebecca stood in the middle of the living room—decorated in feminine shades of cream with gold accents—looking around. I'd thrust my hands into my pockets as soon as we left the library. I hadn't been in any of the other rooms yesterday, and I didn't want to risk leaving fresh fingerprints.

I read Rebecca's face. "Nothing's been taken."

"Not that I can tell."

"Did you see the missing pieces after the party?"

"I can't say I noticed. I was tired by the time the last of the guests and the police finally left. If you hadn't asked to see them, it might have been a few days before I realized they were missing. I don't go into the library often. It was more Ron's room."

"Did you have any visitors after we all left yesterday?"

"No. I ordered a pizza for dinner, but I met the deliveryman at the door."

"Did your maid come in this morning? It looks as though the house has been cleaned after the party." We'd tidied the kitchen but not the rest of the house.

She gave me a look. "She doesn't come on Sundays. And I don't see that the house is any cleaner than normal."

It was a heck of a lot cleaner than was normal in my house. Rebecca herself was the neat-freak and not inclined to let things go until the hired help could take care of it. I didn't think that information would prove useful, but I filed it away just in case.

"How much would you say the missing pieces are worth?" I asked.

She shrugged. "I don't care about the *value*, Gemma. They were important to me."

"You might not care, but the police will. And the thief certainly did."

"The two bowls are a set. Twenty thousand." She waved her hand in the air. I swallowed. "Or thereabouts. I suspect the value of the smaller one will be diminished considerably if it's not part of the set. The kisses? Around ten each."

"Ten thousand dollars for those little things. Wow."

She gave me a strained smile. "Ten dollars, Gemma, not ten thousand. They're not by Dale. I bought them because I like them. I used to have four, but I gave two to my sister's girls when they admired them."

"It's possible that our thief, if there was a thief, didn't know that. Or he or she took them because, like you, he fancied them."

The large living room windows faced the driveway. Something moved, and I pulled back the sheer drapes to see a WLPD car pull up outside.

Rebecca met them at the door. Ryan had brought Detective Estrada. She did not look pleased to see me standing behind Rebecca.

Fair enough—I wasn't pleased to see her either.

"What are you doing here?" Estrada said to me.

"I came to pick up our dishes, and Rebecca was kind enough to offer me a tour of her art collection," I said pleasantly. "It was only then Rebecca noticed some pieces seem to have gone missing."

"Sounds reasonable," Ryan said. Estrada said nothing.

"This way, please." Rebecca led the way through the house to the library. She pointed dramatically to the empty space on the display cabinet. There wasn't so much as an outline of dust to show where the missing pieces had sat.

Rebecca told the police what was missing and that we'd done a brief search of the room.

"You're sure the small bowl and the little ornaments were here yesterday before the tea guests arrived?" Ryan asked.

"I saw them myself," I said.

"Is that so?" Estrada muttered. "What a coincidence."

"Nothing odd about it." I tried not to get my back up. "I admired the house and took a moment to have a peek. I love classic libraries like this one. The chandelier caught my attention, and then I noticed the glass sculptures."

"How much other admiring and noticing did you do?" Estrada asked.

"None. I had a job to do. I went back to it. I shouldn't have to point out to you, Detective, but I will, that if I had stolen the pieces, it is highly unlikely I would bring their absence to Rebecca's attention."

"Wouldn't put something like that past you," she said, "to throw us off the scent."

I looked at Ryan. *Too clever by half*, he'd once called me.

"I'll agree," he said, "that that's highly unlikely."

"Thank you." I couldn't help throwing a glance at Estrada. I might have even smirked. Probably not a good idea.

"We'll send some fingerprint techs around," Ryan said. "I'll have to ask you to stay out of this room until they're done."

I held up my hands. "I've already admitted to being in here. I might have touched the bowl yesterday, and I lifted things up and opened cabinet drawers when we were searching. I poured Rebecca a drink at her request." I pointed to the bottle of Laphroaig and the glass sitting on a side table.

"Convenient." Estrada returned my smirk.

"Make the call, Detective," Ryan said. "Did you have any security here yesterday, Mrs. Stanton? While the party was going on?"

She shook her head. Not a hair moved. "I never thought . . . I've hosted a handful of garden parties over the years . . . I mean, these people, most of them, are my friends. Respectable members of the community. Not the sort to . . ."

"Exactly the sort to drop valuable and rare pieces of art casually into their bag," I said. "Your average street thief would have gone for electronics and jewelry. Did you check your jewelry this morning?"

She instinctively touched the gold hoops in her ears. "I noticed nothing missing. I would have, I assure you, when I got dressed. My jewelry boxes are well organized, as are my closets. I saw no signs of an intruder being upstairs."

"So anyone at the party could have come in," Estrada said.

"The doors were not locked. People were welcome to use the powder room."

"Which is conveniently located right next to this room," I said.

"Gemma's right," Ryan said. "This is unlikely to be the work of anyone whose fingerprints are on file. But you never know. Someone might have a history of kleptomania."

"You think that's all it is?" I asked. "A loose-fingered art collector?"

"If so, it doesn't have anything to do with death of Bellingham," Estrada said. "This could have been handled by a patrol officer. Are we finished here, Detective Ashburton?"

I refrained from pointing out to the good detective that "it is a capital mistake to theorize before you have all the evidence.

It biases the judgment." Without examining the available evidence, or waiting for more to come in, Louise Estrada had decided the theft had nothing to do with the death of Nigel Bellingham. From this point on, she would be biased against any evidence that pointed otherwise.

Fortunately, Ryan wasn't in such a rush. "You said the bowl that was stolen was identical to this one?" He pointed to the remaining piece.

"Yes," I said, "but much smaller. Clearly the thief didn't take the larger one because it wouldn't have fit into their bag, and they couldn't openly march out with it." I thought back to yesterday. Had I seen any good-sized bags? A few women had tote bags, but most carried tiny purses. Renee's bag had been large enough to conceal the bigger bowl as well as the smaller. Then again, of course, there were all the kitchen supplies. Easy enough to slip the pieces into a catering box and retrieve them later, although that had its own risks, as anyone might have gone into the box looking for something or to put something away.

Most of the men at the party were older, not the sort to carry a man-bag. But two had. The chap with the pink shorts and his hair in a bun had a small brown bag thrown over his shoulder, and Gerald carried his ever-present leather satchel. Mentally, I zoomed in on the satchel. When he and Nigel arrived, the satchel had been flat, as though it contained nothing larger than a few pieces of paper. But later, when he'd fussed over Nigel after the disastrous reading? Yes, it had a slight bulge.

"Gerald Greene carries a good-sized leather bag," I said. "Yesterday, after the discovery of Sir Nigel's body, when I came back to the house, he was coming around the corner of the house. He said he'd been on the phone with his mother in England for a long time. Did you think to ask him about his whereabouts after the tea, Detective?"

"We did. He said nothing about any phone call, just that he hadn't seen his boss for some time. Not since the tea ended. I'll check into that; thanks, Gemma. We have his number." Ryan snapped a picture of the remaining bowl with his own phone. "Were these insured, Mrs. Stanton?"

"They were. The insurance company has photos of all the valuable pieces. The kisses weren't at all valuable, so I don't have any pictures of them."

"They're an inch and a half tall. One is clear glass with swirls of white in the interior and gold sparkles and the other blue-green with traces of white."

"You remember them very well, Gemma," Estrada said.

"That would be because I admired them, as I believe I said previously."

Ryan put his phone away. "If you notice anything else missing, Mrs. Stanton, give me a call. In the meantime, stay out of this room and don't move anything until our people have finished."

"Thank you, Detectives," Rebecca said.

"I'll get what I came for and be on my way," I said. "I can see myself out."

I went into the kitchen, ran out the back door, and dashed around the house. I was hiding in the perfectly sculpted shrubbery when the front door opened and Ryan and Estrada came out. They said good-bye to Rebecca. She shut the door, and the police walked to their car. Ryan put on his sunglasses.

Estrada said, "You're barking up the wrong tree, wasting valuable time on a petty theft. I keep telling you, Leslie Wilson is hiding something. We need to hit her and hit her hard. She'll crumble like a dry cookie. You've been told before to stay away from that interfering English woman. I don't know why you can't see . . ." She got into the car, slammed the door shut, and I heard no more.

Chapter 9

Running a business interferes with one's detective work. Not that I am a detective, nor do I want to be one, but sometimes it seems that I can't help myself.

Today, however, I had nothing to do on that front until the evening, so I tried to focus my attention on the store.

By the time the police had driven away and I crept out of the bushes—picking twigs out of my hair—gone back for Jayne's things, loaded them into the car, drove into town, and unloaded the box, it was twelve thirty. Late for opening.

Moriarty greeted me with his customary hiss and display of sharp little teeth. "And top o' the mornin' to you too," I said. He arched his back and spat. I am the hand that feeds him, after all, but that doesn't stop him from open displays of hostility.

As I'd unlocked the front door, I'd spotted Maureen across the street, checking her watch. I had no doubt this minor infraction would be reported to the Baker Street Business Improvement Association with the same seriousness as though I'd been discovered dealing drugs out the back door. Someone else who didn't like me. I was surrounded by enemies.

Maybe not entirely surrounded. The first customer through the door had been in only yesterday and bought the two Anthony Horowitz novels. "My brother was so thrilled with his gift," she said. "I told him I'd rush right over and get him more." She was in her fifties, bright and perky and cheerfully plump with sparkling eyes and an enormous smile. She wore a wide-brimmed straw hat, drooping on one side, red Bermuda shorts, and a garish T-shirt covered in pink flowers. "But first, where is that adorable cat? There you are, you sweet thing." She scooped Moriarty up in her arms. If I tried that, he'd have me calling for an ambulance. He purred and licked her hand. She fussed for a few minutes and then carefully put him down.

"What sort of book are you thinking of?" I asked. "Another contemporary or maybe the original Conan Doyle books, if he hasn't read them?"

"He's always been a big Holmes fan," she said. "He has a set of the originals. He hasn't had time over the past years to read much, but he's laid up right now and thus has all the time in the world to read."

"I'm sorry to hear that," I said, meaning the laid-up part, not the reading part.

She laughed. "Foolish man. He fell off the roof last week when he was cleaning the gutters. His wife told him to hire someone to do it, but would he listen? Oh, no. Not my brother. He knows it all. Except how to safely position a ladder, it would appear. Anyway, he loved *House of Silk*, so I'm looking for something similar. All these years of exchanging birthday and Christmas gifts that he never used, and at last I've hit a gold mine."

I walked her to the shelf, and we chatted while she browsed. She eventually left with *Mycroft Holmes* by Kareem Abdul-Jabbar after giving a preening Moriarty a departing scratch.

"You've earned your day's kibble," I said to him. He lifted his tail and stalked back to his bed.

The next person through the doors was one of the town's well-known busybodies. I knew her by reputation—via Great Uncle Arthur—as she'd never darkened the door of the Emporium before. She snapped up a copy of *The Sign of Four*, narrated by Sir Nigel Bellingham.

"Holmes fan, are you?" I said as I rang up the purchase.

"I'd love to have time to read more, Emma, dear."

"Gemma."

"But I'm so busy with my charities and other activities. I never can find the time to sit down and relax and indulge myself. It's like a curse. Everyone tells me that at my time of life, I can afford to take it easier, but I simply can't disappoint anyone. How is your dear uncle? I haven't seen him around for some time. I was so sorry when he dropped out of the bridge club. We can always use a man around, you know."

Among the ninth and tenth decade crowd, Uncle Arthur is a much sought-after commodity—a single man in full possession of his faculties. *All* of his faculties, he liked to hint on occasion. I pretended not to understand what he meant.

"Audiobooks are great for busy people such as yourself." I gestured toward her purchase. "You can listen when you're in the car. You'll enjoy this one. Sir Nigel does a good job."

"Heavens, Emma. I have no interest in popular fiction. When I do find time to read, I only read works of literature. I'm hoping this'll be worth something on eBay. Not only is the narrator dead, but he signed it himself. Have a nice day. Tell Arthur I was asking after him." She sailed out.

She did have a point. I studied the remaining audiobooks. I took one into the back for myself. Just in case.

Ashleigh arrived to start work at one. Today, she was dressed all in black. Black jeans, black jacket, black boots, black T-shirt. "The whole town is talking about nothing else but yesterday's tea and Mr. Bellingham's death. Gosh, I wish I'd been there. It must have been so exciting. Like something out of CSI."

"Not really. Most police work is extremely boring. Waiting around for the police to finish whatever they're doing and give you permission to leave is even more boring."

"I suppose you'd know. You've been involved in police cases before."

"Never when I can help it. I have to pop next door for a while. If you need something, give me a shout."

I went to Mrs. Hudson's. By now, I was starving. I hadn't had anything today except a cup of tea—that I didn't want and didn't finish—at Leslie's house. I thought sadly of my abandoned Sunday full English breakfast. Every table in the tea room was taken, and people were lined up out the door and down the sidewalk. Mrs. Hudson's serves takeout coffee and baked goods all day, breakfast between seven and eleven, lunch from eleven until two, and afternoon tea from one until closing at four. I tried not to breathe in the enticing scents of bubbling hot butternut squash soup, warm bread, sugared pastries, and melting chocolate as I headed for the kitchen. I failed.

Jocelyn was preparing the chicken salad filling for tea sandwiches, and Jayne was taking a tray of raspberry tarts out of the oven. I grabbed a piece of shortbread and stuffed it into my mouth. "Hey," Jayne said, "I need that."

"I am beyond hungry. I left home at the crack of dawn to help you and your mum, then I missed breakfast because you wanted me to go to Rebecca's, and now I'm going to miss lunch because you made an appointment with the police for one thirty."

"I didn't ask you to sit in when I talk to Estrada."

"Irrelevant," I said.

Jayne passed me a bowl full of fresh greens, purple and yellow cherry tomatoes, dried cranberries, sunflower seeds, and crumbled feta cheese, topped with the tea room's home-made (and justifiably famous) raspberry vinaigrette dressing. "Eat. I don't want another dead body lying around. Yesterday was enough."

I ate. As I did so, I asked if they'd heard anything more.

"The gossip mill is in full flight," Jocelyn said. "Everyone has a theory."

Jayne handed Jocelyn a tray of muffins. "Will you take this out front, please?"

"Last time I looked, we didn't need them yet."

"Please," she said.

Jocelyn raised her eyebrows toward me but did as she was told.

"I called Mom earlier," Jayne said as the door swung behind Jocelyn, "to check in. She's pretty shaken up. I said

I'd take the rest of the day off and come around to be with her, but she said she wanted to be alone."

"It's an upsetting business. Did anything happen since I left her?"

"I don't think so, but she told me the police took away the clothes she was wearing yesterday."

Not good. "Seems a stretch to me. Nigel wasn't knifed or anything like that. There would be no blood spatter to search for."

"Can they get fingerprints or DNA off fabric?"

"Sometimes. Depending on the type of cloth. The killer's more likely to have left traces on Nigel, if he was pushed, rather than the other way around." They were looking for signs of a struggle. Had Nigel grabbed his assailant in an attempt to keep his balance? Had they fought, a la the Reichenbach Falls, at the edge of the cliff? Although in this case, only one person went over.

That they had not asked me or, as far as I knew, anyone else for their clothes meant they were closing in on Leslie. I remembered what Estrada had said as they left Rebecca's home. *Hit her and hit her hard.*

"I don't think that's normal procedure," Jayne said, "to take someone's clothes, I mean. Estrada's coming here to see me. She didn't send someone around to bring me down to the police station. I can't understand why they're so interested in Mom. Did she tell you anything when you took her home, Gemma?"

"She was seen talking to Sir Nigel shortly before he died."

"So? Lots of people talked to him. It was why he was there, to meet fans and encourage them to support the festival. Mom

loves theater. It's natural enough that she'd want to chat with
him if she got the chance. There has to be more than that!"

"You'd better ask her yourself, Jayne."

"Ask her what?"

"Have a talk. That's all I'm saying. In the meantime, I
agree with you. Their interest in your mum seems more than
routine. Something else of interest happened today." I told her
about the theft at Rebecca's home.

"You think that's related to the murder of Nigel?"

"I don't think the idea should be dismissed out of hand.
Coincidences happen, but sometimes they're not coincidences."

"What are you going to do?"

Jocelyn was taking a long time to lay out half a dozen
muffins. I stepped firmly on the loose floorboard between the
counter on which I was leaning and the door. I was rewarded
by the scurry of rapidly retreating footsteps. "Me? It seems
that, against my will, I'm drawn into this. I have an idea,
but this isn't the place to discuss it. Be ready at seven o'clock
tonight for an outing."

"I'm having dinner with Eddie."

"Cancel on him. Wear dark clothes."

"Not again!" Jayne cried.

* * *

I went to the Emporium and found the object I needed in a
drawer beneath the cash counter. I then hid in the restroom to
make a quick phone call. When I got back, Detective Estrada
was being shown into the kitchen by a wide-eyed Fiona.

"I hope this won't take long, Detective," I said. "As you
can see we're very busy."

"It'll take as long as it takes. I don't recall inviting you to this interview."

I pulled up a stool. "I don't mind. Save you the trouble of having to hunt me down."

Jocelyn was also allowed to stay, while Fiona attempted to run the busy tea room by herself.

Estrada leaned against the counter and took out a pen and small notebook. She began with routine questions. Had we seen anyone acting suspiciously? (I refrained from asking what that meant.) Had we noticed Sir Nigel Bellingham arguing with anyone? (Other than getting falling-down drunk and offending almost everyone there, no.) Did we know of anyone who might have a reason to wish Nigel harm? Jayne said no; Jocelyn shook her head. I mentioned that he was ruining Rebecca's party, threatening to turn Pat's play into a farce, standing in the way of Eddie getting the lead role, had publically insulted Renee, and appeared to make a habit of sneering at and belittling Gerald. I'd observed all that having only met the dratted man twice.

"Quite a list of suspects you've given me," Estrada said. "Everyone else is saying he was a charming man, dedicated to the success of the festival, who simply had one drink too many on top of a serious case of jet lag."

"For some reason, it's become expected not to speak ill of the dead," I said. "I think that's foolish in a murder case, and I suspect you agree, Detective."

"We're not yet convinced that this is a murder," she said. "We're still investigating the situation."

"Not a murder?" Jocelyn said. "You mean it might have been an accident or something?"

157

"Possible. The man was highly inebriated—that is not in dispute. So far no one has come forward to say they went with him to the cliff's edge."

"Suicide?" I said. "He was drunk, as you say, and depressed."

She studied my face. "No one has reported him as being depressed."

"That would be because they are not coming to the logical conclusion. He ruined his performance in front of people paying two hundred bucks a shot to see him and was stood up by a much younger man. Actors are emotional creatures. It comes with the job. He was a big star once, knighted by the Queen. These days, he's reduced to performing in a barn in West London, Massachusetts, and appears to be unable to manage even that. After being unceremoniously shoved off-stage at the tea, did he despair of the downward spiral and decide to end it all?"

"I bet that's it," Jocelyn said. "Poor old guy."

I got to my feet. "If we're done here, we've all got work to do."

I'd attempted to distract Estrada from what I feared was her line of inquiry. In that, I failed also. "Your mother told us she was an actress at one time," Estrada said to Jayne. "Is she the emotional type, as Gemma calls them?"

Jayne blinked. "My mom? She's no more emotional than anyone else, I'd say." She gave a tight laugh. "When we were kids, she could get mighty angry at my dad, and then she had a mean arm with the crockery."

"Jayne!" I said. "Don't make jokes."

The color drained from Jayne's face. She had been trying to lighten the mood and instead played straight into

Estrada's hand. "I didn't mean she throws things at people. She . . ."

"You seem to have a lot of questions about Mrs. Wilson, Detective," I said. "Any reason for that?"

"Do you expect me to tell you, Ms. Doyle?"

No. But I had gotten Jayne to stop talking.

"Did your mother ever mention Nigel Bellingham prior to this week?" Estrada asked.

"Not that I can remember." Some of the color came back to Jayne's cheeks, and anyone could see she was telling the truth. Estrada asked if Leslie Wilson had been particularly excited when she heard the news that Nigel Bellingham would be coming to West London.

"She was pleased that the play was going ahead and that they'd scored a famous actor to be in it," Jayne said. "The entire theater group was over the moon. *The Hound of the Baskervilles* will be their centerpiece this season."

At last, Estrada put away her notebook. "Thank you for your time, Ms. Wilson. I'll be in touch if I need anything more." She left.

The three of us didn't say a word. I let a minute or two pass, and then I tiptoed to the door and checked behind it. Louise Estrada did not have her ear pressed up against the wall.

"She didn't thank me for my time," Jocelyn said, "or Gemma either. Did anyone else think some of her questions were weird?"

"I think Fiona is overwhelmed out there," I said. "Go and give her a hand. The food orders must be backed up for miles."

"No one will mind if she tells the customers we're helping the police with their inquiries."

"I don't think that phrase means what you think it means," I said.

"Huh?"

"It doesn't mean you're helping the police with their inquiries in an attempt to be a responsible citizen. It means you're being questioned as a suspect and about to be arrested."

"Oh." She grabbed a fresh apron from the hook by the door and left the kitchen.

"Jocelyn's been watching too many British TV shows on Netflix," I said to Jayne.

"Why does Estrada want to know so much about my mom?"

"I can't say, Jayne. Talk to her. I'll pick you up at your place at five to seven on the dot."

"I still don't know where we're going."

"You will in due course."

*　*　*

I wasn't convinced that the theft from Rebecca's house had anything to do with the death of Nigel, but right now it was the only lead I had. If a party guest had nicked the little ornaments, it was highly unlikely they did it intending to sell them. The bowl was the smaller half of a set, and the imitation kisses were not by Dale Chihuly. If they were valuable, not every common or garden thief would know how to unload highly identifiable (and heavily insured) art. This type of theft was more likely to be, as Ryan had said, done by a kleptomaniac. Someone who stole simply for the sake of it with no desire to profit from the theft. That sort of person, particularly in the rarified world of theater festivals and garden parties, would have a great deal to lose if they should be discovered.

Someone like Gerald Greene with his convenient and large, ever-present leather satchel.

The bookstore closes at five on Sundays, giving me time to go home and take Violet for long walk. Back home, I changed into black trousers with numerous spacious pockets and a dark-gray T-shirt. I slipped a navy jumper over the shirt and put on a pair of trainers—what Americans call sneakers. The trainers were from a midrange, mass-produced line and bought at Walmart. Impossible to trace if I did get sloppy and leave footprints behind me. I slipped the necessary supplies into my pockets.

Violet lay on the bed, her face resting between her paws, watching me.

"What?" I said. "You didn't know a good break-and-enter outfit is what every modern girl needs in her wardrobe?"

I was hoping I wouldn't need Great Uncle Arthur's set of lockpicks tonight. I'd recently lost them.

Actually, I hadn't lost them. I knew exactly where they were: in the police station. Ryan Ashburton had confiscated them.

I arrived at Jayne's at five to seven. Good thing I'd thrown a pair of sweat pants and a black cardigan into the back. Her idea of dressing in dark clothes was a red T-shirt and beige shorts.

"Now are you going to tell me where we're going?" she said by way of a greeting.

"The Harbor Inn. It's the dinner hour."

"We're having dinner at the Harbor Inn? That's nice, but I wish you'd told me. I would have worn something more suitable."

"I brought you suitable attire." I gestured to the back of the car. "Put those on."

She reached around and found the clothes. "Tell me you're kidding, Gemma."

"I have reason to believe Gerald Greene might have stolen the pieces from Rebecca's house. I'm going to check."

"Anyone else would tell the police and let them check."

"Anyone else wouldn't have Estrada on their case."

"Tell Ryan then."

"I can't, Jayne. Not yet. Estrada is looking for a reason, any reason, to have Ryan removed from the case, like she did with the Longton murder. Ryan and I are no longer an item . . ."

"Although you should be," Jayne said.

I ignored that. "To her that's irrelevant. She wants his job. Any suggestion that he's unduly influenced by me will be ammunition in her gun belt. I can't take suspicions to Ryan, only facts. You know what our police chief is like. All he wants in life is for everyone to get along—he should have been a kindergarten teacher. He would have greatly enjoyed writing 'plays well with others' on their report cards. If he has to demote or fire Ryan to stop Estrada from complaining, he will. Therefore, tonight, 'I shall be my own police.'"

"I sense a Sherlock quote."

"'The Five Orange Pips.'"

"Don't think I know that one. Is it . . . ? Why are we talking about Sherlock Holmes, anyway? By check, I gather you mean we're breaking into Gerald's hotel room and searching his things. I assume you know that's a crime, so I won't mention it, but I have to ask why we're doing it when it's still daylight and how you know he won't be there."

162

"He won't be there because he's expecting me to meet him for a drink at McGillivray's Irish Pub right about now. He left me his business card the day they came into the Emporium, and I gave him a call this afternoon while we were waiting for Estrada. It's the same reason we're doing this at seven o'clock rather than in the middle of the night. The inn will be busy serving dinner, and most, if not all, of their guests will have gone out on such a lovely evening. I don't know the man's sleeping habits, and I most certainly do not want to find out, so I can't break in after dark."

Jayne groaned. "How do you talk me into these things?"

"Fear not. You won't be doing anything illegal. All you'll be doing is standing guard."

"I think that's illegal, Gemma."

I pulled into the driveway of the Harbor Inn. It's one of the nicest hotels in West London, a grand old Victorian mansion saved from demolition by a young couple determined to turn it into a successful business. Tonight, the parking lot was almost full, and I parked the Miata between two giant SUVs. I didn't bother to hide my car. If Gerald caught us, the game would be up, and if he didn't, no one would be checking who'd been visiting the hotel tonight.

"I'll admit," I said. "This would be easier in December, under cover of darkness, but I'm counting on everyone minding their own business. People on vacation are usually too busy enjoying themselves to bother about what other people are up to, and the staff will be hopping."

We got out of the car. Jayne took a step toward the entrance.

"Not that way," I said. "They won't tell me his room number, and even if they did, I don't want it on record that I asked."

"Then how do you expect to find it? We're not peering into every window, I hope. Suppose it's on the second floor."

I headed for the west side of the inn. The lobby and comfortable lounge face the ocean to the east. In the summer weather, like tonight, the restaurant extends onto the veranda giving a magnificent view down the hill to the harbor.

To the west of the building, the hillside crowds the house; a thick hedge provides privacy from the property next door, and the farthest wing of the inn faces a patch of woods.

"After the renovations were completed, Andrea and Brian hosted an open house," I said. "That was three years ago, before you came back to West London. Canapés and champagne and a woman playing the harp in the lobby. She was excellent, I remember, although the champagne was on the cheap side. We were given a grand tour of the place. I was most impressed. The inn isn't large, so it has only one suite. It's on the first floor, meaning the one above the ground floor—which as long as I am in America, I must remember to call the *second* floor—at the far corner of the house. Two balconies, one facing east overlooking the ocean and a smaller one adjacent to a grove of old hardwood trees to the north. That would be the room they gave Sir Nigel. I've been told Gerald has an adjoining room. It's highly unlikely the theater people paid the extra one hundred and twenty five dollars a night to give Gerald a sea view with spacious balcony, so it's elementary to conclude that that one must be his." I pointed.

"Very clever. How are you going to get up there?"

"You might notice that they've allowed that maple tree to grow a branch too close to the upper floor windows."

"You can't possibly tell me you remembered the position of that tree from a quick peek three years ago and deduced how much the branch would have grown in the interim."

"Nothing so complicated. At this spot, the woods edge close to the house. Owning and running a business like this requires an enormous amount of work. Andrea and Brian put every cent they have into this place and took out loans for the rest. They watch their pennies and do as much of the work themselves as they can to cut down expenditures. I hoped Brian wouldn't have taken the time to clear the trees until it was absolutely necessary; that's all."

I studied the upper floor. What I suspected was Gerald's room had a small balcony. It was so small, it was more a decoration than a place to sit out and enjoy the fresh air. I felt a small grin cross my face. He'd left the sliding door open to catch the soft evening sea breeze. If I wasn't such a suspicious sort, that's exactly what I would have done had this been my room. He might have locked the screen door, but I hoped that wasn't the case. I felt the wire cutters in my pocket. If I had to, I'd slit the screen where it met the doorframe and count on Gerald not noticing. I'd later send Brian and Andrea enough cash to cover the damage, along with an anonymous note (the letters cut out of a Boston newspaper) advising them to trim the trees back.

I pulled a packet of cigarettes and a lighter out of my pocket.

"This is a strange time to take up smoking," Jayne said.

"They're for you. If someone comes by, pretend you sneaked out for a smoke. If you have to take a drag, don't leave the butt on the ground." I handed them to her.

"I have no intention of taking a drag, as you put it."

"Good. A used and discarded cigarette can carry DNA. Don't worry about dropping ash though. In the highly unlikely event the police investigate this, everyone knows you and I don't smoke. All I need you to do is stand here with your cigarette and look innocent. If anyone comes by, say hello in a strong but not overly loud voice, so I'll know not to come down at that particular moment. If you have reason to believe someone is showing undue interest in what's going on, cough and say that you have to give up smoking one day. That will tell me not to come down by the tree but to walk out the door."

"Have you ever considered going into a life of crime yourself, Gemma? You'd be good at it."

"Unfortunately, I was cursed with a conscience." I pulled a pair of blue latex gloves out of another pocket and slipped them on. "I'll be back before you know it."

I haven't climbed a tree since I was eleven or twelve, playing with my siblings in the abandoned apple orchard behind my grandparents' country home in Suffolk. But like riding a bicycle, it's a skill one never forgets.

These trees had thick, strong branches, and the bottom one was only a few feet off the ground. I swung myself up and then climbed steadily. The only real danger of discovery would be if the occupants of the room on the ground floor suddenly opened their drapes. I was counting on them to be out over the dinner hour. If I'd miscalculated, I'd have some fast explaining to do.

When I was about halfway to my destination, I glanced down. Jayne's head was thrown back as she watched me climb. Jayne and I had been speaking in low voices. If someone was in the rooms on the ground floor, I wanted them to think that a couple of guests were out for an evening stroll or had left the window to their room open. If someone did look out now, they'd be curious about what Jayne was finding so interesting. I couldn't shout at her, so I gestured to her to look away. She did so, and I continued climbing.

I reached the level of the balcony in question. I lowered myself onto the branch extending toward the wall of the inn. It swayed slightly under my weight. Okay, the other danger would be if the branch snapped and I fell and broke my neck. I crawled on my hands and knees along it. The branch swayed and dipped, threatening to bring me too low to grab hold of the balcony railing. I hadn't taken that into consideration. Taking great care, I slowly stood upright. I grabbed the bottom of the railing, and that took enough of my weight that the branch moved a bit higher. I pulled myself, hand over hand, up the railing, and the branch rose more. Finally, I was light enough and the branch high enough that I could swing one leg over the railing. I pulled up the other leg and dropped onto the balcony. It was barely wide enough to accommodate me, but I wasn't planning to sit out and enjoy the evening. I tested the screen door, and it opened easily.

How trusting people are.

I slipped inside. My phone had started vibrating when I was climbing the tree. I checked it now. A call from Gerald's number and a voice mail message. I texted him back: *Sorry, car problems. Be there soon.*

It was coming up to half seven. I didn't know how long he'd wait for me. A long time, I hoped. He was an Englishman in a pub, after all. I hadn't asked him on a date when I'd called this afternoon. I simply said I thought he might not want to be alone tonight, so why didn't we have a drink?

I put the phone away and checked the room. It was small but nicely decorated in a nautical theme. Gerald was not a neat man. The drawers were half-open, showing clothes randomly stuffed in, his shoes were kicked across the room, stacks of paper were tossed onto the desk, and his toiletries were spread all over the bathroom counter. His satchel lay on the bed. I checked the closets and cupboards quickly, finding no Chihuly bowl. There was, unfortunately, a small room safe, and it was locked. I tried the standard combination of 1-1-1-1, and then 1-2-3-4. It opened on 0-0-0-0. *Bad boy.* No precious glass ornaments in there either. Nothing but his passport, English driving license and bank card, and a small stack of well-used pound notes. I didn't bother checking through his passport. That wasn't why I was here, and I needed to be quick.

I picked up the satchel. I could tell by the weight that it didn't have the ornaments, but I checked anyway. It seemed to be empty. I put my hand inside and ran it around the lining. I felt something soft and pulled out—of all things—half a salmon tea sandwich.

I recognized that sandwich! I'd made it myself. I gathered more crumbs from inside the satchel. The remains of a chocolate brownie, a slice of strawberry still sticky with custard filling on its bottom, a dirty Mrs. Hudson's napkin. Gerald had been stealing food. That's why his satchel was fuller at the end of the party than when he'd arrived.

Didn't Sir Nigel pay the man enough for him to eat?

I'd come out after a hard day, dressed like a cat burglar, climbed a tree, and broke into a hotel room, all so I could accuse a man of nicking leftover sandwiches and pastries. If Gerald had simply asked, we would have told him to help himself to the extra food we'd brought for ourselves.

I was about to head off out the window and down the tree when I decided *in for a penny, in for a pound.* I turned the knob on the door adjoining the next room, and it opened.

How convenient.

I slipped into Nigel's room. It had been cleaned since he'd last slept in it, but no one had yet packed up his things. His shoes were laid neatly beside the desk, his shirts and trousers hung in the closet, a laptop was open on the desk. Not expecting to find anything, I opened a drawer.

A *Sherlock: The Mind Palace* coloring book lay on top of his underwear. I shouldn't have been shocked to see it, but I was.

My phone buzzed with an incoming text.

Jayne: *What's taking so long?*

Me: *Major discovery. Almost done.*

Underneath Nigel's socks, I found a steak knife that looked a great deal like the ones used at the inn's restaurant and a saltshaker from Mrs. Hudson's. Jayne probably hadn't even realized it was missing yet.

I used my phone to snap a couple of pictures of the coloring book and the stolen goods in situ. Had the police searched

Nigel's things after his death? If they had, they've have had no reason to know the coloring book had been stolen. I hadn't reported its loss. They might have thought a steak knife and a saltshaker a mite odd to keep among his undergarments. But then again, many Americans thought upper-class English people were all a mite odd. Came from watching too much *Father Brown* or *Miss Marple*.

Nigel must be the one who'd stolen the ornaments from Rebecca's house while the party was under way. I'd been the first to come upon his body, and I hadn't seen any sign of them on him. I hadn't searched him, but I hadn't noticed (and I would have) any bulk in his pockets. If the police had found the items, they would have told us when Rebecca and I reported that they were missing.

Had the killer taken them? If so, why? If not, then Nigel must have hidden them somewhere in Rebecca's house or on the grounds before he died. Did he intend to come back for them later, or was nicking things and hiding them part of his kleptomania? He couldn't have been planning to sell the ill-gotten goods. Not a lot of profit to be made out of one saltshaker with a pink flower pattern and a single steak knife.

I thought back to Nigel's only visit to the Emporium, when the coloring book had been taken. I couldn't remember him being alone at any time. He'd sent Gerald into the tea room in search of a table, but the other theater people, including Leslie Wilson, had been with him in the shop. Still, people's attention got distracted, particularly in a busy place at a busy time, and it would be a matter of a fraction of a second for a light-fingered, experienced thief to snatch the goods and slip them into a spacious pocket. The sort of pocket found in a Harris Tweed jacket.

Another text: *Gemma!!!!*

Me: *Coming. Is the coast clear?*

Jayne: *Yes.*

Chapter 10

"I don't ever want to do that again," Jayne said once we were back in the Miata and driving sedately toward town.

"You didn't do anything," I said, "but stand in a lovely patch of woods on a pleasant evening."

"The tension alone was enough to kill me. I wonder if it's too late to call Eddie and tell him I've finished the work I had to catch up on."

"It's too late."

"It's not even eight o'clock. Where are we going anyway? This isn't the road to my place."

"Take off those clothes I gave you." I pulled into a parking lot.

"Gladly. What are we doing at McGillivray's?"

"Gerald has some explaining to do. Fortunately, I know where he is." I parked the car, took off my jumper, and tossed it and most of the contents of my pockets into the back. I got my handbag—a cute little red leather number—out of the boot of the car and put on a pair of giant gold hoop earrings.

Black trousers, gray T-shirt, red bag, and gold jewelry. Perfect for a pub evening.

Jayne shook her head.

Uncle Arthur, who is exceptionally well-traveled, tells me he's never been to a country that doesn't have an Irish pub. Some towns barely have any people, but they all seem to have the need for an imitation Irish pub.

McGillivray's is the West London version. Just like being back home. Except that you don't have to line up at the bar to get served. I like that.

On a Sunday night, the place was half-empty. The sign on the door informed us that a troupe of Irish balladeers playing "Traditional Songs From the Old Country" would be performing at nine. I hoped we'd be finished by then.

Gerald had taken a booth and sat hunched over a pint of dark ale. The glass was almost full, and I assumed it wasn't his first.

He wasn't alone. That had not been part of my plan.

Irene Talbot looked up as we approached. A bottle of beer, as well as a digital recorder and notepad, was on the table. "Hey, it's the dynamic duo."

"What do you mean by that?" Jayne said. "We don't go around doing strange things, you know. I've been at home . . . all evening . . . I . . ."

I tripped over a loose floorboard and "accidentally" jabbed her in the ribs. "Jayne's had a long day. Those strawberry tarts don't bake themselves. Mind if we join you?"

"Hardly," Gerald said, "considering that I'm here because you suggested it. How's your car?"

"Fine. A stupid little thing. I ran out of petrol." I tittered. "Silly me."

Irene threw me look. I squeezed onto the bench beside her, leaving the seat next to Gerald for Jayne.

"What can I get you?" the waitress asked, laying beer mats on the table in front of us. She wore a black T-shirt and a short red-checked kilt. The first time I'd been in here, I'd told the waitress the kilt was traditionally worn in Scotland, not Ireland. She'd replied, "What's a kilt?" I could have also pointed out that it was not worn that short, and never by women, but I decided to save my breath.

"I'll have a glass of white wine," Jayne said.

"Tomato juice, thanks," I said. "You do know, Gerald, that this woman, as nice as she is, is a reporter."

"I'm not exactly undercover here, Gemma." Irene indicated her recording equipment.

"Just making sure."

"I'm happy to talk to the press," Gerald said. "Sir Nigel deserves to be remembered. He was a giant of English theater, as well as a kind and generous man." He sniffled and buried his nose in his beer.

"Have you worked for him long?" I asked.

"Ten years. Not nearly long enough." He wiped his dry eyes. Gerald might move in the theater world, but he was a heck of a lousy actor.

"Know of any reason anyone would want to kill him?" I asked.

"Gee," Irene whispered to Jayne, "even I was going to approach that question obliquely."

Gerald shook his head. "Everyone loved him. I was telling this lady about the charitable foundation he was setting up in London. 'The Play's the Thing,' he called it. It would give poor children an exposure to theater in a playful yet educational environment." I made a mental note to look up this charity. I'd bet my last copy of *The Sign of Four*, narrated and signed by the late Sir Nigel Bellingham, that if the charity existed, it was just a shell, an attempt to restore some of Nigel's rapidly fading status among his peers. Said peers would be asked to give generously.

"That's so nice," Jayne said.

"Was he murdered?" Irene said. "The police are being noncommittal. They haven't come out and said they're investigating it as a homicide, but Ashburton and Estrada have been questioning everyone who was there."

"What do you think happened, Gerald?" I asked.

"A tragic accident. He wandered too close to the cliff. Lost his footing, perhaps. He wasn't a young man." Gerald hastened to add, "Although he was in perfect health. More than capable of putting on a regular series of performances."

"If you say so." I wondered why Gerald was lying. Was he trying to protect Nigel's reputation out of a sense of loyalty? Perhaps. He'd been close to the man for ten years, although Nigel hadn't been at all nice to him. Some people lied simply for the sake of it. And there was that "not speaking ill of the dead" thing. But Gerald didn't look to me like the sort who'd let a little thing like that stop him.

Was he lying because he'd killed Nigel? He'd have no trouble getting close enough to push the man off the cliff. I thought about the stale sandwich and the pastry crumbs.

If he stole food, what else might he have nicked? A *Sherlock* coloring book?

Was Gerald, not Nigel, the thief? Had Nigel discovered that his PA had sticky fingers and blackmailed the man? They had adjacent hotel rooms, and the door was unlocked. Had Nigel discovered the stolen goods in Gerald's room and taken them as evidence?

Blackmail was a powerful motive for murder.

"Sir Nigel had been married four times," Irene was saying. "I don't suppose any of his ex-wives were out for revenge."

"Out of the question," Gerald said. "They might have been divorced, but he got on extremely well with all of them. They remained great friends."

"That's not what I read in the gossip columns," Irene said. "That incident in the National Gallery got a lot of press in the UK."

"Malicious gossip," Gerald said. "Gross exaggeration. Miss Fotheringham got her heel caught in the carpet, that's all. I thought you were a respectable reporter with a respectable newspaper. If that is not the case, then this interview is over." Rather than leaping dramatically to his feet and storming out, Gerald took another mouthful of beer.

"If any of Nigel's ex-wives had been at the tea party," Jayne said, "they would have been noticed."

"I have several publicity pictures of Sir Nigel on the computer in my hotel room," Gerald said. "I'll send you some, and you can select the ones you want to use. Perhaps one as he appeared in *Roman Wars* would be a good choice. Remind your readers that he had a successful screen career, as well as in theater."

"Didn't he hate *Roman Wars?*" Jayne said. "Do you think he'd want that being his obituary picture?"

Gerald hid a grin. *Oh, yes,* I thought, *Gerald will get his revenge in his own way.* Revenge for what was the question. For being an unkind employer or for being a blackmailer?

"I suppose you have no reason to stay on in West London," Jayne said. "You worked for Nigel directly, right? Not the theater company?"

"As charming as your delightful little town is," Gerald said, "I would love nothing more than to be on my way. Your overzealous police have told me I'm not to leave."

"Then they must be thinking it's a murder. Don't you agree, Gemma?" Jayne said.

"Not necessarily," Irene said. "They like to keep all their options open."

"Let me assure you, I didn't kill him," Gerald said. "I don't know anything more about it than anyone else. I told them that." He finished his beer and raised his hand to summon the waitress to bring him another.

The troupe of "Irish balladeers" arrived and began setting up their equipment. As they talked among themselves, I caught not the merest suggestion of a brogue. They were as Irish as the waitresses' kilts.

Chapter 11

"Have you thought to check with the police in the UK about Gerald Greene, Nigel's personal assistant?" I said.

"I might have. I might not have. Why don't you tell me why I might want to do that?" Ryan Ashburton said.

On past occasions, Ryan has, albeit reluctantly, confessed that he values my observations and my judgment, but police department politics mean he can't openly allow me to be involved in his investigations. I try to keep him informed of what I learn while not fully letting him in on what exactly I've been up do. It's a delicate balancing act.

I'd considered my dilemma last night. It was, according to my deductions, entirely possible Gerald had killed Nigel. I couldn't keep that from the police, so I called Ryan as soon as I got to work on Monday morning. I intended to tell him over the phone, but he said he was on his way to pick up a coffee anyway and would drop into the bookshop.

I've said that I'm a good liar. And I am if I want to be. But there's something about Ryan Ashburton's penetrating blue eyes that makes me blurt out all sorts of things. It was a beautiful sunny day, and I hoped he'd keep his sunglasses on while we talked.

Moriarty is a great shop cat. He loves everyone and is affectionate and friendly. Toward everyone other than me that is. And Ryan. For some reason Moriarty hates Ryan almost as much as he hates me.

Ryan momentarily forgot that, and when the cat jumped onto the table next to us, he attempted to give Moriarty a pat. The man was now sucking blood off his finger while the feline gave me a satisfied smirk.

"I don't know why you keep that cat," Ryan said. "He's a menace."

For once, Moriarty had slipped up and done me a favor. Ryan had been distracted from his interrogation of me.

"The customers seem to like him," I replied as Moriarty stalked off, presumably to gloat over his successful attack on the forces of law and order. "I had a shoplifter in here the other day. Someone pinched one of those coloring books when Nigel and Gerald were here. I noticed it was gone later that afternoon."

"Other people were here too, weren't they?" Ryan studied his finger. The bleeding had stopped already. "What makes you think Greene took it?"

Out of nowhere, I had the sudden compulsion to take Ryan's hand in mine and kiss his finger better. I looked at him, but he'd turned to watch the cat cross the room, tail swishing. I swallowed, and when Ryan turned back to me, I said calmly, "That satchel he carries all the time is big enough to conceal things. I saw him at McGillivray's last night, talking to Irene

Talbot about Nigel, and his bag wasn't with him. I wondered if he only used the bag to carry things for his boss." I hoped that would be enough to have Ryan checking up on Gerald. No need to mention the saltshaker and the knife or that I knew exactly where the coloring book was at this moment.

"I find it hard to believe you only thought to put the missing coloring book and the theft from Mrs. Stanton together last night," Ryan said.

"No more detecting for me," I said. "I had more than enough the last time."

He studied my face for a long time. I smiled.

"I can tell you," he said at last, "that I checked Gerald Greene's phone. He did phone a number in England on Saturday. The call was placed after the nine-one-one call to the police, around the time he told you he'd been talking to his mother. The conversation lasted about ten minutes."

"Worth knowing," I said. "Although it doesn't tell us what he was up to before Nigel died."

"Do you know Jayne's mother very well?" Ryan asked.

My smile disappeared in a flash. "Why are you asking me that?"

"She provided the aprons for the volunteers to wear to the tea, right?"

"What of it?"

"One of those aprons got torn at the tea. A piece of pink edging came off. A picture of the six women, wearing the aprons and posing for the camera, was taken before the guests arrived. The pink trim is intact on every one of them. I hadn't known about any aprons until I saw those pictures, and they all have big pockets . . ."

"So you thought one of the women had secreted something in her pocket? A vial of poison perhaps, slipped out at an opportune moment. Aside from the fact that that's ridiculously fanciful, surely the autopsy showed you Sir Nigel wasn't poisoned?"

"The autopsy hasn't been done yet, Gemma. It's scheduled for this afternoon. In the meantime, we're investigating all possibilities. Estrada went back to Mrs. Wilson's house yesterday afternoon and asked her to hand over the aprons. We hoped she hadn't washed them yet, and we might find some evidence on them. Turns out she had washed them, but I noticed one is torn. I called Mrs. Wilson back, and she says she doesn't know who wore which one. None of the pictures we have show a woman wearing a torn apron."

"You think that's significant because . . ."

"We can't find the edging. I'll admit it's a small piece, but I ordered the garbage collected from the scene searched. Mrs. Wilson says the women took off their aprons and she tossed them into the bag to bring home without checking them. She didn't notice one was torn. I don't believe her."

"Why not?" A chasm was opening up at my feet. I kept my voice calm. I headed toward the door. Maybe if I could get Ryan outside, he'd put his sunglasses back on.

He shrugged. "She has that look, Gemma. She's hiding something. It might be something small, and it might be something big, but it is something. If you know what it is, you have to tell me."

"I don't."

"Louise wants to arrest her."

"Arrest Jayne's mother? You can't!"

"I'm not ready to even call this a homicide yet. No one saw, or claims to have seen, what happened. Louise is a good detective, but she can be impulsive."

We stood by the window. A steady stream of traffic moved down the street and pedestrians browsed shop windows. Across the street, Maureen was opening Beach Fine Arts. She checked to see if anyone was watching, grabbed the terracotta pot overflowing with purple and yellow impatiens from the front of the accessories store next door, and hauled it closer to her property. Maureen didn't believe in doing her own decorating or in spending money on plant life.

"I've do believe I have just observed a crime in action," I said.

"You mean that flowerpot," Ryan said. "I saw it too. The community patrol officer is always getting calls to that store. Calls that originate from the shops in that block. Don't try to change the subject, Gemma. Tell Leslie Wilson to talk to me about what she knows. It bothers me—a lot—that I can't find that pink ribbon. We asked the women who wore the aprons, and none of them noticed any tear on theirs, or so they say. It's the small things that can make or break a case. Until I locate that ribbon, I can't declare this an accidental death."

I was saved from replying when someone came to the door.

Not just someone, but Grant Thompson. He gave me a wave and a smile. The smile faded when he saw who I was with.

"First customer of the day," I said. "I have to open." I unlocked the door, and Grant came in. He and Ryan didn't exactly glare at each other, but they didn't exchange fulsome greetings either.

"Hope I'm not interrupting anything," Grant said.

"We're finished here," Ryan said.

"Glad to hear it." Grant pointed to the theater poster on the door. "I see that's still up. Is the play going to go ahead?"

"I haven't heard otherwise," I said.

"Until this gets sorted, one way or another," Ryan said, "the cast and crew have been told they can't leave Barnstable County. No one except Gerald Greene had any objections."

The three of us stood by the door. Finally, I said, "Detective Ashburton is leaving. Can I help you, Grant?"

"Don't run off on my account," Grant said.

"Wouldn't dream of it," Ryan said, "but duty calls. Think over what I said, Gemma." He left.

Ryan knew I knew something I wasn't telling. He's not the sort to pound the table and demand that I talk, which would have been guaranteed to get him precisely nowhere. I thought about the scrap of pink ruching hidden at home in the safe behind the painting of the opera diva. Was it possible Leslie Wilson killed Nigel? That they struggled, he lost his cravat, and her apron was ripped before she shoved him off the cliff in an act of rage pent up for thirty-five years?

Absolutely not.

I hoped the British police would have something incriminating to report about Gerald.

"Dinner?" Grant said.

"I'm sorry, what?"

"Are you free for dinner tonight?"

I didn't have a chance to answer, as we were interrupted when Donald Morris burst through the door. He'd done without the Sherlock getup today and wore slightly tattered khaki trousers and a T-shirt that proclaimed, "You Know My Methods." He carried his well-worn leather briefcase with his initials embossed in gold, a remnant of his previous life as a family law attorney. He beamed when he saw Grant. "Ah, excellent. I don't want to start a bidding war here, not between two of my closest friends, but if I must, I must."

"Bidding war?" I said. "What on earth are we bidding over?"

"The playbill, of course. I told you about it at the tea. I bet you regret now that you didn't purchase it at the time, Gemma." He formed his face into somber lines. "Most unfortunate news about Sir Nigel. What a tragedy. Still, I can't pretend not to know that the value of my playbill has increased dramatically."

"Playbill?" Grant said.

"Used to promote the Shaftsbury Theater run of *The Hound of the Baskervilles* and signed by Sir Nigel himself. I see you have no customers at the moment. No time like the present. Shall we start the bidding at five hundred dollars?"

"No," I said. "Donald, you know I don't sell anything at that sort of price."

"I thought you might make an exception for such a rare and valuable piece of Holmes, as well as theatrical, memorabilia. Grant?"

"I'm a book dealer, Donald. Posters are out of my range of expertise."

"You'll be eager to have it when you see the quality." Donald led the way to the sales counter, where he opened his case with a dramatic flourish. The item in question lay within. It was in good condition, with no discoloration or tears, and the signatures—Sir Nigel's in particular—were clear and legible.

"I can use it as a wall hanging," I said. "Fifty bucks."

Donald sputtered.

"I might be able to unload it," Grant said. "Fifty-five."

"Gemma," Donald said. "What is your counterbid?"

"Don't have one," I said. "I can't even afford fifty dollars, but I thought it would look nice hanging on the wall next to the *Beeton's Christmas Annual* cover."

"Fifty-five dollars," Grant said. "My final offer. And at that, I'd want to check first and see how common these things are. That play ran only a couple of years ago."

Donald slammed his briefcase shut. "You two have no eye for a good deal."

"Why don't you ask Rebecca Stanton?" I said. "She might be open to using it to honor Sir Nigel's memory."

"Excellent idea." Donald turned and stalked across the floor. He reached the door and then turned. "I almost forgot. Do you have my coat, Gemma?"

"Coat?"

"My ulster. You took it into the kitchen at the tea."

"Oh, right. The police must have it."

"The police!"

"Sorry, I sorta lost track of it, Donald. It wasn't there when I went back to Rebecca's on Sunday. They probably thought it was out of place and took it in. Sorry."

"Do I have to remind you that that's a rare and valuable item of clothing, Gemma? You can't buy genuine ulsters off the rack, you know."

"Sorry," I repeated. "The police'll take care of it. It'll be fine. I'm sure you'll have no trouble getting the fingerprint powder off it."

He screeched, threw open the door, and marched into the street.

Grant and I exchanged a look, and the moment the door slammed shut behind our erstwhile entrepreneur, we burst out laughing.

"About that dinner?" Grant said eventually. "Are you free?"

"No. I mean, no, I'm not. Ryan's visit reminded me of something I have to do. Sorry."

*   *   *

Despite it being a Monday, the store was busy all day, and I didn't get a chance to escape until twenty to four, when it was time for Jayne and my daily business partners' meeting. The tea room was almost full, and my favorite seat in the window alcove had been taken, so we went into the kitchen. Jayne poured tea, Lapsang Souchong today, and I examined the food offerings. They were, to say the least, sparse. "Is this the best you can do? Holmes ate better when he was hiding in a Bronze Age hut in the Great Grimpen Mire." I selected a cucumber sandwich, squished almost flat, and a fruit tart with a broken crust.

"I do run a business here, Gemma. We've been so busy today, I can hardly keep up. Rejects are the best you get. Is the Grimpen Mire a real place?"

"No, but it's based on Fox Tor Mire in Devon, or so they say. I've been there, and it is mighty creepy."

We discussed business for a few minutes, and then I updated Jayne on Great Uncle Arthur's current whereabouts (they'd decided to leave Greece and head for Majorca) before asking, "Have you spoken to your mum today?"

"I called her last night when I got in. I wanted to go around, but she said she wasn't feeling well and had gone to bed early. I said I'd come over after I finish work today, but she mumbled something about a previous engagement. I didn't believe her. I think she's avoiding me, and I'm getting worried. What's happening, Gemma? You seem to know more than I do."

"It's not for me to tell, but I will say that I'm not happy with the direction the police investigation is taking."

Jayne threw up her hands. "My mom is under suspicion for murder, and no one will tell me why that's even a possibility!"

"Are you seeing Eddie tonight?"

"Don't change the subject, Gemma."

"I'm not changing the subject. The theater people are at the heart of this."

"If you must know, we've arranged a late date. He's in rehearsal until seven."

"I bet that's interesting. To watch a rehearsal, I mean. Perhaps we could drop by. Wouldn't that be great fun?" I nibbled on a tart. It might be a reject because of its appearance, but that did nothing to spoil the taste.

"You've never cared about the theater before."

"Sure I have."

"If you're investigating Eddie and his crowd to try to help Mom, I suppose that's good. But I still don't understand what's going on. I suggested calling Jeff and asking him to come for a visit, but she said not to because he's busy. He's always too busy, but that's another story."

I leaned across the butcher's block table, where Jayne rolled pastry and otherwise performed amazing feats of magic with flour and sugar, and took her hand. "If she doesn't want to talk to you about some things, it doesn't mean she doesn't know you have her back. Now, I bet Eddie would be more than delighted to have you drop in on rehearsal. If you bring a friend, all the better. Do they rehearse at the barn?"

"I think so."

I eyed her work clothes of jeans and T-shirt. "I'm guessing you'll want to go home and freshen up. Get your car and collect me at the Emporium at six."

"Don't you want to freshen up too?"

"I'm not trying to impress anyone."

*　　*　　*

The West London Theater Festival operates out of a huge old barn on the outskirts of town. From the outside, it looks like a typical barn surrounded by acres of verdant green fields—with a sloped roof, wide entrance ramp, aging wood, and coat of dark-red paint freshly applied—but the inside is more like a palace for cattle, if ever cows achieve aristocratic status. The moveable seats are wide, plush, and comfortable, the prominent stage well-lit. A chandelier almost as ornate as the one that crashed down at the climax of the *Phantom of the Opera* hangs overhead. A long bar is set up at the back, and gleaming, white-tiled restrooms are installed in what was once the tack room. In the spring and fall, the barn is used for weddings, but in the summer, the theater festival takes over.

I'd provided the favors and decorations for a wedding here last autumn. The centerpieces on each table had been deerstalker hats and magnifying glasses. Every guest—all one hundred of them—received a set of the *Complete Sherlock Holmes* (both volumes), and the after-dinner coffee was served in *Sherlock* mugs ("I am SHERLocked"). They'd approached Jayne about catering, but she hadn't been set up to manage food such as kedgeree and new potatoes or steak and ale pie with Yorkshire pudding, although she had provided the dessert of sherry trifle and the wedding cake—with the topmost layer recreating the front door of the 221B Baker Street of legend in buttercream frosting. Fortunately, the *Sherlock*-mania didn't extend as far as wedding attire. The bride didn't appear as *The Abominable Bride* but wore a simple and attractive cream satin gown. Men's formal fashions haven't changed too much in a hundred years, so although the groom might have wanted to look like Dr. John Watson, his morning suit wasn't entirely out of place at his own wedding.

Today, a scattering of cars were parked close to the building. A tiny Smart car, a flashy BMW convertible, a black Cadillac Escalade, a gleaming Lexus, and a practical tan Dodge Caravan. Except for the minivan, which sported New York license plates, all were from Massachusetts. The big barn doors were locked, but I hammered until someone slid a side door open with a loud creak. A youngish man, dressed in overalls and a baseball cap worn backward, stuck his head out. "We're in rehearsals. Box office is in town, next to the library."

"We're not here for tickets." I put my foot in the door. "We're friends of the festival. Pat Allworth will be delighted to see us." The man glanced over his shoulder, and I took the opportunity to shove the door open. I walked in, and Jayne followed. The stagehand shrugged, not much caring, and strolled away.

The theater was empty save for a handful of people sitting in the front row and one man wrapped in shadows in the back. Our footsteps echoed around the barn as we made our way down the center aisle. Several members of the cast were on stage, dressed in street clothes. Pat was talking to Eddie while gesturing wildly. Eddie spotted us, and his handsome face lit up in a smile. Pat turned. "Gemma. Jayne. I'm sorry, but we're rather busy here."

I took a seat front row center. "Don't mind us. We have some free time and thought we'd pop in. Carry on."

I leaned back and crossed my arms. Jayne slunk into the seat beside me. I nodded to Rebecca, seated halfway down the row. She gave me a curt nod in return.

"I suppose that'll be all right," Pat said. "Very well, let's continue. Ralph, I need a lot more surprise from you when you see Eddie come out of the wings. No, not surprise. I need shock! Astonishment! If you think you can manage that, then take your position."

I had taken Pat's position, and she dropped into the vacant chair beside me.

"You've decided to go ahead with it then," I said.

"We're going to dedicate the run of the play to Sir Nigel. He'd want that, don't you think?"

"That and a bottle of cheap champagne."

She snorted. "Makes no difference really. Nigel had exactly one rehearsal with Ralph, and it was a disaster. He couldn't remember the lines. 'Jet lag,' he said."

I've never seen the play, but I know the story well. As does most of the population of the Western Hemisphere, if not the world. The man on stage was obviously playing John Watson, and this was the dramatic scene where Watson discovers that, rather than being back in London working another case, Sherlock Holmes has been living in a hut on the moor observing everyone and everything.

"Why are you rehearsing out of order?" I asked. "This scene takes place near the end."

"It's critical to create the dynamic between Holmes and Watson, Eddie and Ralph. I always rehearse the important scenes first, to see how the actors play off each other."

On the stage, Ralph was carefully examining nothing. I assumed props would be added later. Offstage, someone whistled, and he leapt to his feet. He lifted his walking stick and assumed a defensive pose. Eddie emerged from the wings. It was just Eddie, wearing purple board shorts and a T-shirt—young and blond and handsome—but he walked with the stiffness of a Victorian-era English gentleman (albeit one hiding out in an abandoned hut) and held his head with all the arrogance of the Great Detective. "It's a lovely evening, my dear Watson," he said in a London accent almost as good as my own. "I really think that you will be more comfortable outside than in."

"Before we break for the day," Pat whispered, "I hope to do Renee and Ralph." She nodded to her left, where Renee sat alone at the end of the row, watching the action on stage. She'd seen us come in but had made no attempt to greet us and was now pointedly ignoring us.

"Where Miss Stapleton mistakes Dr. Watson for Sir Henry and attempts to warn him off," I said.

"That's right. Hey, I've got an idea. Renee is struggling with the accent. Maybe you can give her some tips."

"Why not let her speak in her own voice? The audience knows it's just a play."

"That's what it's all about, isn't it? We don't want the audience to remember that they're sitting in a barn in New England in the twenty-first century watching a bunch of people pretending to be something they're not. We want them to believe they're in the sitting room at 221B Baker Street, or lost on the Great Grimpen Mire."

"Oh." Jayne sighed. "I miss the theater so much."

I was about to suggest that, if the accent was so important, they hire English actors, when Ralph stopped in midspeech. He shook his stick at us. "How am I supposed to concentrate with all this chatter going on? This is an intense scene that requires my full concentration. Or have you forgotten, Ms. Allworth?"

"A good actor," she said, "can perform as the theater falls to ruin around him. However, I take your point. Please continue."

We watched in silence for a few minutes. It was a lot of stopping and starting. Eddie didn't like the way he had to turn to speak to Ralph, and Ralph thought Eddie wasn't being serious enough. Pat kept interrupting to tell Ralph to be more startled! Astonished! She also suggested that Eddie's Holmes might not be quite so sneering toward the eternally hapless Dr. Watson.

The entirety of this scene would fill about two minutes of the play. If they took this long over every piece, I wondered that they'd ever get through it.

Finally, Pat got to her feet. "That's enough of this for today. Thank you, Eddie. You're wanted in costume for another fitting. Ralph, a five-minute break and we'll do a run through of the scene where you meet Miss Stapleton for the first time. Someone tell Harry we'll be ready for him soon."

"Who's Harry?" I asked.

"Plays Stapleton. He wasn't at the tea. Lives in Boston, so went home for the weekend."

Eddie jumped off the stage. He said hi to me, but his eyes were on Jayne, and they had a decided twinkle to them. "Hey, nice to see you. Thanks for coming. I hope this didn't put you off. Early rehearsals are usually a mess."

"It's marvelous," Jayne said, her eyes glowing. "I wanted to be an actor at one time, but I let my mom talk me out of it. I'm regretting that now."

Renee joined our little circle. In contrast to Jayne, her eyes were like chips of ice. "Hollywood's loss, I'm sure. Still, people have to be fed, don't they? Someone has to do the cooking."

"Now, now, put those claws away, Renee." Eddie slipped his arm around her shoulders, but he kept his eyes on Jayne. "Everyone knows you're going to be fabulous in this role. If you can only get that accent right."

She snuggled closer to him. "Maybe you can give me some tips, Eddie, honey. When we can get some private time." She was also looking at Jayne as she spoke. "Non-theater people have no idea how hard it can be."

What an interesting interpersonal dynamic we have here.

"I feel the same way when I order three copies of *The Bee-keeper's Apprentice* and only two arrive," I said in an accent so pretentious it would do the Dowager Duchess of Grantham proud. "Life as a bookseller can be *so* difficult sometimes. I often wonder how I cope."

Renee's eyes narrowed, and she looked at me for the first time. Eddie laughed out loud. He took his arm back and stepped away from Renee. "The wardrobe mistress is waiting for me, and she's a right dragon. We're still on for tonight, Jayne?"

"I'm looking forward to it."

"Me too." He gave her a smile and vaulted onto the stage as though he were Holmes leaping from crag to crag across the moors.

"Take some advice from me," Renee said, "and stay in your kitchen, where you belong."

Jayne, innocent Jayne, who'd missed all the undercurrents flowing around, said, "What do you mean?"

"She means there's nothing a chap likes more than a good home-cooked meal," I said. "I'm sure Eddie's no different than any other man. He must get *so* tired of living in a hotel and eating restaurant food."

Renee glared at me.

"I suppose," Jayne said, "but you know I don't cook at home, Gemma. I do that all day. The last thing I want to do when I get home is take out more pots and pans. If you think he'd like that though . . ."

Renee stalked off.

"What do you suppose got into her?" Jayne asked me.

"Haven't a clue."

Rebecca picked up her purse and got to her feet. "I've seen all I can handle. This is a disaster. A total and absolute disaster."

"Early days yet," I said. "Give Eddie time to get into the role."

"He's had more than enough time. I wanted an actor with gravitas. I got someone who could be on the cover of a magazine providing fashion tips for preteen girls." She stalked off.

"I thought Eddie was doing a fine job," Jayne said.

"Give me a minute, will you?" I said.

When we'd first arrived, I'd noticed the man sitting in the back row of the theater, wrapped in darkness. When the actors took their break, he'd stood up and moved into the aisle, where Pat joined him. I'd seen him at the tea on Sunday. The one with the man-bun and the pink shorts. The hair was still in place, but his clothes were less flamboyant today, beige slacks and a brown golf shirt. I made my way up the side aisle toward them. He'd been at the party, but I hadn't met him. Time to correct that oversight. I needed to know all the players here.

"That was interesting," I said to Pat. "Thanks for letting us watch."

"My pleasure," she said. "I have to get back to your tea room soon."

I offered the man my hand. "Gemma Doyle."

"I'm sorry," Pat said, "I didn't realize you hadn't met. Gemma Doyle. Leo Blackstone."

"Pleased to meet you," we chorused.

"Gemma owns a Sherlock Holmes-themed bookstore in West London," Pat said. "It's a delight."

"I'll have to check it out." He could barely control his total lack of interest.

Notably, Pat did not tell me what Leo Blackstone did or why he was here. I rectified that omission. "What brings you to rehearsal today, Leo?"

"Curiosity," he said.

I couldn't tell much about him by his appearance or the way he talked. American, for sure. His fancy Rolex and Italian loafers indicated some money. The man-bun and permanent tan probably meant California, perhaps Arizona or Florida, so the Escalade, which was the sort of vehicle he would drive, would be a rental. The fat gold wedding ring he wore indicated he wasn't on the make, and his attitude toward Pat eliminated that as a possibility anyway. Their behavior toward each other indicated that they weren't friends; they might be relatives who didn't know each other too well, but I could see no traces of family resemblance. He was likely here on business, and his hair style, dress, and demeanor indicated something in the arts. Because he was here, it must be theater. Judging by the tan, he was more likely to work in movies than the stage, but there was no reason he couldn't have an interest in both.

I put him down as a financial backer of the play. I don't know much about how these things work, but it seemed odd that someone would come all the way from California to check on his investment in a small, local repertoire company.

"So far," he said to Pat. "I like what I'm seeing. You're lucky that young man was ready to step in to take the main role. I think he'll do a good job. Nigel had the name, but we don't want to re-create an old chestnut. But . . . early days yet. Catch you later. Nice meeting you, Gemma." He walked away. The interior of the barn was well-lit, and plenty of light crept between slats in the walls, but as he opened the door, he was framed in a burst of brilliant sunlight. What do they call people who finance theatrical productions? *Angels.*

"Is the loss of Nigel likely to mean a financial setback for the season?" I asked Pat.

"I won't say I'm not worried. The publicity from having his name attached to our production would have been immeasurable." Her jaw tightened. "Despite that, I have to confess I wasn't entirely comfortable having him in the main role. His, shall we say, best years seemed to have passed."

"Losing him is not a disaster, then, as Rebecca seems to think."

"I've always been a boundless optimist. You have to be, to be a director of live theater. I like to believe it's all turned out for the best. Although," she added hastily, "not for poor Sir Nigel."

We turned at a burst of laughter from the direction of the stage. Eddie had come out, wearing his Holmes frock coat and carrying his walking stick. He was performing for Jayne, using the stick as a sword. He lunged and parried and then dropped to his knees and held it out to her, head bowed. Jayne clapped her hands and laughed.

From the wings, Renee threw daggers.

"Time to get back at it," Pat said. "People, stop that foolishness. I need Harry out here, and I need him now. Renee, get that pout off your face before it freezes into position. Eddie, that hem's loose. If you tear it, Alice'll tear a strip off you."

Chapter 12

Jayne dropped me back at the store and went home to change once again for her date with Eddie. She glowed with such happiness, I hated to be the one who might end up sticking a pin in her balloon. I didn't mention that Eddie was now firmly at the top of my suspect list. I don't think Sherlock Holmes ever said "cui bono," but if not, he should have. *Who benefits?* The first question that must always be asked in any murder inquiry. Who benefits from the death?

Eddie Barker clearly did. The starring role in the festival's centerpiece play now rested in his well-manicured, tanned hands. Not only did he land the role, but the death of Nigel would attract even more theatergoers. People like to be involved, no matter how peripherally, in a celebrity death. The more mysterious, the better.

I did a quick inventory as I came into the shop. Business had been brisk.

"Lots of people are talking about that play," Ashleigh told me. "They saw the poster in the window and think we're involved. Are we?"

More than I would like. "No. Although I might see about selling tickets. If people come in here, there's no point sending them down the street to the box office."

"Maybe we could provide some of the props," she said, "and sell copies of them at the theater."

"What kind of props? The play, from what I saw, is set in the nineteenth century. The characters won't be sipping tea out of *I Am SHERLocked* mugs or reading Lyndsay Faye or Anthony Horowitz."

She shrugged. "Maybe you could get some old stuff in. Like capes and hats or something."

"I think I have enough stock, thank you."

Her face fell, and I added quickly, "That's a good suggestion but not entirely practical. Keep thinking, and don't be afraid to bring your ideas to me."

"Businesses need to expand if they are to grow," she said.

"Right." I didn't add that I didn't want to grow. I was happy with the Emporium exactly the way it was.

"There's an active chapter of the Baker Street Irregulars in Boston. They call themselves 'The Speckled Band.' I looked that up last night. I bet they'd love to shop at your store. If you aren't keen on my idea of selling franchise rights to the name, why don't you open a second location of the Emporium?"

Perish the thought. The bell over the door tinkled, thankfully putting an end to that line of speculation.

Donald Morris came in. I was pleased to see that he wasn't carrying the folder with the playbill. I gave him a smile. "Twice in one day. To what do I owe this honor, Donald?"

"About sixty," he said.

Not this again. "I told you earlier, my top offer is fifty bucks."

"Not sixty dollars, but the book *About Sixty*. Do you have it?"

"Oh, yes, I do." I walked with him to the nonfiction shelf. "I thought you had this already. I remember you buying it when it first came out."

"It will be gift," he said, "for a fellow Sherlockian who's in the hospital."

"Nice of you to think of him." I took the book off the shelf. There are sixty stories in the original Holmes canon. In this collection, a Sherlockian makes the claim as to why each story is the best. A clever idea, I thought, although some of the arguments had to be stretched mighty far. I handed Donald the book. "Did you find a buyer for your playbill?"

"Mrs. Stanton was delighted to have it. Naturally, I'll never reveal the amount she paid for it, but she is a very generous woman. It will have a prominent place during the run of *The Hound*, in Sir Nigel's honor."

After Donald had made his purchase, I debated calling Grant and saying I was free for dinner after all. Instead, once Ashleigh had left and I closed the shop for the day, I phoned Leslie Wilson.

"I'm checking in," I said when she answered. "Everything okay there?"

Her sigh came down the phone. "Detective Estrada came by yesterday. She took the aprons my volunteers wore and asked me all the same questions. Why did Nigel and I go for a walk? Why did we think it necessary to leave the garden for the privacy of the woods? Did I—?"

"Let's not talk about this on the phone. Are you at home?" It was unlikely the police or anyone else was tapping Leslie's phone, but nevertheless, I didn't want this conversation to be on record.

"Yes."

"I'll be there in half an hour."

Violet loves nothing more than a ride in the Miata. She could use a treat today, so I took her with me. I don't like leaving her at home alone all day, but when Uncle Arthur's traveling, I have little choice. In the off-season, I can close the shop for an hour in the afternoon and take her for a good walk, but in the busiest times, I can't usually get away. At one time, I'd considered taking her to work with me some days. She was well behaved and would stay in the office without barking to be let out or trashing the place. Let's just say that Moriarty and Violet's initial meeting was not a success, and I was forced to abandon that plan. When he's home, Arthur's with her most of the day, and he walks her regularly, which does the both of them a lot of good: exercise for Uncle Arthur and a proper doggie social life for Violet. For some reason, all the elderly ladies and their equally elderly dogs have the same walking schedule as Arthur and Violet.

Leslie opened the kitchen door when she heard me drive up, and Rufus ran out ahead of her.

"I brought my dog," I said. "She's friendly. Is it okay to let her play?"

"Rufus loves to make friends."

I opened the door, and the two dogs greeted each other in a flurry of wagging tails and inquisitive sniffs. Violet then went on to investigate all the marvelous new smells in Leslie's yard, and Rufus followed her.

"Have you told the detectives you walked with Nigel to the cliff edge?" I asked as Leslie and I watched the two animals get acquainted.

She hung her head. "It's too late, Gemma. How can I possibly say I forgot that little detail?"

"You have to, Leslie. They're concentrating on you because they think you're hiding something. And they're right. If you let them know what it is you're hiding, they might move on."

"Might. Or they might decide to arrest me."

"If you want," I said, "I'll come with you when you talk to them."

She shook her head. "No. I didn't kill Nigel. I had no reason to. And no one can prove I did."

"I think that's a mistake, but it's your decision. But you have to talk to Jayne. She's worried. She's beginning to realize that you're of far more interest to the police than anyone else who was at the party. She wants to know why."

Leslie threw up her hands. "How can I tell her about my past? About this secret I've kept all these years?"

"Better than worrying her half to death and driving a wedge of distrust and suspicion between you."

Violet cornered a squirrel in an old oak and leapt frantically against the tree trunk trying to reach it. From sixty feet above the ground, the squirrel laughed.

"I know you're right, Gemma. But it's hard. Detective Estrada asked me about money."

"What about it?"

Leslie waved her arm around, indicating the house falling into gentle disrepair, the overgrown flower beds, the old car that was as much rust as metal. "When Rick died, he left a lot of medical bills and not much else. I have my pension from the bank, and that pays my expenses, if I live simply. It's obvious to anyone that I don't have a lot of extra cash. Jeff has been after me to sell the house. I have no mortgage on it, and he says I'd make a handsome profit. I know it's the practical thing to do, but I simply can't." She looked around her, taking in the old house, the spacious gardens, the peace and quiet. "I love it here. Rick and I were so happy. This is where we raised our children. I have to live somewhere, and I'm not ready to move into a soulless condo. I'm happy with my life the way it is. Although I'd love to have a pack of grandchildren. Don't tell Jayne I said that."

"Why does Estrada care about your finances?"

"I think she suspects I was blackmailing Nigel."

"Why would you do that? She doesn't know about your son. Does she?"

Leslie shook her head.

"Then she's fishing. Was Detective Ashburton with her?"

"No. She came here alone to get the aprons."

"Don't talk to her again. Next time she comes, tell her you want your lawyer to be present."

"Won't that make me look like I have something to hide?"

"It will make you look like a citizen in danger of having her rights violated. I don't know what game she's playing at, but I don't want you playing along." I touched her arm. "I'm doing what I can to get to the bottom of this. Don't worry."

Her brave smile looked so much like her daughter's.

I called Violet, and we got into the car and headed home.

*   *   *

Not good. Not good at all.

Louise Estrada was clearly focused on Leslie Wilson as the killer. Ryan was always telling me Estrada was a good cop and a good detective. I had yet to be convinced of that.

Ryan also told me I got Estrada's back up and I should attempt to make nice.

Somehow, whenever I try to make nice, it goes awry.

I had to ask myself if Estrada was focusing on Leslie because I was defending her. Might Estrada not even realize she was letting me, unwittingly, push her buttons?

Surely we both had the same goal in mind? To find out what happened to Sir Nigel Bellingham at the edge of that cliff on Saturday afternoon.

I had to remember that Ryan himself wasn't completely convinced of Leslie's innocence either.

I pulled into my driveway but didn't get out of the car. Instead, I called Gerald Greene. I tried to sound as though I was just making a friendly call. Checking up on a fellow countryman alone and far from our native shores. "How are you doing?"

"Doing? How do you think I'm doing? I'm stuck in this miserable town. I want to go home."

"Are the police still saying you can't leave?"

"Yes. Fortunately, I have a hotel room. Sir Nigel's and my rooms were paid in advance. Mrs. Stanton wants me to leave so she can get a full refund, but I don't see why I should have to. As it is, I have to pay for my own meals and other expenses here. My salary ended with Sir Nigel."

"How about a drink at the bar in your hotel?"

Long pause.

"My shout," I said.

"Brilliant idea," he replied.

I agreed to meet Gerald in fifteen minutes and backed out of the driveway. I brought Violet with me, hoping I could find out what I needed to know from Gerald quickly and still have time to go for a walk along the water's edge.

A strong wind was blowing off the ocean, and the sun was low in the sky to the west, but I didn't want to leave the dog in the car, so I tied Violet to a tree at the side of the parking lot of the Harbor Inn and told her I'd be back as soon as I could. She didn't object and settled down on the cool grass for a short nap.

Gerald was waiting in the lobby and got to his feet when he saw me. "Good evening, Gemma."

"Thanks for agreeing to meet me," I said.

"Anything for an English woman," he said, as though he were doing me a big favor by letting me buy him a drink. His accent was educated, veering toward upper-class. He'd had a comfortable childhood, I thought, and had gone to a good university. Good, but not Cambridge or Oxford. He was in his early sixties, late in life to be working as a PA to a crotchety old man. Either he'd fallen on hard times and taken whatever job he could get or he was such a fan of the theater that he wanted to move in its orbit, no matter what the level.

Gerald headed toward the French doors leading outside, but I stopped him. The restaurant at the inn is excellent, and they have a beautiful patio bar for those wanting to enjoy the summer evening, but the lounge is far more private at this time of year.

"Why don't we stay inside," I said. "It's a bit chilly out tonight."

He shrugged, and I led the way.

Sherlock Holmes and Sir Arthur Conan Doyle would have been comfortable in this small room. Well-worn leather couches and wingback chairs around low tables. Striped wallpaper, rich red carpets. A large (although gas and now unlit) fireplace.

We were the only customers in the place. I nodded to the bartender as we came in, and we took two chairs in a corner. The waiter took our orders. I requested a glass of Sauvignon Blanc, and Gerald asked what they had in the way of Highland Single Malt.

Unfortunately for my pocketbook, they had Macallan's, and Gerald said he'd have that. He leaned back with a sigh. "This is most inconvenient. Not only do I now suddenly find myself unemployed, I'm trapped in a foreign country without adequate funds." His small eyes darted around the room, and he picked at the lint on his trousers.

"The West London police are good at their jobs," I said. "I'm sure they won't detain you much longer." I knew no such thing, but I wanted to put him at ease.

He leaned back with a sigh. "I can only hope so."

"This isn't a bad hotel in which to be detained, as you put it."

"No. But I have to confess, as long as I have no immediate prospects for employment, I can't fully enjoy myself." Meaning he was broke.

"What brought you to work for Sir Nigel?"

"I've always loved the theater," he said. "When my . . . uh . . . circumstances were more favorable, I dabbled in amateur theatricals. I directed some minor productions over the years. Quite excellent they were. Many reviews said one would never believe them to be amateur theater." The nervous mannerisms stopped, and he looked at me for the first time. He might have even smiled at the memories.

"Sounds marvelous," I said.

The waiter brought our drinks. "Can I get you something to eat?" he asked.

"No," I said quickly, cutting Gerald off. I had no interest in sitting over a meal with the man.

He left, and Gerald and I lifted our glasses. "Cheers," we said simultaneously. He took a long, deep drink and closed his eyes in pleasure.

"How did you come to work for Sir Nigel?" I asked.

"Even in amateur theater, at least at the level in which I moved," he boasted, "you meet many professionals. Including some of the great actors of our age. I had dinner in London with Helen Mirren once, you know."

"That must have been exciting. What's she like?"

"As beautiful and charming and gracious as I expected. Of course, I wasn't seated next to her, so we didn't get a chance to chat intimately, but she did say hello. Maggie Smith herself came to one of my plays. She came backstage after and spoke to the actors. I shook her hand." He beamed proudly. "And then there was the time Hugh Grant—"

"Nigel?" I prompted.

"When I was . . . uh . . . seeking employment, a friend from the old days mentioned that Nigel . . . I mean Sir Nigel, had lost his PA and needed another. So I applied. We hit it off instantly." His eyes turned away from me once more, and he peered into the depths of his glass.

I felt rather sorry for Gerald. Reading between the lines, it was obvious that he'd desperately wanted to be a stage director, but he had little or no talent (or, to be fair, luck). He'd had some family money that allowed him to indulge his love of theater as a hobby, but that had eventually run out, leaving him needing to make a living with no marketable skills. I smiled across the table at him. I saw no signs of indulgence or bad habits (except for a preference for good whisky at someone else's expense), so I surmised he hadn't gambled or drank away his inheritance. Bad investments, perhaps, or maybe just not enough to last into his old age and not the sense to realize it in time. Then again, maybe none of it was his fault. He'd phoned his mother the day of the afternoon tea. If Gerald was sixty, she had to be eighty, at least. Care of an aging parent can require a lot of money.

"I assume you'll be packing up his things," I said.

"I've done so. Such a sad task." He tilted his glass back and forth and studied the liquid swirling about. His eyes were completely dry. "You must still have contacts in England, Gemma. Do you know anyone in theater? I'm an excellent PA. I was more to Sir Nigel than a PA, really—more like a friend and confederate. I was, you might say, the Watson to his Holmes."

"The day you and Nigel came into my shop, I later noticed a coloring book had gone missing. I was at the Stanton house after the party, when Rebecca discovered that some small art items of varying value had disappeared. By which I mean they'd been stolen."

His eyes flicked up in surprise. Then he ducked his head again.

"You know anything about that, Gerald?"

"Why are you asking me?"

"Because I suspect that if the police searched Nigel's things, which you so conveniently packed up, they'd find some of the missing items. Maybe a few other things that don't belong among a gentleman's traveling necessities."

"You come by your name honestly, I think."

"Gemma?"

"Doyle."

"The relationship to Sir Arthur is tenuous," I said.

He took a deep breath. "Nigel Bellingham was what psychologists call a kleptomaniac. What others might call a common or garden thief. When I hung up his jacket on Wednesday before going to dinner, I found your coloring book in a pocket. That evening, a steak knife from the restaurant where we'd dined. Part of my job, Ms. Doyle, was to keep Sir Nigel out of trouble and his tendencies from becoming common knowledge. In the parlance of what I see on American TV, I *cleaned up* after him."

I refrained from pointing out that that phrase was normally used on crime dramas to mean getting rid of the bodies. "Mrs. Stanton's items?"

"She will find them in a plant pot by the front of her house. Hiding in plain sight, really. Nigel went to the loo before they sat down to tea. He was in the house a long time, and I was getting suspicious. When he came out, I took him around the side of the house and patted down his pockets. I found several small glass ornaments, which I took to be of considerable value. I confiscated the items and later stuck them beneath a flowering plant."

"Is that what you were doing when the police first arrived?"

"I sought some privacy to ring my mother, as I told you. At the same time I took the opportunity to dispose of the items in question. A coloring book and a steak knife is one thing. Fine art, no matter how small, is entirely another altogether. If he'd been found with those things on him, he might have been arrested. He certainly would have been disgraced."

I sipped my wine. "All of which sounds beyond the performance of a PA's normal duties. If you'd been the one found with the items, between taking them off Nigel and hiding them, you would have been in a lot of trouble."

"I call it other duties as assigned," he said.

"Were you blackmailing him?" I asked.

"You're very blunt, Ms. Doyle."

"So I've been told. I prefer not to beat about the bush when both parties know what's being discussed."

Earlier, I'd considered the possibility that Gerald was the thief and Nigel was blackmailing him. I dismissed that idea now. Gerald, as I earlier observed, was no actor. He was habitually a nervous man, but as he talked, he didn't get more agitated, his gaze settled on me without trying to will me to believe him, and he engaged in none of the traditional "tells" of a poor liar.

"I was not blackmailing him. I was, however, highly paid for my discretion."

"Was that explicit? I mean, did he tell you that?"

"He never said a thing. I was, I'll admit, surprised at the interview when he told me what the salary would be. Far, far higher than I'd expected. I assumed he wanted the best and was prepared to pay for it. He went to a dinner party the first night of my employment. The next morning, when I was tiding his clothes, I found a seventeenth-century snuffbox in his pocket. The pattern continued. Nothing was ever said between us. I returned the items whenever I could."

"You say you were highly paid, but you're worried about spending a few more days in West London in a prepaid hotel room?"

He sighed, and for a moment, I thought he wouldn't answer. It had been a brazenly personal question, after all. But I find that once people start trying to explain their actions, they rarely stop. "I was raised in the Kent countryside. I had a good childhood, and I have fond memories. I'm hoping to buy a small property there for my retirement years. Another benefit of working for Sir Nigel was that my living expenses were light. I lived in a small apartment in his house and traveled at his expense. I put every bob I could into my savings."

"Be that as it may," I said. "He didn't seem to treat you very well."

"I assume you're asking if I killed him."

I lifted my eyebrows.

"On the contrary, his death is a severe blow to my plans. If we're being honest here, Ms. Doyle, I'll tell you that I hated the man. He was arrogant, rude, and sneeringly condescending. I kept telling myself one more year . . . one more year . . .

and then I'd have enough saved to retire and buy my house. I did not kill him."

I believed him. Gerald might love the theater, but he wasn't much of an actor. His early attempt at a suitable expression of mourning was a complete failure.

"I hated him, in some ways, but I also felt sorry for him. He had achieved great heights in his chosen profession, and equally great was his fall. His friends abandoned him. Dinner party invitations dried up. No one would work with him. His parents are long deceased. He hadn't spoken to his only sister in years. His ex-wives would have nothing to do with him. All he had left was a bottle and a collection of pilfered items. You have no idea, Gemma, how excited he was when he got the offer to perform here, in *The Hound*. It was, truth be told, sad to see."

* * *

I'm well aware that the Internet is not always the best the place to go for factual knowledge, but for gossip, nothing beats it.

I had only one drink with Gerald and left him ordering another. I gave the bartender enough money to cover it. I untied Violet, and we drove to the beach for a long walk. I'd have enjoyed an evening swim in the warm waters of Nantucket Sound, but I knew that if I went home for my swimming costume, I'd never leave the house. Violet enjoyed the walk, as she always does, and as it always does, watching her play in the surf and chase sandpipers gave me a lot of time to think over what I'd learned today.

When we got home, I searched for Gerald Greene on the Internet. I eventually found a list of productions over the years from an amateur theater company in Reading, and Gerald had credit as director for ten years' worth of performances. Not that I had reason to doubt his story, but I never take anything on face value. The website featured pictures of the actors who'd appeared, but none of the director. I found no further information on Gerald, and Greene is such a common name in the UK, it was not worth my time trying to investigate his past without a lot more to go on.

I next searched IMDb for information on Edward Barker. He was, so the page reported, recently divorced from an actress named Garnet Hogan, to whom he'd been married for three years. I clicked on Garnet's info and wasn't at all surprised to see that she was a small, fine-boned, blue-eyed blonde in her early thirties. Her list of recent credits included two supporting roles as the best friend in moderately successful Hollywood romantic comedies.

Was Garnet on her way up and thus ready to dump Eddie, stuck in small off-Broadway roles? Or did jealousy at her success on his part get in the way of the marriage?

Wouldn't have been the first time that happened.

I searched the gossip blogs, looking for nothing more than dirt. A familiar name leapt out at me. *Well, well, what do we have here?* Before he married Garnet, Eddie's name had been linked to that of none other than Renee Masters. The dates were close enough that it would appear they broke up shortly before his marriage. If Eddie dumped Renee for Garnet and now he was single again, Renee might be wanting to get the relationship back on track. Which would explain Renee's hostility to Jayne.

I didn't find anything scandalous about the other actors. Ralph Carlyle had a solid career in repertory theater. Solid, steady, and respectable, with few highs and not many lows. He was married with four children and lived in New York City.

The bio listed him as thirty-eight years old, which is what I'd estimated when I met him. Far too young to play Watson to Nigel Bellingham's Holmes—the two men were supposed to be similar in age—but just right against Eddie Barker.

Harry O'Leary, who played Stapleton, had a few minor movie roles as a child but now only acted in summer theater. Tanya Morrison, who played Mrs. Hudson as well as Mrs. Barrymore, had also been in movies in her youth, the last of which was many years ago. She was now retired and living on the Cape with her husband of thirty years. She took the occasional part at the festival to keep her hand in. Her bio mentioned that she donated her salary back to the theater company.

Other than Renee and Eddie, they seemed like a boring bunch.

But, I reminded myself, murder can sometimes be a very mundane business.

Chapter 13

"How'd it go?" I asked Jayne.

"How'd what go?" The rush of color into the tips of her ears told me she knew exactly what I was talking about.

I took a sip of my tea. I hate drinking out of a takeaway cup, but I was en route to the shop, and I've found through experience that balancing cup and saucer while unlocking the door can end in disaster. Moriarty seems to instinctively know when I'm least able to defend myself from flying claws.

"Your evening," I said, "with the handsome and eligible Eddie. He is single, by the way—officially divorced with no children on record. I checked on that."

She glanced up from the tart shells in front of her. "Gemma, I did not ask you to do that."

"I have your interests at heart."

She shook her head. "I asked him, okay? He told me all about it. His wife decided there were better career options for her in Hollywood than in New York, so she dumped him. At first, he was crushed, devastated. Lots of acting couples, he told me, have cross-country marriages, but she didn't want to go to the trouble of working things out. He realized why when she set up housekeeping with some third-rate character actor the week she arrived in California."

I decided this was not the best time to point out to Jayne that she was too trusting for her own good sometimes. No doubt Garnet would spin a different story. "Where'd you go for dinner?"

"The café. It was lovely."

"Did you see Andy?"

"Yes. He gave us the best table and sent out a bottle of wine on the house. He's such a nice man. I know you think he's got a crush on me, Gemma, but we're just friends. He was so nice to Eddie."

If that was true, I figured Andy was a loss to the theater world.

"And after dinner?" I wiggled my eyebrows.

Jayne flushed. "We bought ice cream cones and went for a walk along the boardwalk." She sighed. "It was so romantic. And then—not that it's any of your business, Gemma Doyle—he drove me home and gave me a kiss at the front door. That was all."

"He rented a Smart car? That must cost a pretty penny."

"He likes to have his own transportation because he doesn't want to be dependent on others for getting him around. It's a superfun little car. Hey, how'd you know that?"

"I saw it outside the barn and figured a vehicle like that would suit him." Here on Cape Cod, Eddie was trying to make a good impression. What better than playing the role of a responsible, environmentally conscious consumer? Not a bad look for a visiting actor. Jayne always told me I was too cynical. Maybe he really was a responsible, environmentally conscious consumer.

The soft smile faded from Jayne's face. "I called Mom after you and I went to the rehearsal. She didn't answer, so I left a message. She still hasn't called me back. I'm getting seriously worried. She's hiding something from me, something mighty important, and you know what it is, don't you, Gemma?"

"Ashleigh comes in at one. I'll take a break at four to take Violet for a short walk. Let's have our partner's meeting at my house today. Four fifteen."

"Don't change the subject!"

"I'm not changing the subject. I'll invite your mum too." I gave her a wave with my tea mug and left her to her bread dough and pastries.

Speaking of pastries, I'd had time this morning to relax over the British online newspapers with a breakfast of yogurt, muesli, and fresh berries, but one of those brownies would suit me nicely for elevenses.

It was quarter to ten, and the tea room was almost empty. The business breakfast crowd had filled up and left, the late-morning tourists were yet to arrive, and it was a long time until lunch.

Today was Jocelyn's regular day off, and Lorraine, the part-time staffer, was taking a rare moment of quiet to adjust her shoe. Lorraine was an older woman, retired from running her own successful shop on Baker Street. She claimed she soon began to miss the human interaction of the retail trade and signed on to work at the tea room part-time over the summer. What Lorraine called human interaction, I knew, meant gossip.

While Fiona selected the fattest brownie and slipped it into a paper bag, I spoke to Lorraine. "Business has been good all over town this season. It must be the great weather we're having. Everyone seems to be happy, particularly the store owners on Baker Street. I suppose the hotels and B and Bs are saying the same. Your sister owns a B and B doesn't she?" *As if I didn't know.*

"Yes, and she's thrilled. She's already booked solid for the whole season."

"Brilliant. What's her B and B called again?" *Also, as if I didn't know.*

"Sailor's Delight."

"Is that so? I think I heard mention of that place only the other day."

"Some of the actors from the festival are staying there. Judy's absolutely thrilled. Imagine Renee Masters and Edward Barker staying in her house. She'd never heard of either of them before, but she looked them up, and now she's bragging to all her friends. She was disappointed that Sir Nigel Bellingham was staying at the Harbor Inn—him, she had heard of—but with what happened to him, she's glad he wasn't with her. She wouldn't want the police poking around her house, looking for clues. Nothing like police interest to put the guests off, or so Judy says."

I took my brownie from Fiona and gave Lorraine a slight twitch of my head. I moved away from the counter, and Lorraine followed. I could scarcely come right out and ask what I wanted to know, but I could dangle the bait. Either it would be snatched up by ravenous jaws or left dangling. "I bet your sister has some fun things to say about her guests."

She sniffed. "Guests are entitled to their privacy, you know."

"Goes without saying." I smiled at her.

"She occasionally talks to me about things in complete confidence. Nothing important, you understand."

"I'm not interested in common gossip."

Lorraine looked shocked at the very idea. "Of course not."

"But, well, with the death of Nigel Bellingham, I can't help but wonder if the guests have been acting at all strangely. Other than Renee and Eddie, who else is staying there?"

"Pat Allworth, the director, and one of the other actors, some older guy. I don't know his name. That's all the rooms Judy could give them. She has regular guests who come every year, and she didn't want to have to put them off. She didn't know what to do. She's never been asked by the festival before, and she hated to turn them down, because they're likely to be a reliable source of income. If we'd known then what we know now, Judy might have suggested they double up." She giggled. If I had whiskers, they would have been twitching. Another gentle nudge, and Lorraine would snatch up the bait.

The door opened, and two women came in. Unfortunately, they took seats rather than going directly to the counter. I edged slightly sideways, putting Lorraine's back to the room. "Double up? Has anything been said about the festival being short of money?" That might be an avenue worth exploring. Was Nigel's contract so cast-iron, he couldn't be fired even for being drunk and unable to perform? I couldn't think of a way I'd be able to persuade anyone to let me have a peek. I am not, as the recent incident at the Harbor Inn showed, entirely above a touch of breaking and entering, but I didn't need to be in possession of any more information I couldn't tell the cops. If the festival was in severe financial difficulties, that would be something the police needed to know.

Lorraine giggled. "I don't know about that. About the inner workings of the festival. All I mean is, some of those folks don't spend every night in their own beds." She gave me a wink.

"Huh?"

"Judy and I like to have a little chat every morning. Now that our kids have jobs and families and Dad and his new wife are spending all their time in Florida, we're all we have. You'd think that as Nancy—that's my oldest girl—is only living in Yarmouth, not more than half an hour down the highway, she'd have some time for her lonely mother, wouldn't you? But no, not that girl, she's too involved in her own career. Too important to have a good long chat with her mother in the mornings. Judy says it comes from—"

"Who's not sleeping in their own bed?" I ignored Fiona, who was trying to direct Lorraine's attention to the newcomers.

Lorraine gave me a wink. "I don't like to gossip, dear, but if you think it's important . . ."

"Definitely important."

"That Edward Barker, so handsome, isn't he? Just this morning, Judy told me that when she went to do up his room yesterday, his bed hadn't been slept in."

Not slept in? Was that relevant? It was unlikely he was out all night hiding evidence in the murder of Nigel or scouting out locations in which to commit other dastardly deeds.

"Oh, look," I said, "you have customers. Better get back to it."

Seeing she was losing me, Lorraine quickly added. "That's not all."

"It's not?"

"Judy says whereas his bed wasn't slept in, Renee's showed signs of double occupancy. And a lot of . . . tossing and turning . . . went on during the night."

"Excuse me!" One of the customers had gotten to her feet and was waving her napkin in the air. "Can we have some service here?"

"Be right with you," Lorraine called. She dropped her voice. "You won't tell anyone, will you, Gemma? That's between you and me. Judy will have my hide if she finds out I've been gossiping about her guests."

In that case, I thought, Judy would be well advised not to engage in gossip herself.

Lorraine bustled off without waiting for me to agree. Or not.

That was one tidbit of news I did not want to know. It was highly unlikely, to the point of improbably, that if Renee and Eddie were tiptoeing between rooms in the dead of night as though they were starring in a French farce, it had anything at all to do with the death of Nigel.

Unfortunately, it did have a heck of a lot to do with the romantic entanglements of Jayne Wilson.

I had learned something and, as much as I might want to, I could not unlearn it.

* * *

As planned, I went home at quarter to four. On the grounds that food and drink can be relied upon to smooth all social occasions, I popped into the market to pick up a few things. I prepared a pitcher of iced tea; arranged a selection of cheeses, bread and crackers, and plump green grapes onto a large wooden platter; and poured nuts into a bowl. I made the tea with powder from a packaged mix, although Jayne would disapprove, but we English have never learned to drink our tea cold.

I'd phoned Leslie from the store and invited her around to my house to talk over the day's developments. She said she hadn't heard from Estrada or Ryan again and was about to hang up on me. Leaving me with no choice but to lie and say I had something to tell her.

The only thing I'd learned today was that Eddie was dating Jayne and at the same time sleeping with Renee, but I didn't think Jayne would thank me for telling her mum. I didn't think Jayne would thank me for telling her either, so I decided to keep that tidbit of information to myself.

Jayne was the first to arrive. She eyed the snacks suspiciously. "Who else is coming?"

"I told you—your mum."

"Is that all?"

"Yes. Why?"

"You've put enough food out here to feed an army. Or an entire theater company at the very least."

"You think so? I wanted to be sure we had enough."

"An entire wheel of brie, at least a pound of Stilton—and that stuff's not cheap—and another pound and a half of cheddar. Never mind the slices of salami and ham, the hunk of pâté, a whole baguette, and two types of crackers." Jayne helped herself to one grape. "I don't think I've ever seen so many cashews in a single place at any one time."

"I'm not accustomed to entertaining."

"No kidding, Gemma." She gave me a grin. "But thanks."

We both jumped at a knock on the mudroom door. Violet hurried to answer, and I followed. Leslie gave the dog a pat and me a quick hug. I led the way into the kitchen. Leslie stopped so abruptly, Violet ran into the back of her legs. Her smile disappeared when she saw her daughter munching on a thin slice of cheddar. "Jayne, I wasn't expecting to see you here."

"Will you look at that?" I said. "Poor Violet is desperate to go outside." At that moment, the dog had hurried to assume a polite seated position at Jayne's feet, hoping for a piece of cheese. "Come on, Violet. Violet! Walk!" I grabbed the leash off the hook in the mudroom, snapped it onto her collar and dragged the dog out the door. "Can't be helped, sorry. Enjoy some cheese and crackers. Don't wait for me."

At last, Violet got the hint, and we hurried down the driveway.

I stayed away for about an hour, and when we got back, Jayne and her mother were gone. The pitcher of iced tea was almost finished. It looked as though two, maybe three grapes had been eaten. Oh, well, I'd have a cheese and ham sandwich for dinner. And for lunch tomorrow. And probably for several days to come. Maybe the rest of the week.

Perhaps the theater crew would like some.

A piece of paper lay on the counter, tucked under the bowl of nuts.

Thanks, it said in Jayne's neat handwriting. That was all it needed to say.

*   *   *

It was now coming up to six o'clock. I put the leftover food into the fridge and headed back to the shop. I wouldn't call Jayne to ask how things had gone. I'd leave it up to her to tell me when she wanted to. If she ever did.

"I brought you a sandwich," I said to Ashleigh.

"Gee, thanks." She took the parcel and peered through the plastic wrap. "Hey, this doesn't look too bad."

"I might not be much of a cook, but I can make a sandwich, thank you very much. Why don't you take your meal break now?"

"It's not six yet."

"If you go early, you can have an extra fifteen minutes. I have to go out again at seven."

"Do you actually work here, Gemma, or just pop in now and again?"

"I have important matters to attend to. Is that a problem?"

"Nope. I'm not complaining. Although I was rushed off my feet about an hour ago. I hope we didn't lose any customers when I couldn't help them quickly enough." Moriarty leapt onto the counter. He rubbed his entire body against Ashleigh's arm, and she gave him a hearty pat. "Such a pretty boy! You might need an extra assistant for the rest of the summer. I can do the interviewing if you're too busy with important matters. Who's a good cat? I have an eye for serious employees." Her tone of voice didn't alter between praising the cat and addressing her boss.

I decided to ignore her attempt to imply that I was not a serious employee. "That won't be necessary. We'll manage."

"If you say so. I hear the women's wear shop up the street is still hiring."

"Take an extra half hour. Be back by seven fifteen."

Gripping her sandwich, Ashleigh scarpered before I could change my mind. Moriarty jumped off the counter.

She was right, and I knew it. I was neglecting my store, getting involved in a murder investigation that the police would say was none of my business. The bookshop had been busy this afternoon, and it wasn't fair to Ashleigh to expect her to manage on her own. As I waited on customers and rang up purchases, I vowed to keep my nose out of the investigation into the murder of Sir Nigel Bellingham.

By the time Ashleigh returned, five minutes early, I'd changed my mind.

The police might think this inquiry was none of my business, but in suspecting Leslie Wilson, they'd made it my business.

I let Ashleigh take over the cash register and escaped into my office to make a quick phone call.

"I'm calling to apologize for turning down your invitation to dinner last night," I said to Grant Thompson.

"I know you've been busy," he said politely.

"Are you free tonight?"

"Let me check my busy schedule." He was silent for about two seconds and then said, in a voice pitched so I'd know he was teasing, "Will you look at that? I happen to have a slot available this very evening."

"Blue Water Café? Eight thirty?"

"That'll work."

"My treat, but first, I'd like your help with something."

"Name it." He didn't even sound suspicious as to my motives. I like that in a man. Ryan would have immediately had his guard up. *Why was I thinking about Ryan when I was setting up a dinner date with Grant, anyway?*

"I'll explain in the car," I said. "Pick me up in ten minutes. I'm at the shop."

"Ten minutes? You don't give me much time to put my makeup on."

"You don't need it," I said. Only after I'd hung up did I wonder if he'd think I'd been flirting.

* * *

I waved good-bye to Ashleigh as I walked through the store. Ashleigh was chatting to a customer while other people browsed the bookshelves. One woman had a heavy stack of gaslight mysteries, including books by Rhys Bowen and Victoria Thompson, tucked under her arm.

"Oh, Gemma," Ashleigh called, "if you have a moment, this lady has a question about that second edition of *The Sign of Four*."

Grant pulled up out front. He'd taken eight minutes to get here. I like punctuality in a man also.

All the street parking in our block was taken, and I spotted Linda Novak, the town's parking enforcement officer, heading this way, ticket pad at the ready. "No time," I called over my shoulder.

"Sorry about that," I heard Ashleigh say to the customer as I sprinted out the door. "Gemma's sister must have gone into labor. She's way overdue."

I jumped into Grant's Ford Explorer, and he pulled into the slow-moving traffic.

"Where to, madam?" he asked as I fastened my seat belt.

"Sailor's Delight B and B. Do you know it?"

"I know where it is. Want to tell me why we're going there?"

"You're considering making a hefty donation to the West London Theater Festival for next year's season, but first you want to talk to the people involved about the state of the festival's finances."

"Why am I doing that?"

My initial assumption on talking to Lorraine, that the festival was in financial difficulties, had turned out not to be true, at least not to Lorraine's knowledge. But it was an avenue worth exploring. "You'll think of something," I said. Yesterday, rehearsal had ended at seven. I was hoping the same would be the case today. Pat Allworth would be likely to head back to her B and B to change before going out for dinner. Pat, I assumed, was an employee of the festival, the same as the actors, costume designers, and stage hands. Anyone who put up the money to produce the season or stood to make a profit, such as Rebecca Stanton, wouldn't simply tell Grant all, not with five minutes' notice that he wanted to donate. But Pat might give us her impressions. She should know if the festival was on sound financial footing or facing potential disaster.

In addition, I wanted to find out what I could about the state of Nigel Bellingham's contract. Had he fiercely negotiated a generous compensation package, or had he taken whatever was offered out of desperation?

That might give me an indication as to his state of mind lately, which would be relevant if I were to conclude he'd killed himself.

"I suppose," Grant said, "I could say I'm hoping the play will renew interest in first edition British novels of the late nineteenth, early twentieth century. Thus bringing me business."

"I knew you'd think of something," I said. He took his eyes off the road long enough to give me a warm smile. The smile soon faded.

"But that's not true, Gemma. I don't have extra money to invest in theater of all things. If I did, I'd rather buy books. I hate to get their hopes up and then let them down."

"I'm sure you'll do it gently. Oh, good! It looks as though our quarry is here."

The Sailor's Delight is a huge Georgian-style house surrounded by a large and beautifully maintained garden. Portico supported by white pillars, symmetrical facade, two brick chimneys, black shutters, red door. Nooks and crannies, bay windows, attic gables, and a wide side porch.

The Smart car, the convertible, and the minivan were parked outside. The trees lining the parking area threw long shadows. I touched the bonnet of each of the cars as I passed. The BMW was stone cold, but the Smart car and the van felt warm beneath my hand.

Grant rang the bell, and the door opened almost immediately. If she'd been thirty pounds heavier, Judy would have been the spitting image of her sister Lorraine. They were almost certainly identical twins, but the lines on Judy's face were fewer and not as deep, indicating she didn't frown quite so much, and her eyes sparked with genuine welcome. "Good evening. I'm sorry if you're in need of a room, but I'm full up."

Grant gave me a sideways glance. I said nothing, so he cleared his throat. "I'm hoping to catch one of your guests. Pat . . . uh . . . Pat."

The woman in question came into the front hall. She wore a loose tunic splashed with a colorful flower pattern over black leggings and flat leather sandals, much the same outfit as she'd had on at rehearsal the other day. "That would probably be me. Oh, Gemma, hi. I just got in, haven't even been upstairs yet. What brings you here?"

Eddie had followed Pat. He gave me a nod.

"I've brought someone to meet you," I said. "This is Grant Thompson, rare book dealer and collector."

"We met at the tea party," Pat said. "Nice to see you again."

"I'd like to talk to you about—" Grant began.

Pat cut him off. "Give me a minute, will you? I've something I have to deal with here." She turned to Judy. "I can't stand a prima donna, but that's what I seem to be stuck with. I'll see what I can do. You wouldn't know anything about this, would you, Eddie?"

"Me?" Eddie blinked innocently.

"What's happening?" I asked.

"Renee's having a hissy fit over something," Pat said. "She finished her scenes earlier, checked her text messages, and ran out of the theater in tears without so much as asking if she was free to go. To which I would have said no, she was needed in wardrobe. She came back here and locked herself in her room. Judy knocked a few minutes ago to ask if she'd like anything, but Renee won't answer. Frankly, as far as I'm concerned, she can sulk all she wants until she's needed at rehearsals. But she likes to think she's a delicate flower, so I'll say some soothing words."

"Maybe she went out for a walk?" I said. "And Judy didn't see her leave?"

Eddie laughed, and Pat gave me a look. "Excuse me, but creatures like Renee don't *walk*. Thus she rented that ostentatious convertible to get her back and forth to the gym."

Pat headed for the stairs, followed by Eddie. For no reason but that I like to know what's going on, I followed them. Grant followed me. At the top of the stairs, Eddie said, "I'll be in my room if you need me." He continued down the corridor, unlocking the door at the far end and letting himself in.

Pat tapped lightly on the actress's door. "Renee, sweetie, it's me, Pat. Open up."

Silence. I took a step closer and sniffed the air. A large bouquet of fresh garden flowers sat on the piecrust table at the end of the corridor under a window. The window was open, and the fragrance of the flowers drifted lightly on the breeze. Judy had a heavy hand with scented cleaning equipment and commercial air freshener, but something stronger lay over this end of the hall. I sniffed again. Spilled brandy and the unmistakable scent of illness.

I stepped forward and rapped loudly. I put my ear closer to the door but heard nothing moving inside the room. "Renee! Some people are here to talk to you."

Silence.

"Maybe she's in the shower," Grant said.

"The shower's not running," I said. "The radio and TV are not on so she should hear us. If she was in the bath or undressed, she'd call out for us to wait. Something's wrong." I grabbed the doorknob and twisted. Nothing happened. "Judy, get this door unlocked!" I hammered on the door. "Renee! Wake up." Judy didn't arrive, so I turned to Grant. "Kick the door down."

"What?"

"Do it. Now. Kick the spot immediately below the handle." All the blood rushed out of Pat's face. "You don't think . . ."

"I do," I said, pulling her out of the way.

Grant stepped back. He braced himself. "Always wanted to do this." His foot shot out, and the door splintered. He grunted and struck it again. The door crashed inward. I pushed it aside and ran into the room.

Renee Masters lay sprawled across the bed, facedown. I leapt over a bottle of brandy rolling on the floor to reach her. "Pat, call nine-one-one." I rolled Renee onto her back. She let out a low moan and her eyelids flickered, but she didn't open her eyes. A small amount of vomit was soaking into the pretty white bedcover with a trim of pink roses. "Grant!" I shouted. "Get the shower going. Keep the water cold."

"What's the heck's going on?" Eddie ran into the room.

"I need a pen. Who's got a pen?"

"You're going to take notes?" Eddie said.

"Don't be a fool. A pen, anything long and thin. I'm not putting my fingers down her throat, but she needs to be sick."

"Looks like she already was," Eddie said.

"Not enough."

"Will this do?" Pat pressed a spoon into my hand. "It was on the tea tray."

I pried open Renee's mouth and shoved the bowl of the spoon in. She gagged and swatted at me. "Leave me 'lone. Go 'way. Let me die."

I heard the sound of an ambulance approaching. "Grant, bring me a bucket of cold water."

"Where am I going to get a bucket?"

"You'll think of something. The flower vase in the hall."

"I'll get it," Pat said.

I shoved Renee's head over the side of the bed, and she retched onto the floor. I couldn't help but notice that the pretty cream-and-pink carpet was a perfect match to the bedding.

Grant threw a vase of cold water onto Renee. His aim wasn't good, and I ended up soaked.

Then the paramedics were in the room, and I left them to do their jobs.

I waited in the hall with Pat, Grant, Eddie, Judy, and other B and B guests who'd been attracted by the commotion. It wasn't long before the stretcher came out. Renee was covered by a blanket and her eyes were closed, but her chest rose and fell in a steady rhythm.

"Anyone here a relative?" the young female paramedic asked.

"I'll accompany you to the hospital," I said.

I was standing next to Eddie. As the stretcher passed, Renee's eyes flicked open. She extended her hand toward him. He made no move to take it.

As I fell into step behind the stretcher, I heard Eddie say to Pat, "Anything for attention."

* * *

Either we had gotten to Renee in time or she hadn't taken much since she stayed awake on the trip to the hospital. I'd found a container for prescription pills—empty—among the bedclothes and given them to the paramedics, as well as pointing out the brandy bottle on the floor. A cell phone had been beside the pill bottle. That, I had pocketed.

"I assume the police have been contacted," I said to the paramedic as she checked her patient.

"Yeah."

"You'll want to suggest they inform Detective Ashburton. This woman was recently a witness in a possible homicide."

When we arrived at the West London Hospital, I was directed to the waiting room while Renee was whisked behind a curtain.

I took a seat and pulled out Renee's phone. Conveniently, it was not password protected. I never fail to be amazed at how lax some people are over matters of security and privacy.

Amazed, but highly satisfied.

I checked her messages.

At three fifteen, Renee had texted Eddie, *Hey hot stuff. Let's blow this pop stand after reh*

Three thirty: *Dump her and we can go back to B 4 afternoon delight*

Between three thirty and three forty: three outgoing texts containing significant suggestive content.

In all that time, Renee received no incoming texts.

Then nothing until six fifteen, presumably when the actors were given a break: *I saw U checking messages. Answer me.*

Six twenty: *Don't U ignore me, Eddie. I no U R hiding in costume rm*

Six twenty-two: *It's that blond baker, isn't it?*

Six twenty-four: *She's as empty as her so-called cake*

Another long gap until six forty-seven: *Eddie. Please. We're so good together. Don't you remember?*

Finally, a response. At six forty-nine, Eddie replied, *Always fun to have a romp for old times' sake. We're still finished. Don't make a big deal of it.*

And thus ended the text messages. Poor, desperate Renee, dumped by text.

Lucky for snooping Gemma, the entire conversation laid out before her. All afternoon Renee and Eddie were in the same building, but they conducted their correspondence by text message. Sherlock Holmes would have been reduced to listening at doors or relying on third-hand accounts.

"I shouldn't be surprised, but I am. What on earth are you, of all people, doing here?"

I slipped Renee's phone into my pocket. Louise Estrada stood over my chair, hands on hips, glaring down at me. At the end of the corridor, Ryan was talking to a nurse at the ER reception desk.

"Lovely to see you too, Louise," I said.

"Don't mock me, Gemma. They told us you're the next of kin. How the heck did you manage to make them believe that?"

I lifted my hands. "I never said anything of the sort. Someone needed to be with Renee, and as I was the one who administered treatment to her when we found her, I volunteered to accompany her in the ambulance."

"And you just happened to be there when she was found."

"As a matter of fact—yes. That's exactly what happened."

"They say we can talk to her in a couple of minutes." Ryan joined us. "She'll be fine. They got to her in time. Or, it would appear, you got to her in time. Want to tell us about it, Gemma?"

"I'd be happy to."

Pat and Grant burst into the room. "She's going to be okay," I said to the director.

Pat let out a puff of air and fell onto the lumpy couch beside me. "Thank heavens. I might have called her a prima donna, and I might not have sounded all that sympathetic, but the last thing I need is to lose another actor in this production."

"Miss Stapleton doesn't have too big a role in *The Hound*," I said. "Doesn't Renee have a much bigger part in *Cat on a Hot Tin Roof*?"

"Yes, but *The Hound of the Baskervilles* is our centerpiece this season. Why—?"

"Save it for later," Estrada said.

"I need a coffee. I'll be back soon." Pat got to her feet and walked away.

Ryan said, "First, is there any doubt, Gemma, that this was a suicide attempt?"

I shook my head. "Not in the least. She took sleeping pills—I don't know how many as I don't know how many had been in the bottle—and chased them down with brandy. It's possible someone could have forced her to consume the pills and the liquor, but obviously that wasn't done in this case."

"It's obvious, is it?" Estrada said.

"Yes, it is. Aside from the fact that no one stayed in the room to wait for events to come to their logical conclusion, Renee told me to go away. She attempted to stop me helping her and resisted when I did so. In short, she did not want me to save her life."

Estrada and Ryan exchanged glances.

"A suicide attempt is often a confession," he said.

"But not in this case," I said.

"Oh, please," Estrada said. "Bellingham insulted her at the tea party, loudly and publicly. We've been looking into her, we've been looking into them all, and it's clear that her career is pretty much stalled, if not on a substantial downward direction. His insults pushed her over the edge, and she lashed out the first chance she got."

"Sounds reasonable to me," Grant said. "I mean, your theory sounds reasonable. Not the lashing out part."

"What are you doing here, anyway?" Ryan asked.

Grant stood straighter, lifted his chin, and subtly puffed up his chest. He casually laid his arm on my shoulder. "Gemma and I paid a call on Pat before going out to dinner."

Ryan glared at Grant's hand. He pulled back his own shoulders. For a moment there, I expected the two of them to lower their heads, paw the cracked and faded linoleum of the hospital floor, and issue bellowing challenges.

"Grant's thinking of making a substantial donation to the theater company," I said. "I suggested he speak to Pat to find out how the festival is doing financially. I know rehearsal ends at seven, so we'd be likely to get her at the B and B if we dropped in."

The two men eyed each other for a moment. Ryan was the first to break the stare-down. "Gemma, do you have anything to say about the theory that this suicide attempt was a confession?"

"Why are you asking her?" Estrada said.

I ignored her. "I don't think Renee tried killing herself over anything to do with Nigel. I notice Eddie didn't bother to come to the hospital."

"He said we don't need a crowd. He told me to call when we have news." Pat returned, bearing a cup of machine-dispensed coffee. It looked as unappealing as it smelled. "Speaking of news, I don't want this to get into the papers. The last thing we need is word getting around that our cast is unreliable."

"I would have thought the last thing you'd want would be another one of your actors dying," I said.

"That too," she replied.

"I have a feeling Renee will be happy to tell you what drove her to desperation," I said.

"What do you know that you aren't telling me, Gemma?" Ryan said.

I smiled at him. He did not smile in return. Not for the first time, I wished Ryan Ashburton was not a police officer. But he was. I sighed. "If I can have a word in private?"

"I don't . . ." Estrada said.

"A quick one." Ryan and I moved farther down the hallway.

I didn't tell him I'd been reading Renee's phone. "She used to date Edward Barker. They broke up a few years ago when he married someone else. And before you ask how I know, it's common knowledge, available for anyone to read thanks to the marvels of the World Wide Web."

"Dare I ask why you've been checking up on these people when you've been told not to get involved?"

"In this case, I'm innocent. He's going out with Jayne. I'm protecting her interests."

"Whether she wants you to or not, I'd guess," Ryan said.

I ignored that comment. "Renee seems to think that, seeing as to how Eddie's single again, they're going to get back together. He, apparently, disagrees."

"The oldest story of them all." Ryan couldn't help himself. He glanced at Grant.

"Yup."

A doctor came out of one of the curtained cubicles. She spotted Ryan and headed straight for us. "Detective. Ms. Masters can talk to you now."

"How is she?" I asked.

"She'll be fine. More embarrassed than anything, I think, and she'll have a killer headache. It doesn't seem as though there were many pills in that bottle, so it was mostly the effects of all the booze taken at once."

Ryan gestured to Estrada to join him, and they followed the doctor.

"Out of danger," I told Pat and Grant.

"That made for an exciting evening," Grant said. "Ready to go, Gemma?"

"Why don't you and Pat conduct your business now," I said. "I'm sure Pat will want to talk to Renee when the police are finished, won't you, Pat?"

"Darn right, I will. It's too bad talking is the worst I can do. That girl deserves a good spanking."

I sat down. "I'd like to give her my best wishes too."

"Perhaps you could call on her tomorrow. She'll be exhausted tonight." Grant checked his watch. "It's after eight thirty. If we don't leave now, we'll lose our reservation."

"Reservation?"

"At the Blue Water Café?"

"Do we have a reservation?"

"I assumed so. It was your idea to go there tonight, and it's almost impossible to get a table on the deck without one. Didn't you make the reservation?"

"I guess I forgot. Sorry."

"No matter," he said. "The mood's been thoroughly ruined. I could use a coffee, though. And not something out of a vending machine. Do you think the cafeteria's still open?"

"No idea."

"I'll check. Do you want anything?"

"No, thanks."

"I'll come with you." Pat threw her cup into the trash.

It was a fairly quiet evening in the West London Hospital's ER. A nearly hysterical mother came in with a girl of about twelve, bleeding copiously from the side of her head, and an elderly man was hustled past, screaming that they, whoever they might be, were after him.

While waiting, I amused myself by checking to see if Renee had had any contact with Nigel Bellingham prior to his death. According to her phone, they had never spoken or texted. She had also never been in touch with Gerald Greene. I didn't bother to read her correspondence with Pat or anyone else in the theater group. That would be too intrusive. Even for me.

Pat and Grant came back, carrying their coffees, at the same time Ryan and Estrada emerged from the curtained cubicle.

Estrada checked her phone. "That Reynolds kid's been brought in again," she said to Ryan.

"You take it. I'll finish up here."

She pointedly ignored me as she left.

"You can go in now," the nurse said.

Pat got to her feet.

"But only one of you, and only for a moment."

"Tell her I hope she's feeling better tomorrow." I handed Renee's phone to Pat. "I picked this up off the bed at the B and B. I'm sure she'll want it."

"Now can we go?" Grant said.

"I think so."

Ryan was on his own phone, but he caught my eye and lifted one hand, telling me to wait. I wandered over to see what he wanted.

"How can I go on without him?" Renee moaned from behind the thin curtain.

"Because you have to, you silly thing," Pat said. "Heartbreak is a part of life. I can't see that he's worth it anyway."

"But I love him."

"Pooh. Waste of time, love is. Take it from me. You know what's worth living for?"

"What?"

"Fame, that's what. A chance at the brass ring."

Renee groaned. "You can't possibly mean performing in this two-bit town. In a barn no less! I haven't been offered a good role in months. Years. I'm washed up. Finished. My mom paid for that car rental as a birthday present. I'd rather have the rent on an apartment in the city, but how can I tell her I've been evicted?"

"Something big is coming, Renee. Believe me. I need you to stick with me. You won't be disappointed."

"She's right here." Ryan offered me his phone.

I tore my attention away from the drama going on behind the curtain. "What?"

"Jayne," he said. "She wants to speak to you."

I took the phone. "Hello?"

"Mom's ready to talk to the police," Jayne said.

"That's good."

"Only Detective Ashburton though. She doesn't trust Estrada."

"I don't know that she can specify the conditions, Jayne." I glanced at Ryan. He gave me a nod.

"And not at the police station. She's scared, Gemma. Scared and embarrassed and ashamed. The police station will only make her feel worse. I told Ryan that, and he said we could talk someplace else. She wants you there."

"Me?"

"Yes, you."

"I haven't had dinner yet. How about my house? It just so happens I have the makings for a lot of sandwiches."

"I was hoping you'd say that."

"Fifteen minutes."

"We'll be there."

"Oh, Jayne, one more thing. Have you heard from Eddie in the last little while?"

"He called about half an hour ago suggesting a walk along the harbor and then a quiet drink somewhere. Isn't that so romantic? But I said I needed to be with my mom tonight. Why are you asking?"

"No reason." I handed the phone back to Ryan.

Once we'd gotten this little matter of disabusing the police of the notion that Jayne's mother had murdered Nigel Bellingham out of the way, I'd have to get to work coming between Eddie and Jayne.

I was not looking forward to that.

Chapter 14

"I have to say," Grant Thompson said, "you are not a dull date, Gemma."

"Sorry to dump you like this," I said, "but what we have to talk about is highly confidential."

He moved as though he were about to kiss me on the mouth but changed direction at the last minute and dropped a peck on my cheek. I wondered if that had something to do with the fact that Ryan Ashburton was standing by his car, watching us and tapping his foot.

On the drive from the hospital to my house, I had only enough time to ask Ryan what Renee had to say for herself. "You know I'm not going to tell you any private details, but as we overheard when Pat was talking to her, it was all about a boyfriend who'd done her wrong and her career not doing well. Louise out-and-out asked her if she'd killed Nigel Bellingham, and she seemed to have no idea why we'd even think that."

He pulled up in front of my house. I undid my seat belt and put my hand on the door handle.

"Gemma," he said, "this isn't exactly a suitable time to talk, but I have to ask. Are you dating Grant?"

"No." If I'd stopped to think about it, I wouldn't have known what to answer. Instead, the word popped out, and I realized I was glad it had. "We're friends. We have things in common: love of books, memories of jolly old England. We were going to have dinner together tonight, but that's all." I didn't bother to mention that I was using Grant to do some investigating on my behalf. I took a deep breath and focused on Ryan's face. "Does it matter to you if I were?"

"It does, Gemma. I . . ." He stared into my eyes. "I want to be with you. I've never not wanted that. But as long as you keep getting involved in my work, I don't see how that can be."

I touched his face. The bristle scratched the pads of my fingers. "I can't help the things I observe or the conclusions I come to. I want to, sometimes, you know I do, but it never works out. I can't stop my mind working the way it does."

"If you did try to change your whole personality—to hide your intelligence, your perceptiveness, your incredible memory—you'd be bitter and miserable. So I guess all I can say is that I want you to be happy, Gemma. And if I'm not the guy who can—"

We jumped at a rap on the window. I turned to see Jayne's face peering in. "Geeze, you two, my mom's about to spill her life's secret, and you're making out in the car like a couple of teenagers."

I opened my door. "We're having a personal conversation. We are not making out."

"Coulda fooled me. Mom's inside. I knew you wouldn't mind us letting ourselves in." Jayne kept a spare key to my house as I did to hers.

*   *   *

We gathered in my kitchen. Jayne fussed with coffee and tea things, and I put together sandwiches while Leslie told Ryan her story. About her affair with Nigel thirty-five years ago, his rejection of her, coming home brokenhearted and pregnant to marry Jayne's father.

"When I heard Nigel was coming to West London, I was conflicted. It reminded me of all my pain, but in some way, it also reminded me of those exciting, heady days when I believed the New York theater world lay at my feet. I didn't have any expectations of us picking up our"—she made quotations marks with her fingers—"'romance.' I wouldn't have wanted that in any case. It was so long ago. Another lifetime. But I was looking forward to seeing him, and perhaps that's why. Because it was in another lifetime. A chance to remember my youth and my dreams and the fun times. New York in the early eighties, the most exciting city in the world, struggling to make it on Broadway. My acting career didn't end well, but it's a life experience I'm glad I had. I haven't spent a lot of time over the years worrying about what Nigel Bellingham was up to, but I did keep casual track of his career. I was well aware that he probably never gave me so much as another thought since the last time we were together, but I guess I thought—hoped?—he'd at least remember me if prompted. I should have realized that he loomed far larger in my memory than I would have in his.

I volunteered to pick him up at the inn on Wednesday and bring him into town. He didn't recognize me. Okay, I've changed more than a little bit in the last thirty-five years. Other people were with him, so we didn't have a chance to talk. It was chaotic in the shop, and when I did try to tell him my name, he brushed me off."

I sliced the sandwiches and arranged them on a plate. Jayne poured coffee and set the table. Violet, as always so aware of human emotions, sat beside Leslie's chair. Jayne's mother twisted a tissue between her fingers and occasionally let her hand drop to the top of the dog's head, seeking—and finding—comfort there. Leslie wasn't crying, but her eyes were red, and deep lines had appeared around her mouth.

"I tried to talk to him at the tea on Saturday. When he first arrived, before the guests gathered around him, I grabbed a chance to speak to him privately." Leslie lowered her head. Jayne put a hand on her shoulder.

"I told him who I was. I told him my name, and I told him we had once meant something to each other." The tears began to flow. I put the tray of sandwiches on the table and then took myself to the far side of the room where I stood against the counter.

No one picked up a sandwich.

"Take your time, Mrs. Wilson," Ryan said.

"He could have said something polite like 'How have you been?' or lied and told me that I hadn't changed a bit. Instead, he said he met so many people over the course of his life, how could he possibly remember one . . . average-looking, middle-aged woman?" She fumbled for a napkin and blew her nose. "He . . . he told me to get him a glass of wine."

The look on Jayne's face was something I have never seen before and hope never to see again. I do believe that if Sir Nigel Bellingham had walked through the door at that moment, Jayne herself would have killed him.

Ryan gave Leslie a minute and then asked in a soft gentle voice, "What happened then?"

"I left him to get his own blasted drink," she said, "and I went back to work. I was furious, as you can imagine. Humiliated, at first, but as the afternoon progressed, I began to realize that I wasn't the one who should be ashamed. I'd had a wonderful life, married a man who loved me beyond words and whom I loved in return. I had two beautiful children." She reached up and took Jayne's hand in hers. "I've been so very lucky. Nigel Bellingham, Sir Nigel, was a lonely, bitter old drunk."

She wiped the tears away and put the napkin down. Sensing the worst of the emotion was over, Violet wandered away to check her food bowl. Discovering it still empty, she sighed heavily and dropped beside it with a thud of disapproval.

"I decided to leave it alone," Leslie continued. "Let the miserable man stew in his glass of Prosecco. I could still, I told myself, enjoy the afternoon and the festival and have nothing more to do with him." She shook her head. "But you know me, honey, always got to get the last word."

Jayne nodded silently.

"After his fiasco of a speech, I tried to help, but he was rude to me all over again. Everyone abandoned him and left him sitting at the patio table all by himself. Even the likes of Gerald and Pat were either too embarrassed or too angry to go near him. So I went over, full of righteous indignation, and told him I had something to say to him, and he was going to listen to me."

"You went into the woods," Ryan said.

"I didn't want anyone else hearing what I had to say. Once he was on his feet, he seemed to want to walk, so I followed. We went into that patch of woods and down to the cliff edge to watch the waves. I had no intention of telling him about Jeff. But, well, once more I had to get the last word in, and so I did. And then, I swear, Detective Ashburton—Ryan—I walked away and left him standing alone at the edge of that cliff."

"Did anyone follow you?" Ryan asked. "Did you see anyone else in the woods at that time?"

Leslie shook her head. "No, but I wouldn't have been likely to notice. I was totally wrapped up in my own thoughts. It's my fault he died, and I am sorry."

"Don't say that, Mom!" Jayne said.

Leslie gave her a small smile. "I'm not confessing, honey. All I'm saying is that, knowing the state he was in, I shouldn't have left him alone."

"Babysitting him wasn't your responsibility," Jayne said.

"Isn't anyone going to have something to eat?" I pulled out a chair and sat at the table. "Now that we know the circumstances which led to Nigel standing on that cliff, we have to discuss what might have happened next."

Ryan attempted to hide a grin. "We do, do we?"

"Yes, we do." I selected a ham and cheddar on a baguette. "In this case, I'm prepared to accept the premise of Occam's razor." I took a big bite.

"What's that?" Jayne asked.

Ryan answered while I chewed. "The theory that the simplest explanation is almost always the correct one. Meaning, don't complicate things if you don't have to." He helped himself to a sandwich. "Although, at the moment, I don't see what the simplest explanation might be."

"He killed himself," I said. "He jumped off the cliff under his own free will. No one else was observed in the woods. I did see, at the time in question, a young couple heading to the water's edge, but they were not going in the same direction as Leslie and Nigel. I assume you questioned everyone who was there."

"We did. Not only the people who were still on-site when we arrived, but everyone on the guest list, as well as all the theater people and the volunteers. Mrs. Stanton assured us that no one would have gotten onto the grounds without either a job to do or a ticket. The Stanton property is fenced and posted, but it's possible someone crept unobserved over the fence. There are no alarms or security apart from in the house and immediate grounds. She told me the occasional group of teenagers looking for a place to party or tourists who don't think signs apply to them wander in following the cliff's edge. We have looked but can find no signs of illicit entry on the day in question."

"No reason for anyone to do so," I said. "Not to kill Nigel anyway. Now that we know the theft of the Chihuly bowl and imitations was not random . . ."

"How do we know that?" Ryan said.

"What theft?" Leslie asked.

Jayne guilty dipped her head, and Ryan gave her a suspicious look.

"Oh," I said. "Didn't I tell you? Sir Nigel was a kleptomaniac, and Gerald was highly paid to cover it up and return the pilfered items when possible."

"Gemma!" Ryan said. "How do you know that, and why didn't you tell me?"

"Slipped my mind," I said. "Sorry. I called Rebecca and told her she could find her items in a plant pot. I didn't think to remind her to tell the police she'd found them."

"We checked with the police in England, and Greene has no record of anything more serious than a parking ticket. I interviewed him myself. He said he was devastated at Bellingham's death and had no idea why anyone would want to do him harm. He told me nothing about any theft, but he mentioned that Bellingham had a considerable drinking problem. Part of his job, he said, was to get Sir Nigel home safely and without incident after a bender."

"Sometimes," I said. "People talk more freely over a drink in a bar than under the bright lights in the police interrogation room. Figuratively speaking, of course."

"Helps if the questioner knows what questions to ask. How did you?"

I hesitated and took another bite of my sandwich to cover up my hesitation. This was the point at which I should tell Ryan that I knew Nigel was a thief because I'd found stolen goods in his hotel room. There was, however, absolutely no way of giving him that information without having to confess how I knew it. And if I did that, not only would Ryan feel he had to do something about my confession to breaking and entering (like arrest me), but we would be distracted from my main point.

"Gemma found—" Jayne said.

"We can come back to that later," I said quickly. Ryan gave me *that* look, but he didn't press the point.

"Saturday afternoon," I said. "Nigel was extremely drunk, not an unusual occurrence as we have learned, and he totally humiliated himself in front of his colleagues and a group of people who'd paid a lot of money to meet him. His career was on the skids, as anyone could see by the fact that the hero of *Roman Wars* was reduced to doing summer repertory theater in West London, Massachusetts. A younger actor had stepped in and saved the performance. And then, on top of all of that, he had it thrown in his face that he was such a failure in life, he had son he didn't even know about. A depressed man. A cliff. The conclusion is obvious."

"I drove him to his death," Leslie said.

"Don't you even think that, Mom," Jayne said. "It seems to me that all his problems were of his own making."

"No one at the theater seems to be missing him," I said, "other than Rebecca Stanton, who wanted a big name actor to front her festival. The professionals are happy Nigel's gone, although they'll never come right out and say so."

Ryan let out a long sigh. "I agree with you, Gemma. We've seen nothing to indicate that anyone else, other than you, Leslie, joined Nigel at the cliff top. Not that absence of evidence . . ."

". . . is evidence of absence," I said.

"The autopsy results showed a man in poor condition," Ryan said. "His lungs were what you'd expect from a lifetime smoker, and his liver was a mess. He'd had a bad heart attack a year or so ago and probably a smaller, earlier one. That is confidential, by the way."

"Understood," I said.

"Putting all that together—bad health, failing career, drunk, and embarrassed. Occam's razor does point to suicide. We have more lab results to come in, some record checks to finish, and further analysis to do of statements from people who'd been at the party. If that doesn't show me anything indicating otherwise, I'm going to declare this a suicide. The missing piece of pink ribbon has been bothering me, but I'll have to assume it blew off the cliff and out to sea after it came off your apron, Leslie."

I said nothing.

"Poor Nigel," Leslie said with a shake of her head. "What a sad end to a brilliant career."

"I'll do what I can to keep the details of your confidence, Leslie," Ryan said, "but as you were the last person, as far as we know, to see Nigel Bellingham alive, I can't keep you totally out of this. I have to tell my partner and my chief why I'm closing the investigation. I will only say, unless they push me, that you and he talked about your mutual past and you left him sad and despondent. If they insist on knowing the details of that conversation . . ."

"I understand," Leslie said.

Jayne wrapped her arms around her mother. "I'm here for you, Mom. Always."

"I've finished with your Sherlock Holmes tea set, Jayne," Ryan said. "You can pick it up at the station at any time."

"I'm not eating all those sandwiches myself," I said.

Chapter 15

A nd that was the end of that.

Two weeks passed, and I heard nothing more about Sir Nigel Bellingham other than from Emporium customers expressing their shock and dismay at his passing. Advance ticket sales for the theater festival were better than expected, and Leslie informed me that several nights were completely sold out. A good deal of the excitement at being involved in the festival had left both Leslie and Jayne, but they still pitched in when they could.

Jayne continued to see Eddie, and I continued to worry about that. I'd debated telling her that he was sleeping with Renee while beginning a relationship with her, but I decided to hold my tongue. Recently, I'd told a young woman in love that her intended's only interest in her was for her inheritance: it had not gone well.

I've been told people don't always appreciate the benefit of my observations and conclusions.

Thus I resolved to stay out of it and to hope that, when the run of the play finished, Eddie would be on his way to newer pastures, both professionally and romantically.

I hadn't seen Renee again, but Jayne told me she'd recovered from a bout of food poisoning (the reason the festival put out for her visit to the hospital) and had thrown herself enthusiastically into rehearsals. Everyone, Jayne said, was thrilled with how it was going.

The chief of police called a press conference, which was well attended. Irene Talbot had told me that media attention around the death of Sir Nigel Bellingham had been intense.

I didn't bother to go, as earlier Ryan had called to tell me the chief and Louise Estrada had agreed to close the investigation on his suggestion. I read the chief's statement in the next day's *West London Star*. The police had concluded that the man had slipped and fallen to his death "while under the influence." Ryan told me that forensic investigators had found no sign of anyone "slipping." The earth at the cliff edge was not scuffed and disturbed enough to indicate a misstep followed by a desperate attempt to keep one's footing. But with no proof that Nigel had jumped, the police thought it best to be discreet.

Gerald Greene was told he was free to leave. He did not stop by the Emporium to say good-bye.

Wednesday afternoon, I went next door to have my regular daily partners' meeting with Jayne. I settled in the window alcove, and Fiona brought a pot of tea and a selection of sandwiches. "No brownies today?" I asked. "I feel like a bit of chocolate."

"Sold out," she replied.

Jayne dropped onto the window bench. "Another good day. You?"

"*The Hound of the Baskervilles* opens tomorrow night, and theater patrons are streaming into town. As we'd hoped, many of them are Holmes fans, and the Emporium is high on their list of places to visit."

Jayne poured the tea, and we toasted each other with delicate china cups.

"Seen much of Eddie?" I asked.

"We had dinner Monday," she said, "but that'll probably be the last time for a while. He's acting every night, and when he finishes, it's too late for me to be going out."

"You don't sound terribly disappointed at that," I said.

She shrugged. "It's been fun to be with him, but I don't see that anything can come of it. To be honest, Gemma, we have nothing in common. Eddie doesn't seem to be interested in much in life other than Eddie. Not in the difficulties of owning and operating a bakery and tea room. He's super excited about tomorrow's opening. He says this performance is his chance at the big time."

"Summer stock in Cape Cod? Unlikely," I said.

"Actors have their dreams." She smiled at me. "I'm happy here at Mrs. Hudson's and in West London. I'm happy my mother isn't going to be charged with murder. I'm happy I have a good friend, as exasperating as she might be at times. How about you?"

"All of those things," I said, returning her smile. "Ambition is highly overrated. Although I have no idea to what friend you might be referring."

"I'll drink to that," she said, toasting me once again with her teacup. "What's Ashleigh supposed to be today, by the way? I can't imagine where she got that poodle skirt."

"I fear she's planning to dress as though she's in one of the plays for the rest of the summer. *Cat on a Hot Tin Roof* and *The Hound* are easy, but I don't know what she can wear that will put people in mind of *The Odd Couple.*"

"She'll think of something."

"That's what I'm afraid of."

The door opened, and Leslie Wilson bustled in. "I knew I'd find you two here." She dropped beside Jayne and pulled an envelope out of her purse. "Surprise!"

"What's that?" Jayne asked.

"Three tickets to tomorrow's opening of *The Hound of the Baskervilles*. Rebecca Stanton told me to invite you two, with thanks for your help at the tea and for finding her stolen items. They were precisely where Gemma said they'd be."

"That's nice of her," Jayne said. "I'd love to see the play. Gemma?"

"I want to see how they manage to misinterpret *The Hound of the Baskervilles.*"

"I'm not sitting next to her if she's going to complain and point out discrepancies all the way through," Jayne said to her mother. "Is the third ticket for you?"

"Yes. Remember, this is opening night, and dress accordingly. Everyone will be dressed to the nines."

"What goes for the nines in Cape Cod in summer," Jayne said.

"More like the sevens," I said.

*   *   *

Thursday evening, I made an attempt to dress to the nines.

I left the shop in Ashleigh's hands at five, dashing out before she could show me the website she'd found about how to set up a mail-order business. I went home, took Violet out, and then hopped into the shower. I washed and blow-dried my hair, fluffed the curls into some semblance of style, and tied the edges off my face with rhinestone clips. I brushed a touch of blush onto my cheeks and put a dab of pink lipstick onto my mouth. I don't have a lot of fancy clothes—I rarely go anyplace that requires them—but I do have the perfect "little black dress" that's been with me since I left London. Fortunately, it was a warm night so I could do without the dreaded pantyhose and leave my legs bare. I added the small gold-and-diamond earrings that had been my parents' wedding gift to me and a long gold chain. Last of all, I slipped into a pair of black high-heeled Ralph Lauren sandals that I'd bought on impulse and never worn.

I then ruined the outfit by tossing my small black leather bag over my shoulder. Although women's clothing is nothing at all like it was in the Great Detective's day—thank heavens!—it's still highly impractical at times. I never carry a clutch bag as I don't like having my hands occupied, but I need someplace for my phone and keys, a bit of money to buy a drink at intermission, and an emergency tissue. Expensive little black dresses don't come with pockets.

Violet eyed me. She did not look impressed.

"Don't wait up," I said.

My phone beeped, telling me Jayne and Leslie were on their way to pick me up. I went outside and waited for them at the curb.

When we arrived, a long line of cars was pulling into the driveway leading to the theater barn. The building itself was fully lit, a brilliant yellow glow against the encroaching purple darkness of the night sky. Young men and women in safety vests waved flashlights to direct cars to their parking spaces.

Fortunately for the sake of men's Italian shoes and women's heels, it hadn't rained recently. The theater parking lot isn't paved.

"Don't you two look great," I said once we were out of the car.

"I don't often get a chance to dress up." Leslie wore a long dress of soft blue, all swirling silk and touches of lace.

"You're definitely a nine," I said.

"A nine?"

"As in dressed to the nines. Jayne, I'll give you nine and a half." She beamed at me, looking fabulous in a wide knee-length skirt in shades of red and gold, a deeply plunging gold shirt under a tight red jacket, and ruby-red shoes with four-inch heels. Her blonde hair was piled on the top of her head with a few tendrils left loose to curl softly around her face.

"Not too bad yourself." Jayne slipped her arm through her mother's, and we headed for the barn.

Rebecca Stanton stood at the main doors, greeting patrons. She wore a designer gown of swirling red satin that probably cost in the thousands; gold and diamonds flashed from her throat, ears, and wrist. She and Leslie exchanged air kisses.

"Looks like it's going to be quite the night," I said. "Congratulations."

"Don't congratulate me until the play's over," she said. "The proof is in the pudding."

"'The proof of the pudding is in the eating,'" I said.

"Pardon me?" She raised one perfectly sculpted eyebrow.

"That's the correct quote. People often get it wrong."

Jayne stuck an elbow into my ribs.

"Although," I admitted, "quotations have been known to evolve over time."

"We're holding up the line," Leslie said. "Let's go in and find our seats."

I had to remind myself we were in a barn. The press at the bar was heavy, conversation and laughter echoed off the slatted walls, and the soft lighting made everyone look good. A handful of tourists were dressed in everyday wear, but like us, most people had gone to some trouble. Jewelry sparkled, and the scent of perfume mingled with aftershave and freshly laundered men's dress shirts.

"The play hasn't even started," I said, "and the magic of the theater is already all around us."

Leslie beamed; the light of true love shone in her eyes.

Which, I thought to myself, is perhaps why I am not a big fan of theater. I don't care for deception, in any form.

I told myself to relax and enjoy the evening.

"I'll join you two in a minute," Leslie said. "I see someone I want to talk to. Here's your tickets, in case I don't get back before they call us to sit down." She handed them to us and slipped away.

"Good evening, Gemma, Jayne. May I say you look quite lovely tonight?" Donald Morris stood at my side. He wore a proper nineteenth-century morning suit: stripped trousers, tailcoat, waistcoat, high white collar, and gray tie. Even a gray top hat.

"Good heavens," Jayne said. "Wherever did you get that outfit?"

"I've been saving it for a suitable occasion." Donald, I thought—and not for the first time—was a man out of his era. He would have been happiest waving a walking stick to hail a hansom cab on the foggy cobblestones of London or the teeming streets of New York City.

That reminded me. "Did you get your ulster back?" I asked.

"I did. It was, I was unhappy to find, in the police evidence locker. The officers were pleased to discover the owner and returned it to me."

"No harm done then," I said.

"Are you looking forward to the play, Donald?" Jayne said.

He sniffed. "We will see. I hope they don't add any of those oh-so-clever modern touches to this interpretation. I'll be content with nothing less than a faithful rendition."

"So you're not a fan of the Benedict Cumberbatch series," Jayne said.

"On the contrary. I love it. A modern interpretation for our times. Faithful to the original, yet also suitable for the twenty-first century. It doesn't attempt to be some sort of ham-fisted crossover."

Grant Thompson joined us. He carried a glass of wine and was dressed in a gray business suit. "Ladies. Donald. Quite the night. Can I get you something to drink, Gemma?"

I opened my mouth to agree when Jayne jumped in. "No, thanks. We're fine."

"Isn't that Andy Whitehall over there?" I said. "Why, so it is. Oh, look, he's seen us. He's waving. He seems to be trapped in conversation with that old couple. Go and rescue him, Jayne." She hesitated, and I gave her a light shove. "Off you go. Maybe he'd like to go for dinner after the play or something."

"Sounds like an idea," Grant said.

"Excellent!" Donald said. "I'd love to join you. Where are you sitting, Gemma?"

I checked my ticket for the first time. "Front row, it looks like."

His face fell. "Oh. I'm in the back. The sightlines will not be good. Can't be helped now. I'll meet you at the main exit after curtain. I see Matthew Berkowitz from the Boston chapter of the Baker Street Irregulars is here. I've been meaning to ask him about . . ." Donald hurried away.

"I'm also in the cheap seats," Grant said.

"Pays to have friends in high places," I said. "Rebecca gave the tickets to Leslie."

"Speaking of Rebecca, I read that the police closed their investigation into Nigel's death, so I didn't think you'd have any more interest in what I learned about the financial affairs of the festival."

"Oh, I'm so sorry. I forgot to tell you not to bother."

He grinned. "Not a problem. I got a nice cup of tea out of it. I ran into Rebecca on Baker Street the afternoon after that trip to the hospital with Renee, and I dropped hints that I was considering investing in the festival next year. She invited me to Mrs. Hudson's to talk about it. I'm afraid lying isn't something I'm good at, so I pretty soon confessed that I didn't have a lot of spare money. She waved that trifle away and said she was more interested in getting volunteers. And"—he blushed ever so slightly—"young single men are hard to find to volunteer for anything. I got the impression she doesn't much care if the festival makes money or not. She'll put in whatever she has to to keep it going. It's the appearance she's interested in, and the standing in the wider community she gets from being the chief patron of a successful festival. A strong stable of eager volunteers means the festival has respect among the people who matter. Matter to Rebecca, anyway."

I thought of her standing proudly at the entrance tonight, resplendent in satin and diamonds, greeting guests as though they were visitors to her house.

"I should have known I'd find you here," said a voice behind me.

I turned to see Ryan Ashburton, also looking very dapper in a business suit.

"Wouldn't miss it," I said.

"Evening, Detective," Grant said. "Are you here on business?"

Ryan shook his head. "I've come with my mother. She bought two tickets the day they went on sale, but my dad's hip's bothering him something bad today, and he didn't want to go out. Being a lady of a certain age, Mom was prepared stay at home with him rather than come alone, so he asked me to escort her." He gestured to a steel-haired woman in her early seventies, chattering to a group of her peers. She glanced up, saw me watching, and turned sharply away.

I'd met her when Ryan and I were together. Looks like she still hasn't forgiven me for our breakup.

People continued to arrive, and the lobby was soon bursting at the seams with excited people and loud chatter. I shifted from one foot to another, hoping we'd be seated soon. I was seriously regretting wearing these shoes. Only now that it was too late to do anything about it, I remembered why I'd never worn them.

My gaze continued to travel across the room, and I saw someone I definitely didn't expect to see.

Gerald Greene, heading our way.

"What on earth are you doing here?" I said. "I thought you'd gone back to England."

"I did, but I wanted to see how the play turned out, so I flew over for a few days. It was my first ever flight in business class—what a treat! I'm staying at the Harbor Inn, at my own expense." He read my face and preened. "I've come into some money since we last met. Sir Nigel left the majority of his estate to his charitable foundation, but to my considerable surprise, he was kind enough to mention me in his will. His estate turned out, again to my surprise, to be quite extensive. Some properties in Chelsea and Kensington he'd bought in his salad days for rental income. His mother, obviously a wise woman, had insisted he invest every cent he made from *Roman Wars* into property."

"Wow!" I said. "That would have appreciated a lot over forty years."

"He also had a country home in Cornwall, and it, along with a small income, he left to me."

"Congratulations," Ryan said.

"Such a great man," Gerald said. "So thoughtful. I see Mrs. Stanton. I must give her my wishes. Please excuse me."

The three of us stared at his retreating back.

"If I hadn't closed this case," Ryan muttered.

"You'd ask *cui bono*," I replied.

"Who benefits?" Grant added. "Gerald appears to have. Do you think he knew he was mentioned in the will?"

"No way of finding out now," Ryan said. "Gemma?"

I thought back to my conversations with Gerald. "Unless he's a far better actor than I took him for, I don't think so. The last time I spoke with him, he was bemoaning the fact that he was penniless and out of a job. Of course, I've misjudged people before."

"That comes as a surprise to me," Grant said.

"I try not to make a habit of it," I said.

Bells began to ring, calling us to be seated. A buzz of excitement washed through the barn.

"I'll see you at intermission," I said, and we went our separate ways.

Leslie, Jayne, and my seats were in the front row, slightly off to the left side. Leslie sat between Jayne and me. The mayor took the seat to the right of Jayne, her husband on her other side. Farther down the row, I recognized the chief of police between Mrs. Chief and the head of the town's arts council and none other than one of our state's senators was at the far end of the row. Rebecca would be thrilled: all the town's dignitaries had shown up.

A man dropped into the chair on the other side of me. I shifted the bag over my shoulder and turned to greet him. "Mr. Blackstone. Good evening. Are you excited about the play?"

His hair was tied into its habitual man-bun, and he wore tight dark-blue jeans turned up at the ankles, a pink shirt with a red bow tie, suspenders, and the sort of cloth cap with a brim that was once only worn by men of the British working classes. What passes for evening wear in the hipster world, I assumed. "Excited?" he drawled. "I long ago gave up being excited about anything. But I am looking forward to it. I have a lot riding on this production."

"Investor, are you?" I asked, not really caring.

"You might say that. How much remains to be seen."

"How are *The Odd Couple* and *Cat on a Hot Tin Roof* coming along in rehearsals?" I asked for no reason but to be polite.

"Don't know. Don't care."

The lights began to dim, and conversation slowly died to a halt. I settled back in my seat. Beside me, Leslie tittered in excitement.

Instead of the curtain rising, Rebecca Stanton came out of the wings. She walked slowly to center stage, her red gown flowing around her slim figure. A single spotlight threw sparkles off her diamonds.

She waited patiently for everyone to give her their full attention and then thanked us for coming and the mayor and the town of West London for its support of the arts. We all clapped enthusiastically. Rebecca then told us that the run of *The Hound of the Baskervilles* would be dedicated to the memory of Sir Nigel Bellingham. Another round of applause.

Rebecca left the stage and appeared moments later on the floor in front of me, heading for her seat, front row center.

The lights dimmed, and the curtain opened.

221B Baker Street in all its glory. Fireplace and mantle. A "patriotic" *VR* shot into the red wallpaper. A tattered red rug, two worn leather couches. A table containing a coffeepot and one place setting.

Eddie Barker—I mean, Sherlock Holmes—sat at the table with his back to where Dr. John Watson stood by the mantle, examining a walking stick.

They paused, the audience breathed, and then Sherlock said, in a deep rumbling English voice, "Well, Watson, what do you make of it?"

And the play began.

It was, I have to admit, well done. The sets, lighting, and costumes were excellent, and the actors rose to the occasion, although I did think Renee Masters played Miss Stapleton a bit too much like a high school girl desperate for an invitation to the dance.

As Sir Henry Baskerville was exclaiming over his missing boot, I flinched as an elbow got me in my left arm. I glanced at the man beside me. He was holding his hands up in front of his face, as though he were watching the action through a camera.

Curious.

I followed the play closely, but my mind divided itself into two, and I considered Leo Blackstone. I don't know much about theater, but I'd have thought if he was investing in this production, he'd also be concerned about the other two plays; instead, he expressed no interest in them. I'd had a glance at the program book and read the list of sponsors of the season. I hadn't seen his name, and no one was listed as anonymous.

A burst of light and noise startled me out of contemplation. The curtain had fallen for the intermission, and people were rising from their seats.

Leo stood up, and I jumped to my feet. I bit back a grimace as my Ralph Lauren heels reminded me not to do that. "Can I buy you a drink?" I asked.

"Never say no to that," he replied.

Being at the front of the theater, it took a long time for us to get to the back and the bar. The line was three deep when we arrived.

Ryan spotted me and began to come my way. I gave him a tiny shake of the head, and he turned around abruptly.

"Visiting from California, are you?" I said to my new best friend.

"Yup."

"I've never been to California. I hear it's lovely."

"Yup."

"Is the weather as nice as they say? Two white wines, please." I handed over my money, and the bartender poured our drinks.

"Sometimes." Leo couldn't have sounded more bored with my company if he'd tried.

I pretended I hadn't noticed. "What brings you to Cape Cod?"

"I'm interested in this play. Thanks for the drink, Ms. . . . uh . . ." He turned and walked off. Other than grab him by the arm and whirl him around, I couldn't think of a way to get him to talk to me.

Leslie swept down on me. Her eyes glowed. "Isn't it marvelous? They've done a fabulous job, don't you agree, Gemma?"

"It's fine." I wanted to speak to some of the cast and crew members, but I knew they wouldn't exactly welcome me backstage in the middle of the play. Instead, I sipped my wine. Leslie left in search of more responsive conversation.

"What are you up to?" Ryan asked me.

"Nothing," I said.

"Who was that guy you were talking to?"

"I'm not entirely sure. But I intend to find out."

"Gemma, I know that look. All too well."

"What look?"

Jayne joined us before Ryan could answer. "Eddie sent me a note." Her blue eyes sparked with the same intensity as her mother's, and she was almost dancing on her tiptoes with excitement. "Inviting me to join him backstage after the performance for a small party. Isn't that fun? Do you want to come?"

"Come where?" I asked.

"For a drink backstage. I'm sure Ryan's welcome too."

"I don't know yet," I said. I put my drink down and wandered off.

"Did you find that a bit strange?" I heard Jayne say to Ryan.

"I find many things Gemma does a bit strange," he replied. "Which is why," he might have added in a very low voice, "I love her."

* * *

The play continued. They'd done a good job of recreating the mood of the moor with dry ice and careful lighting. As Holmes and Watson cried to each other through the mist, on one side of me, I felt Leslie shiver in delight, while on the other, Leo continued framing the stage with his hands. The tormented howl of the great spectral hound needed some work, I thought. It sounded more like Moriarty when his food bowl isn't filled fast enough. I closed my eyes and thought back over the events of the previous weeks.

"It is a formidable difficulty, and I fear that you ask too much when you expect me to solve it," Sherlock said, pressing tobacco into his pipe and relaxing in his chair once again in 221B Baker Street. "The past and present are within the field of my inquiry, but what a man may do in the future is a hard question to answer. Come, Watson, might I trouble you to be ready in half an hour, and we can stop at Marcini's for a little dinner."

The curtain fell, and the audience broke into thunderous applause.

"Bravo!" someone shouted from the back.

The curtain rose, and the company stood before us, bowing deeply. Grinning, the minor actors stepped forward, and then they swept back for Ralph Carlyle, Tanya Morrison, and Harry O'Leary. Eddie took Renee's hand and led her to the front of the stage. He bowed, and she curtsied.

"You didn't care for it," Leo said to me.

"What? Oh, no, I thought it was an excellent production." I remembered to start clapping. "I was thinking of something else. Would it matter to you if I didn't like it?"

"It would. But everyone else seems to have enjoyed it. Very much, I'd say." I glanced down the row. Rebecca Stanton was beaming.

Pat Allworth was "reluctantly" dragged out of the wings. It was the first time I'd seen her this evening. She wore a knee-length black dress under a sequined black jacket, and the shoes with metal stars on the bottom of the heels were on her feet. She bowed, and then Eddie lifted her hand and kissed it. The audience continued applauding. Many people, Leslie and Jayne among them, were on their feet.

Pat's eyes swept the front row. They passed over me and came to rest on the man beside me. He gave her a thumbs-up, and she broke into a huge smile.

I turned to him. "Are you going to do it?"

He looked startled. "What do you know about it?"

I smiled.

"Guess it won't be a secret for much longer. I'm convinced." He got to his feet, and I did also.

I spoke over my shoulder to Leslie. "You and Jayne go on ahead, I'll catch up."

At the end of our row, Leo turned right and headed backstage. I turned left. I needed to find Ryan. Jayne and Leslie, followed by Rebecca, slipped past me and also went right.

The crowd poured into the aisle, and I made no progress. I was stuck in a traffic jam. I saw Ryan at the back of the theater. He was standing, but his mother was still seated. She waved her arms about, and he smiled down at her as he listened. I tried to catch his attention, but he didn't look my way. I pulled out my phone, switched it on, and waited impatiently while it booted up. Then I sent a text: *Urgent. I need you backstage ASAP.*

Ryan reached into his pocket. We were supposed to turn our phones off during the play, but he had his on vibrate in case he got a call from work.

He read the screen and looked toward the front of the barn, searching for me. I waved my arms over my head until he caught my eye, and I jerked my thumb over my shoulder toward the stage.

Ryan leaned over and said something to his mother.

I turned and fought my way upstream, against the crowd. "Excuse me, excuse me. Forgot something. Pardon me. Hi, Mrs. Herrington. Yes, loved it. Excuse me. Sorry, was that your foot?"

At last I broke free of the elegantly dressed masses and found a small set of steps leading to a door at the side of the stage and slipped through it. I emerged into the sitting room of 221B Baker Street. The curtain was down, and the cast and crew and their guests had gathered on the stage. The table on wheels that had earlier held evidence of Holmes's science experiments had been converted into a bar cart. Champagne flutes, silver ice buckets, and foil-topped bottles. The wine, I couldn't help but notice, was at the cheaper end of the scale, and the glasses were plastic. Tanya Morrison, still dressed in long skirt and apron as Mrs. Hudson, was pouring drinks.

Everyone was laughing and babbling in excitement. They were obviously pleased at how it had gone.

Eddie had his arm draped around Jayne's shoulders. On the far side of the stage, next to the mantel, Renee pretended not to notice. Alone of all the company, she was not smiling.

A glass was pressed into my hand. "Congratulations," I said to Eddie. "It seems to have been quite the success."

He tossed his head and laughed. He was still dressed and made up as the Great Detective, but that one movement brought him crashing back to twenty-first-century Massachusetts. "It must have been quite something in the old days," he said in his laid-back California drawl, "when everyone had to wait up all night until the morning papers brought out their reviews. Pat's checked Twitter, and people are already raving about the play. What did you think of my accent, Gemma? I worked hard on it."

Jayne edged slightly away. "I'm going to make sure my mom gets a drink."

"She looks fine to me," Eddie said, but Jayne left us.

"Your accent? Passable," I said. "Excuse me." Ryan hadn't yet appeared. I sent another text: *Stay in the shadows until needed.* I slipped my phone into my bag without waiting for a reply. I held onto my glass but did not take a sip.

Fortunately, no one seemed in a hurry to leave. The cast and crew were delighted with their evening's work and spent a lot of time congratulating each other. The wine might have been of lesser quality, but it was free, so they were happy. The wardrobe mistress approached Renee, now laughing with excessive enthusiasm at something Ralph had said, and pulled a needle and thread out of her shirt. She ordered Renee to stand still and then dropped to her knees and began stitching a ragged hem.

The side curtain moved and Ryan stepped onto the stage, followed by Grant, Donald, Gerald, and Andy. I hadn't asked Ryan to bring an entourage.

Ryan stayed in the wings as I'd asked, but the other men headed toward me. "What's up, Gemma?" Grant asked. "Donald saw Ryan heading this way, and he told me to come along."

"I don't want us to get scattered," Donald said. "I thought we were all going to dinner. Are we having drinks here first?"

Andy saw Jayne standing next to her mother. A smile crossed his face, and he went to join them.

"No one invited me to this party," Gerald said, "but I thought I'd come anyway. Someone has to remind everyone that this was Sir Nigel's night, and he is sorely missed."

"The drama's not over yet." I marched across the stage, my heels echoing off the boards. When I reached Rebecca, Pat, Leo, and the group around them, I lifted my glass in a toast. "A triumph."

"A triumph!" voices called.

"I wouldn't go quite that far," Rebecca said. "It was good, I'll admit, but Sir Nigel would have provided the gravitas we needed."

"I don't think everyone agrees. You don't, do you, sir?" I asked Leo.

"Nigel was a . . . competent actor in his day. But unfortunately, his day was long past."

"Now, see here," Gerald protested. As if, before receiving his inheritance, he wouldn't have said, and probably had, the same thing.

"Drunken old letch," Renee said. "We're better off without him."

"Don't move," the wardrobe mistress warned her, "or I'll sew your dress to your leg."

"With Nigel in the role, the movie wouldn't have gone ahead, would it?" I was talking to the small circle of Pat, Rebecca, and Leo, but I projected my voice to the far reaches of the stage. If there is one thing a stage is good for, it's acoustics.

"What movie?" Rebecca said.

"No, it wouldn't," Leo answered. "Who are you, and what do you know about that anyway? Has someone been talking?"

"Everyone's been talking," I said. "Rumor travels, and it travels fast. As for who I am, consider me an interested party. The police closed the investigation into Nigel's death, assuming that he had taken his own life . . ."

A murmur spread across the stage. People exchanged curious glances. "The police said it was an accident," Harry said.

"Because they weren't positive it wasn't suicide, although that's what they believed, and out of respect for the man's memory," I said. "But I'm increasingly becoming aware that neither accident nor suicide was the case."

"Suicide," Harry said. "That's news to me, but I can't say I'm all that surprised."

"Of course it was, Gemma," Leslie said. "We all agreed. I told Detective Ashburton . . . I told him Nigel was upset when we talked after the tea. I left him alone at the cliff edge, drunk and sad and lost."

"You left him there, Leslie," I said, "but he wasn't alone for long." I looked around the space making sure I had everyone's attention.

I did. "Mr. Blackstone here wants to make a movie out of this production."

Notably Pat, Renee, and Eddie didn't look at all surprised. Ralph Carlyle, who'd played Dr. Watson, clapped his hands; the stage crew shrugged; the wardrobe mistress struggled to her feet with a grunt; and Tanya Morrison said, "Count me out. My film days are long over." Rebecca said, "I don't see what that has to do with me."

"Nothing, as it happens. Except that Leo and his backers aren't about to pour money into a production featuring a washed-up old actor, no matter what his past fame. Therefore,

I have to ask who knew about the movie deal and who had the most to benefit from it."

"I hope you're not suggesting," Eddie said, "that I killed Nigel to get his role. I don't know anything about this movie you're talking about. No one takes a second-rate summer stock play, no matter how good, and turns it into a movie. And as much as we might all want to pretend it isn't, this festival is second-rate."

Rebecca glared at him, but she said nothing.

"There's not much in the world of popular entertainment hotter these days than Sherlock Holmes," I said. "Movies, TV. Books and more books, as no one knows better than I. Even coloring books, tea sets, and embroidery thimbles."

"What of it?" Eddie said. "It's all been done before."

"So it has. Therefore, a fresh interpretation is needed. Tell us about your vision, Leo."

"Might as well," he said. "I was going to make the announcement tonight anyway. I and my partners intend to bring a stage version of *The Hound of the Baskervilles* to the big screen. Not any version, but this version. Staged as it is, in front of an audience, only slightly adapted for the camera."

Renee squealed. Eddie said, "That's fabulous."

"As Ms. . . . uh . . ."

"Doyle," I said.

"As Ms. Doyle pointed out," Leo said, "people can't get enough of Sherlock. There's no point in trying to make another modernized version, not to compete with the likes of Robert Downey Jr. or Benedict Cumberbatch."

"I prefer *Elementary*, myself," the wardrobe mistress said. "I suppose you'll be needing adjustments to the costumes for close-ups. I hope you're planning to compensate me for my extra work."

"That discussion can be held for another time," Leo said. "*The Hound* is probably the best known Holmes story—"

"Best known, arguably, but definitely not the best," Donald said. "Nothing can compare with the drama of the climactic scene of *The Speckled Band* when Holmes—"

"Thank you, Donald," I said. "Another discussion for another time. Please continue, Leo."

"Therefore, my partners and I thought we'd simply return to the source. A fully authentic rendition of the original story, in the intimate and unusual setting of live theater. When I heard that Pat Allworth was putting on such a production, I told her what we were considering. All in confidence, of course." He turned to Pat. "I assume you broke that confidence and spoke to Ms. . . . uh . . ."

"Doyle," I said. "Pat never said a word to me."

"How did you find out then?"

"As I heard Sherlock Holmes himself say this very evening, 'The world is full of obvious things which nobody by any chance ever observes.' I observed." I looked around the room. Everyone was staring at me. From the shadows, Ryan made a circle in the air with his right hand in a hurry-it-up gesture. "Which brings us to the main point. Nigel Bellingham would not have suited this movie, wouldn't you agree?"

"Totally," Leo said.

"Therefore, he had to be gotten rid of. One way or another." Everyone began talking at once.

Gerald's voice rose above the clamor. "Are you saying, Gemma, that someone killed . . . murdered . . . Sir Nigel?"

"I am."

More clamor.

"That's preposterous," Pat said.

"Who do you think you are to make an accusation like that?" Rebecca said. "The police closed the case. It was an accident. A tragic accident."

"I don't want to hear this." Leo took off his cap and rubbed at the thinning hair on the top of his head. "I don't need these sort of rumors before we've even signed the contracts."

Renee headed for the bar cart.

"Nevertheless," I said, "hear it you will. Rebecca, it was important to you that Nigel be in the play, wasn't it?"

"As I keep telling everyone, yes, it was. I saw him perform in *The Hound* ten or fifteen years ago in London, and he was simply amazing. He was a great actor. A legend. I'd met him many years ago, when I was working in New York and took the liberty of writing to him and asking if he'd grace our little festival. He would have made us the talk of Massachusetts, if not the entire east coast."

"Ten or fifteen years ago, he was a lot younger in more than years. You must have been disappointed when you saw what he'd become."

Rebecca's back stiffened. "I'll admit he hadn't aged well. But I instructed him to buckle up and rise to the challenge."

"I'm afraid you can't simply instruct an alcoholic not to be so. I assume you were paying him out of your own pocket."

She glanced around the stage. "What of it?"

"It's your money to spend, but others in the company didn't agree with your casting decisions. Pat hired Eddie to play Sherlock, not Nigel."

"Eddie was the understudy," Rebecca said. "Pat knew I intended Nigel to have the role. I'll admit that she objected at first, but she came around. For the good of the festival."

"For the good of your image, Rebecca, but that's beside the point. Look at Ralph there," I pointed. The actor glanced around himself in confusion. "He's far too young to be Watson to Nigel's Sherlock. No, Pat might have made agreeable noises, but she never intended for Nigel to take the part."

"The festival is important to me, I have to admit," Rebecca said. "There's so much competition with so many other theater companies, it's hard to stand out. I needed something—someone—to set us apart from all the rest. To my delight, Sir Nigel tentatively accepted my offer to appear in *The Hound*, pending his recovery from an illness."

"From a stint in rehab, more like it," Harry said.

She stared him down. "I didn't know that, now did I?"

Harry shrugged.

"Perhaps not," I said, "but you quickly realized he wouldn't do your production any good. As you pointed out, competition is tough. A couple of bad reviews—even worse, mocking reviews—would be a disaster."

Rebecca's eyes blazed enough fire to match the light off her diamonds. "I'll admit I was somewhat disappointed when I met Nigel. But I can survive. My livelihood doesn't depend on this theater."

"No, but your reputation, as you see it, does."

She sputtered, but I turned my attention to Pat. "You weren't happy with him in the role right from the beginning."

"That's also not exactly a secret. I knew no one would cast him anymore and why. He'd be a disaster, as you said, movie or stage. Yes, I wanted Eddie all along, but Rebecca insisted. She's the boss, after all, the one with the deep pockets."

Eddie grinned and lifted his glass in a salute.

I studied the stage. Some of the actors looked delighted at the news that they were about to become film stars. A few didn't appear to much care. Most of the crew were grinning from ear to ear at the prospect of union-scale wages.

"You," I said to Eddie, "knew about this proposed movie deal, didn't you?"

"Me?" His big smile faded. "I had no idea until now."

"That's not what you told my friend Jayne. You said this was your chance at the big time."

"I was trying to impress her." He glanced around the stage. "Don't tell me none of you have ever tried to make things sound more important than they are to impress a date?"

"Never!" Andy said, sneaking a sideways peek at Jayne.

"Impress is one thing," I said, "but no one would logically conclude that a role in a play in a barn, as successful as it might be, would lead to great things. Yes, you knew. You also would have known that understudies don't get a chance at the brass ring, as long as they're trapped in the role of understudy."

"I . . ."

"Renee, you knew, didn't you?"

The actress tossed back her glass of wine. "So what if I did? I wasn't ever going to get the starring role, now was I?"

"No, but you wouldn't have a movie role at all if there was no movie because Leo wouldn't do it with Nigel in the role of Sherlock."

"Leo has Hollywood written all over him," Harry said. "I had an inkling something was up. I didn't expect it would have anything to do with me. I figured he was here looking to cast someone in a movie."

"Any idea who that someone might be?" I asked.

"Eddie, of course."

"Hey!" Eddie said. "Don't start accusing me."

"He could have been interested in me, you know," Renee said. "I'm not chopped liver here."

"You can count me out," Tanya said. "I'm finished with the movies, and I don't want any part of it. I agreed to this to give me something to do. You'll have to cast someone else in my roles."

"As far as I've determined," I said, "prior to this evening, three people knew for sure why Leo was here, apart from Leo himself. Eddie, Renee, and Pat. But . . . only one of them knew about it on the day of the tea. The day Sir Nigel died."

"Hey!" Eddie said.

"You're off your rocker, lady," Renee said.

"Do tell," Harry said.

"I've had enough of this," Pat said. "In case you've all forgotten, we have a performance to put on tomorrow. Someone close those bottles and get rid of the glasses. This party is over."

"Pat told Renee when she was in the hospital after her . . . food poisoning incident. Presumably as way of encouraging her to get over her blues. Renee then told Eddie, in what was probably an attempt to distract him from his amorous pursuit of Jayne Wilson. Only after Renee's bout of food poisoning did Eddie start talking about this play being his big chance."

"As if I care what he gets up to." Renee couldn't help glaring in the direction of my friend.

"Pat spent a lot of time at the tea with Leo," I said. "Fussing over him, even."

"I was attempting to be a good hostess," the director replied. A light layer of sweat was beginning to appear on her face. She shifted uncomfortably on her heels, and her eyes darted nervously around the stage, doing everything they could to avoid mine.

"Most commendable, I'm sure. At what point, Leo, did you tell Pat you were not going forward with the deal?"

"When the drunken fool couldn't even finish one line. I had my doubts about him anyway. I wanted a fresh face." A glance at Eddie. "My backers want Holmes to be a young athletic man, not an old codger past his time. I came here intending to suggest that Nigel be given a lesser role. Barrymore, perhaps."

"He never would have agreed," Gerald protested. "He would have regarded that as an enormous insult."

"So he would," I said. "I think we can agree with Gerald that Sir Nigel would have refused."

"Pat told me Rebecca was adamant that Nigel have the role," Leo said. "She suggested we put on a special performance for the filming with Eddie playing Holmes. Without seeing Nigel's contract, I couldn't agree to that. My backers were having cold feet as it was. I told Pat I was going to have to withdraw the offer."

He paused. No one said a word. Pat's face had gone completely white.

I turned to the director. "Rebecca realized Nigel wasn't going to work out. If you'd waited a little longer, she would have agreed to replace him."

Pat wiped her hands on the side of her dress and glanced around the room. We were a strange assortment: actors in nineteenth-century costumes, the crew in jeans and T-shirts, Rebecca in satin and diamonds, Jayne and her mother and I in our best clothes, the men with their suits and ties. But we all had one thing in common: everyone watched Pat Allworth.

"All I've worked for," Pat said at last, "all I've ever wanted was to direct a film that played to a larger audience than a backwater film festival. And it was going to be ruined by some aging actor who should have died years ago, and no doubt would soon enough."

"So you did something about that," I said.

The look she gave me was one of pure hatred. Then she faced the watching crowd. "Things may have worked out to my satisfaction, but I guess I was just lucky. Let's get out of here. We have a performance to put on tomorrow, people."

I let out a long breath I hadn't realized I'd been holding. I'd lost. I'd been so sure of myself, so confident in my reasoning, I'd played all my cards, expecting Pat to simply confess. As if life was a classic English crime novel and I was Sherlock Holmes or Lord Peter Wimsey.

Pat Allworth smirked at me.

Ryan Ashburton stepped out of the shadows. "I've been noticing your shoes, Ms. Allworth."

What the heck?

All the blood drained from Pat's face. I looked at Ryan, his face set into determined lines. I looked at Pat's feet. At the black mesh shoes with gold stars fastened to the stiletto points.

"I'm going to have to ask you to come with me, Ms. Allworth," Ryan said. "I've been wondering what created that unusual star pattern I saw at the crime scene."

Chapter 16

"That was interesting," Donald said. "Now are we going to supper?"

"I want the film dedicated to the memory of Sir Nigel," Gerald said. "A portion of the profits paid into his estate would be a kind gesture."

Renee pulled out her phone. "I'm calling my agent right now. We'll be renegotiating contracts here."

"I don't want anyone forgetting that we have a sold-out performance tomorrow," Rebecca said. "For now, all this movie stuff is incidental. The stage play is the most important thing."

"Are you still going ahead with it, Leo?" Eddie said. "I mean without Pat?"

Leo threw up his hands. "I have to talk to my backers. 'There's no such thing as bad publicity,' as we all know. But some of my sponsors might not be so confident. The news that Pat Allworth killed—"

"*Allegedly* killed," I said. "Such has not yet been proven in a court of law."

"My partners will not be making a distinction, Ms. . . . Ah . . ."

"Doyle."

"That Pat killed, allegedly or not, Sir Nigel Bellingham in order to see this film get made will be all anyone in LA or New York will be talking about tomorrow. Some people might think it's in poor taste to carry on with it."

"Poor taste." Harry laughed. "When did that ever stop anyone from making a movie?"

Ryan had left a few minutes ago with a handcuffed Pat Allworth. She had not protested her innocence or claimed she'd been misunderstood but walked offstage with her head down and her hands behind her back. Ryan told me I'd be needed at the police station tomorrow to make a statement.

He also told me, not in words, that he had something to say to me.

Leslie had followed them out, saying she'd give Ryan's mother a lift home. One by one, the actors and stage crew drifted away, most of them shaking their heads.

Eddie snatched a bottle of wine out of the cooler and held it up. "Care for a nightcap, Jayne?"

She glanced at Andy, standing by her side. "I don't think so. Right now I need to be with my friends."

"Understood," the actor said, pouring himself a drink.

"The news that Sir Nigel didn't die in a senseless accident but that he was murdered by his own director should send the value of his memorabilia through the roof," Donald said. "Too bad you didn't purchase my playbill, Gemma. I wonder if Rebecca would be agreeable to giving it back."

"She bought it, did she?" Grant said. "In that case, the first round's on you. Is the Blue Water Café still open, Andy?"

"I'll make sure it is." He touched Jayne's shoulder. "That's if you want to come for a drink, Jayne?"

"Great idea." She gave him a big smile, and the one he returned was almost dazzling in its intensity.

Overhead lights began to go off.

We filed out. Behind me, I heard Eddie say, "It's been quite a night. Feel like a drink, Renee?"

The barn was dark and empty. Only the emergency lighting and one lamp over the door broke the gloom.

All the magic was gone, leaving nothing but an old barn at night.

* * *

I joined my friends at the Blue Water Café for one drink but declined to stay for dinner. They peppered me with questions about when and how I'd come to realize that Pat Allworth had murdered Sir Nigel Bellingham, but I wasn't in the mood for talking about it.

I pushed back my chair and said I'd walk home. Grant leapt to his feet and offered to escort me, but I gave him a soft smile and said that wouldn't be necessary.

He studied my face for a long time and then sat back down.

I hadn't gone more than a few yards before I took off the heels and walked the rest of the way in my bare feet, vowing to drop the shoes in the hospital's donation box tomorrow. I strolled through the quiet streets and let myself into my saltbox house. I put Violet out and made myself a cup of tea. I switched the light above the door on but left most of the interior lights off. I changed out of my evening clothes into shorts and a T-shirt.

When Violet was back inside, I took my tea and my book into the study and curled up in the wingback chair. I eyed the portrait of the black-haired opera singer next to the fireplace. Tomorrow, I'd get the pink ribbon out of the safe and burn it in the kitchen sink.

I sipped tea and read. It was well after midnight when my phone beeped.

Ryan: *Finished here for now. Still up?*

Me: *I'll put the kettle on.*

He couldn't have been far away because, by the time I reached the kitchen, white lights were washing my driveway, and Violet was running to the door.

Ryan still wore his good suit, but he'd taken his tie off and undone the top button of his shirt. Stubble was coming in thick on his jaw.

"Tea or coffee?" I said.

"I'm coffee'd out. Orange juice would be nice if you've got some."

"I do," I said.

I made myself a pot of fresh tea and poured his juice. We sat at the kitchen table, and Violet curled up beneath.

"Did Sherlock Holmes ever say 'singing like a canary'?" Ryan asked.

"Not in the stories by Conan Doyle, but I'm sure somewhere, in some modern pastiche, he does. Can I assume that's what Pat's been doing?"

He nodded. "When the average person, meaning not a professional criminal, commits a crime, they want nothing more than to rationalize their actions. We catch a surprising number of them because they can't resist telling someone what they've done. Once they're arrested, they can't wait to get it all off their chest to make sure we know how justified they were. As you surmised, Pat realized that the Hollywood people wouldn't go ahead with making a movie of her play if Nigel Bellingham was in the lead. Since she wanted to direct a movie, Bellingham had to go. She'd told Leo she could handle Nigel and ensure that Edward Barker would play Holmes. Eddie has the looks for the movies."

"Does he?" I said. "I hadn't noticed."

Ryan didn't look as though he quite believed me, but he continued. "Leo dug into Eddie's bio and theatrical credits and liked what he saw. Then when he arrived at your tea, Nigel was being introduced as the star. He told Pat the project couldn't go ahead, and she decided it would be up to her to make an unannounced change in casting."

"Foolish. All she had to do was give it some time. Rebecca would have realized soon enough that Nigel couldn't pull it off."

"Pat figured she couldn't wait. Leo told her he was catching a plane back to LA the next morning."

"I don't understand about the shoes," I said. "One minute Pat was laughing at my deductions, then you noticed her shoes and she collapsed like a house of cards."

He shook his head. "A serious mistake on my part. We found one unusual print at the scene, very close to where Nigel had gone over the cliff."

"A small star."

"Precisely."

"I didn't see it. If I had, I would have recognized it. I'd noticed those shoes with the unusual heel earlier."

"It was half-covered by a dead leaf. The leaf must have blown to the ground after Pat left the scene. I didn't know what it was. Louise thought it might be the tip of a cane. We spent a lot of time checking into who at the tea carried a cane. Two elderly people did. Neither of them had the slightest reason to want to kill Bellingham and, even if they had, not the ability. They showed us their canes. No star pattern. We decided the mark had been made earlier by a trespasser onto the property. Then tonight, on the stage, I got a good look at Pat's shoes, and I knew."

I thought back. I hadn't seen Pat again that day after finding Nigel at the bottom of the cliff. I'd heard her crossing the lawn but not seen her. "She wasn't wearing the shoes when you questioned her at the house?"

"Nope. She must have changed out of them."

"Common enough for women to carry an extra pair of shoes," I said. "Why we wear ones that are so uncomfortable we have to slip out of them the first chance we get, I will never know. Too bad you didn't mention this to me."

"Yes," he said, "if I'd shown you a picture of the pattern, this would all have been over a long time ago."

"Did you interview Leo after the killing? What did he have to say for himself then?"

"Louise spoke to him." Ryan lifted one hand when he saw the beginning of an expression cross my face. "He said nothing about any movie. He told her he was from LA and was in Massachusetts visiting his parents. Which turned out to be true, but not the main reason for the trip. He said he came to the tea because he likes to support regional theater. He told Louise he'd never met Nigel before, which was true, and didn't speak to him that day—also true. So Louise went on to interview the next person."

"He told you enough facts that you could dismiss him as a suspect. If he'd only mentioned wanting to film the play and working with Pat to that aim, it would have saved us a lot of time and trouble."

"Speaking of Louise, she said to tell you good job."

"Through gritted teeth, no doubt."

"You two may not get on," Ryan said, "but she's a good enough cop to be pleased when we catch a killer. No matter who made that happen. If you hadn't gathered us all backstage after the play, I never would have noticed the shoes. My view was blocked when everyone took their bows."

I attempted and failed to suppress a yawn.

Ryan put his empty glass on the table. "I'd better be going. It's late. Pat contacted a lawyer, and she'll be at the station bright and early tomorrow morning."

"This morning," I said.

"Right." He got to his feet.

I stood also, and Violet hurried to join us. We walked with Ryan to the mudroom door. He put his hand on the knob and hesitated.

Then he turned. He put his arms around me and gathered me to him. My heart pounded. He bent his head, and I tilted mine up. He kissed me, long and deep.

Violet barked. She didn't care to be ignored.

Acknowledgments

I've said many times that the best thing about being a writer is all the friends I have made in the Canadian crime-writing community and beyond. Thanks to Barbara Fradkin, Mary Jane Maffini, Linda Wiken, and Robin Harlick in particular for our annual summer writers' retreat. (Much retreating is done, little writing!) Thanks also to my fabulous agent, Kim Lionetti, and the gang at Bookends, and to the people at Crooked Lane, including Sarah Poppe, who always brings a keen but fun-loving editor's eye to my manuscripts.

Thanks also to the Sherlock community, who've accepted my work in the spirit in which it was intended.

Read an excerpt from

A SCANDAL IN SCARLET

the next

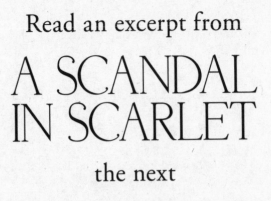

SHERLOCK HOLMES BOOKSHOP MYSTERY

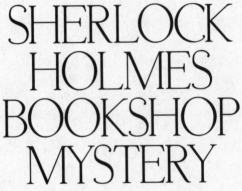

by VICKI DELANY

available soon in hardcover from
Crooked Lane Books

CROOKED
LANE

NEW YORK

Chapter One

I love owning a dog. I love being owned by a dog. No matter how tough the day has been or how low my mood might be, being greeted at the door by a joyful, exuberant animal is one of life's greatest pleasures. It's hard to stay tired or grumpy or in a thoroughly foul mood in the face of those bright eyes, perky ears, lolling tongue, shivering body, and tail wagging hard enough to knock the knickknacks off side tables.

I don't, however, love having a dog when I get home late, tired and hungry, and have pet-owner duties to perform before I can look after myself. Still, you have to take the (very occasional) bad with the (almost always) good.

"You won't mind missing your walk just this once, will you?" I said to Violet, the cocker spaniel.

She lowered her head and whimpered. "Okay," I said. "You win. Give me a minute to change my shoes and we'll go out. Walk!" I was rewarded by a dance of pure joy.

I was tired. Bone tired. It had been a hard day at work. My shop assistant, Ashleigh, had come down with a dose of summer flu and I had to manage the Sherlock Holmes Bookshop and

Emporium myself in the middle of the Cape Cod tourist season. Tourist season means lots of customers and long hours.

Today, the hottest new Sherlock Holmes pastiche novel had been released, and my shop's order had somehow gotten lost in the chaos. I'd been turning away disappointed customers all day. Some, I feared, would order online and never return to my little shop at 222 Baker Street.

Next door, at number 220, Mrs. Hudson's Tearoom, Fiona, one of the waitresses, was down with the same bug as had felled Ashleigh. There was a crisis of some sort involving blueberries, and Jayne Wilson, part owner and head baker, had burst into tears and threatened to walk out the door. Forever. All while the lineup of eager afternoon tea drinkers stretched out the door and down the sidewalk.

Shortly before nine o'clock in the evening, as I was contemplating flipping the sign on the door to "Closed" a few minutes early, a customer came in. I greeted her warmly and told her to let me know if she needed any help.

As it happened, she did need my help. She needed a full explanation of which stories were contained in which volume of the *Collected Stories of Sherlock Holmes*. She needed to know which short story collections were not too scary and which one contained a story by Hank Phillippi Ryan (*Echoes of Sherlock Holmes*). She wanted a full plot description of each of the Laurie R. King books and asked if she'd find it too unbelievable that Sherlock Holmes had been to Timbuktu, as described in *Sherlock Holmes, The Missing Years: Timbuktu* by Vasudev Murthy. Was it realistic, she asked, that Sherlock would have had children, as was the premise of several series, including *The Daughter of Sherlock Holmes* by Leonard Goldberg? I answered all her questions with a smile and tried not to glance at the clock over the sales counter. Soon the smile turned into a grimace, and I pulled out my phone to check the time. More than once. And not subtly either.

Still she chatted. She picked up and examined every book and then put them back in the wrong place. I ran after her, trying not to be too obvious about reshelving them. Eventually I didn't worry about being too obvious about it. She liked the Benedict Cumberbatch interpretation of Sherlock, she told me, but Robert Downey Jr.'s not so much. Too frivolous, she thought. Didn't I agree?

I agreed with everything. Absolutely everything.

All the time she fussed over the shop cat, Moriarty. He wound himself around her legs, he purred, he preened. He allowed her to pick him up and stroke him. Between barking out rapid-fire questions, she complimented him on his regal bearing, his sleek black coat, his friendly personality. Moriarty peered at me from under her arms. He didn't even bother to try to hide his self-satisfied smirk.

At quarter to ten, the woman put the cat down. "That was so interesting. Thank you. I'll have to think about it."

And she left. Unencumbered by any purchases.

I twisted the lock on the door behind her and glared at Moriarty. He yawned mightily and stretched every fiber of his lean body before heading off to his bed under the center table, letting me know that his work was done for the day and he was looking forward to a good night's sleep.

I, unfortunately, had things to do once I closed the shop. I'd arranged to have a drink after work with my friend Irene Talbot, a journalist with our local newspaper, the *West London Star*. I managed to send her a text saying I was delayed while the non-shopper fussed over Moriarty. I hoped Irene would tell me not to bother, but her reply said she was waiting.

Once I'd switched off the lights and locked up, I dragged myself down to the Blue Water Café. Irene, so I discovered, had been offered a position at a newspaper in St Louis. It was a good job, but, she moaned, could a Cape Cod girl ever be happy in the landlocked flatlands? She didn't really want my advice; she needed to use me as a sounding board. I had a drink I didn't want and sat in my chair on the restaurant's deck, bouncing her words back to her. It was a beautiful Cape Cod summer's night; we were sitting outside in the warm evening, looking out over the dark sea, but I could barely keep myself awake.

At long last Irene said, "Maybe I should talk to Joe McManus. He went to Chicago."

"Excellent idea," I said, having no idea who Joe McManus was or what might be wrong with Chicago. I waved for the check, said my good nights and staggered home.

I was thinking fondly of my lovely, soft, comfortable bed when I remembered Violet had been alone most of the day. I live with my great-uncle Arthur, and Violet is technically his dog. But right now Arthur was cruising somewhere in the Mediterranean. Our next-door neighbor, Mrs. Ramsbattan, has a key to the house; if I can't get away from the store during the day, she comes over to fill the water bowl and let Violet out into the enclosed yard. But Mrs. Ramsbattan is almost Uncle Arthur's age, late eighties, and she needs the assistance of a cane, so Violet doesn't get a walk.

That task is left up to me. I took the leash off the hook by the mudroom door. Beautiful liquid brown eyes stared lovingly up into mine.

It wasn't terribly late when we left the house, not much after eleven, but this is a quiet part of a quiet town. Blue Water Place, our street, is a stretch of nice houses and well- maintained gardens. Some of the homes are new, many are renovated, and a handful date from centuries past, such as the 1756 salt box in which Great-Uncle Arthur and I live.

Once I was outside, feeling the caress of warm salty air on my skin and the scent of roses and the sea in my nose, I began to enjoy the walk. Violet wandered back and forth across the sidewalk, sniffing under bushes and at patches in the grass, finding sensations only she could interpret. A startled squirrel darted up a knurly oak as old as my house.

The stretch of harbor at the foot of Blue Water Place is a family-friendly boardwalk of ice cream shops, souvenir stores, and small markets. The lights of the Blue Water Café twinkled in the distance, and lamps from small fishing boats or pleasure craft bobbed gently as the ocean rose and fell.

We turned left at Harbor Road, heading away from town. The lights from the restaurants, shops, and the fishing pier fell away. The fourth-order Fresnel lens of the West London Lighthouse flashed its rhythm of three seconds on, three seconds off, three seconds on, and twenty seconds off. We walked down the silent street, the only sounds the swish of the occasional passing car and the gentle purr of the incoming surf against the rocky shore.

Some of the houses facing out to sea along this stretch of the road are very old. Old by American standards, that is. Not so old for someone born and raised in England, as I was.

The oldest surviving house in West London is now a museum. Built in 1648 by Robert Scarlet and family, who settled in

Massachusetts in 1640, it's called Scarlet House in their honor. The property consists of kitchen and herb gardens and a working barn. The home itself has been carefully restored to its original condition and furnished with authentic period furniture and household utensils. Costumed volunteers work at tending to a few sheep and goats or sharpening scythes in the barn, and baking bread or making cakes over the open kitchen fires. It's hugely popular with school groups in the spring and tourists in the summer and fall.

As we passed the museum, Violet stopped so suddenly I bumped into her. Her ears stood up, and she woofed, low in her throat. Her head turned from side to side, and her nose twitched, pulling scents out of the air. This was not the stance she used when she detected the presence of a cat or a squirrel. She barked again. I sniffed the air, and at last my feeble human senses caught up with Violet's. The slightest trace of smoke drifted on the air. Then it was gone. The breeze was blowing inland, bringing us fresh air off the sea.

"What is it?" I said to Violet. She was staring intently at the white picket fence around Scarlet House. The wind shifted slightly, bringing another trace of smoke toward me. Violet barked.

I quickly retraced my steps and peered over the gate. An out-of-place electric light burned over the front door, and a soft glow came from the barn around back. Otherwise, all was in darkness.

Then I saw it. In the front window, a flash of red and yellow. Even as I watched, not yet entirely sure of what I was seeing, the light began to move and to grow.

Fire.

I threw open the gate and ran onto the property. I fumbled

in my pocket and found my phone. I dropped the leash, pressed the emergency button, and punched 9-1-1.

"Fire, police, or ambulance?" said a calm voice.

"Fire. Scarlet House, the museum on Harbor Road. I can see flames."

"Are you safe, madam? Is anyone inside the building?"

"I'm fine. I'm just passing. I'm outside. I'll check."

"Please don't—" she said. Her words were cut off as I shoved the phone back into my pocket.

Violet was barking now, the sound constant and frantic. The animals in the barn bellowed their panic. I ran toward the house. A large padlock was looped through a wooden latch. I pounded on the door. It felt warm beneath my touch.

"Fire! Fire! Is anyone in there?"

No reply.

Hardly any time at all passed before sirens could be heard coming down the street. I continued hammering on the door. It was highly unlikely someone would be inside at this time of night, but it was also highly unlikely the empty building would catch fire. The flames were building now, eagerly gobbling up the old wooden furniture and dusty rugs, biting into the ancient wooden beams. I'd read somewhere that a fire doubles in size every minute. This one was moving faster than that. The entire house would be gone soon.

"Step aside, ma'am," said a voice. A hand touched my shoulder. I turned to see a man dressed in full bunker gear. His intense dark eyes studied me. "Is anyone in there?"

"Not that I know of. I was passing and smelled smoke. I'm trying to alert them just in case."

"I need to you get out of the way. Please. You and your dog."

I looked around. In the—what, five minutes?—since I'd stepped into the yard, the scene had changed totally. Firefighters ran across the lawn, dragging hoses behind them, shouting orders. As though night had ended early, bright light flooded the yard, and red and blue emergency lights filled the street. More sirens approached. The curious were emerging from nearby houses, many dressed in pajamas.

"Is that your dog?" the firefighter said.

Violet stood in the center of the lawn, barking her head off. Her leash trailed on the ground behind her. I smiled at her. She knew better than to get too close to the burning building, but she wasn't going to run off and leave me alone.

"Yes, she is. The barn. Animals are in there."

"We'll take care of that, ma'am." His voice was polite but firm. He didn't need any help from me.

I hurried toward Violet, scooped up her leash, and led her off the museum property. There was nothing she and I could do here but get in the way. I wasn't, at the moment, particularly curious. I've been at fire scenes before, and I know how the firefighters operate.

Police were attempting to string tape around the property and keep onlookers back. I spotted a person I knew and headed toward her. "Evening, Officer Johnson."

Stella Johnson half-turned. "Gemma Doyle. Hi. Can you move away, please?"

"Happy to. I wanted to let you know that I'm the person who spotted the fire and called it in."

"Detective Estrada's on call tonight. She'll be here soon, and you can tell her what you saw."

"Uh, maybe not. She'll be busy, and I have nothing of importance to say. I smelled smoke and saw flames in the window and called nine-one-one. I knocked on the door, so it might have my fingerprints. That's all. I saw no one on the grounds or on the street in the minute or so prior to seeing the fire. I'll go down to the station in the morning and make a statement."

"She'd rather talk to you now."

"I have absolutely no doubt about that. You can tell her I was so traumatized I had to go straight home and lie down."

Johnson studied me. "A less traumatized witness I've yet to see."

"I don't display my feelings openly. You know what we English are like. Stiff upper lip and all that. Or so they say. Besides, my dog is traumatized." Johnson eyed the animal sitting calmly at my feet. Violet wagged her stubby tail. If she could have smiled, she would have.

I gave the leash a slight tug, and we set off home. I might have walked faster than I had earlier. Detective Louise Estrada was not, shall we say, my best friend. She'd be more likely to accuse me of starting the fire in order to attract attention to myself than to hear what little I had to report.

I gave no more thought to the fire or speculated on what might have caused it. The investigators would find out soon enough.

Chapter Two

Rather than me having to go down to the police station, the police came to me the following morning, in the much more pleasant form of Detective Ryan Ashburton. I opened the back door, wiping sleep from my eyes, to find Ryan and an extra-large takeout tea waiting for me.

I took the offered mug without a word and lowered my face to it. Warm, scented steam enveloped me. "Mmm."

I stepped back and Ryan came in. He greeted Violet with as much enthusiasm as she greeted him. Mutual admiration over, she ran past him into the yard to see what the neighborhood squirrels had been up to in the night.

"To what do I owe the honor of this visit?" I sipped my tea. English breakfast, with a splash of milk, no sugar, prepared properly.

"You're the hero of the hour," he said.

"I am?" I didn't feel much like a hero with bedhead, watery eyes, wearing yellow polka-dot shorty pajamas. No doubt I still had impressions of my pillow pressed into my cheek. It was eight AM. I'd slept soundly, undisturbed by dreams of fire and smoke.

Ryan pressed a kiss onto the top of my head and then dropped into a kitchen chair. I took the other while trying, no doubt fruitlessly, to tidy my mop of wild curls.

"You called nine-one-one last night. The fire at the museum."

"Violet and I were out for our nightly walk, and I saw flames in the window. Modesty forces me to admit that Violet noticed it first. The wind was blowing inland, carrying the smoke away from me. If she hadn't alerted me, I would have walked on past. I was planning to go up the hill at the next intersection and return home that way."

"I'll get the mayor to give the medal to Violet then."

The hero of the day ran into the kitchen. Ryan gave her a scratch on the top of her head. She'd prefer that to a shiny piece of tin and a colored ribbon any day.

"Do you know what caused it?" I asked.

"The arson investigator was on site first thing this morning. Looks, he says, like a candle had been left to burn down. Louise is talking to the museum staff, and I said I'd handle you."

I grinned at him. "As if."

Ryan Ashburton was a good-looking man at any time, but never more so than when he laughed, and he laughed now. Six foot three and solidly built, he had chiseled cheekbones, short black hair and expressive blue eyes, and a strong jaw that seemed as though, no matter how recently he'd shaved, it always had a cover of stubble.

He and I had a complicated connection. We'd been in a serious relationship once, on the point of getting engaged. (Of that fiasco, all of it my fault, the less said the better.) He had moved to Boston for a few years and had come back a couple of months ago when the job of lead detective for the WLPD came open.

And we found that our feelings for each other hadn't faded.

But I'd run afoul of the West London police before, through absolutely no fault of my own. Things had not gone well for Ryan when the Chief and Detective Estrada thought that I exerted an undue influence on him. Ryan's career was important to him, and thus to me, and so we stood at a crossroads. Sort of in a relationship, but not fully.

"Were you able to . . . uh . . . deduce anything, Gemma?" he asked now.

"I smelled smoke and saw flames. I put those facts together and decided, in an instant, that the museum was on fire. Sherlock Holmes couldn't have done better."

He didn't rise to the bait. "You didn't see or hear anything else?"

"Nothing. I saw no one, I heard nothing out of place other than the fire itself. I called nine-one-one the moment I realized what was happening. I knocked on the door, in case anyone was inside, a vagrant who'd fallen asleep or something like that. The door was locked, and no one answered. The firefighters arrived and I left." I studied his face. "You don't look overly concerned about this, so I'll assume no one was inside."

He shook his head. "No. And we're pretty sure it wasn't arson."

I sipped my tea. "Have you had breakfast yet? I can do scrambled eggs, and I bought some sausage from the farmer's market on Monday."

"I'd like that," Ryan said.

Violet, who hadn't yet had her breakfast, barked in agreement.

* * *

By the time Ryan left, it was time for me to get ready for work. Ashleigh had texted to say she was feeling better and would be at work today as scheduled. I was very pleased to hear it.

At five minutes to ten, I went into Mrs. Hudson's Tearoom for a muffin and another cup of tea. Uncle Arthur and I own half of the business, and Jayne Wilson, who serves as the manager and head baker, owns the other half.

"Morning, Gemma," Fiona said from behind the counter when it was my turn to be served.

"I'm glad to see you back," I said. "Feeling better?"

"Much. Did you hear about the fire last night?"

"I did."

"If you have a minute, Jayne wants to talk to you. She told me to send you in."

"Thanks." I accepted a raspberry muffin, always my second choice. Apparently the Great Blueberry Crisis was not yet resolved. I went through the swinging doors into Jayne's domain. By now I knew the picture of total chaos that greeted me was anything but. Jayne knew what she was doing and always did it with competence and efficiency. Occasional moments of complete panic don't last long. Yesterday's near meltdown had been a rare event. I might be a partner in the business, but at this side of the counter I'm very much a silent partner. A kitchen, of any sort, is not a place in which I feel entirely comfortable.

Unless I'm eating some of Jayne's baking, that is.

"What's up?" I said.

A lock of blond hair had escaped its net, and Jayne brushed it out of her eyes with a flour-dotted hand. At the moment she was stirring pale yellow batter in the industrial-sized mixer. Jocelyn, her assistant, rolled out pastry and cut it into small circles to make the base for miniature fruit tarts. Loaves of bread for lunchtime sandwiches and trays of scones to be served at afternoon tea were cooling on racks. Something fragrant was about to come out of the oven.

Heaven, I sometimes thought, must smell like Jayne's kitchen.

"Did you hear about the fire last night at the museum down by the harbor?" Jayne asked.

"I did."

"No one was hurt, thank heavens—not even the animals— but the house suffered a lot of damage."

"Much of their fabulous old furniture was destroyed," Jocelyn said. "Some of it dated from the seventeenth century."

"I don't' have much time," I said. "I have to open the store. What do you want to talk about?"

"My mom's a volunteer at the museum," Jayne said.

"Of course she is." Leslie Wilson was a West London stalwart. Any committee to do with the promotion of arts and culture in town, Leslie would be on it.

"The museum committee had an emergency conference call meeting this morning. They need to raise funds to repair the house and restock what was lost."

"They move fast."

"That they do. Mom said they're going to move the educational programs into the barn and the back fields in the meantime, but they're determined to reopen the house as soon as possible."

"Very admirable. Dare I ask why you're telling me this?"

"It'll cost money, Gemma. A lot of money. The museum's important to the town. It attracts visitors, visitors who then shop on Baker Street."

"Or have afternoon tea," Jocelyn added.

"I know that," I said. "I'd be happy to make a donation."

"Mom says they're planning an auction as a start," Jayne said. "They're going to ask all the shops to donate something."

"I can put in a basket of books."

Jayne was thirty-two, the same age as me, short and thin and extremely attractive with soft blond hair, a heart-shaped face, good cheekbones, and perfect skin and teeth. She hefted the bowl of batter in her arms. She was a lot stronger than she looked. While she talked, she scooped sticky globs of batter into prepared cake tins. "Think bigger, Gemma. Much, much bigger."

I tried to think bigger. The Emporium was primarily a bookstore. We specialized in the Sherlock Holmes canon and modern pastiche novels and story collections, as well as nonfiction about the life and times of Sir Arthur Conan Doyle and historical novels set in the gaslight era. As well as books, we sold a wide variety of Holmes-related merchandise and things to do with the many TV shows and movies about the Great Detective. I didn't deal in anything truly collectable, except the occasional second edition Holmes book or damaged first.

"Maybe Arthur can think of something," Jayne said.

"I'll ask. What are you giving?"

She turned to me with a grin. *Oh no.* "We've agreed to host the auction here, at the tearoom."

"We have, have we?"

"Yes, Gemma. We have."